THE
FIRST
QUESTION

Alex Fallows

ISBN: 979-8879676549

Also by Alex Fallows

CHEEK TO CHEEK

Chapter 1

The first question you probably want to ask me, is why I put up with it. That's the first question everyone wants to ask us; women like us. Why we put up with it. And don't get me wrong; it's a perfectly reasonable question. It's the obvious question, in fact. I'm damn sure that's what I would want to know. So, go right ahead and ask me. But please, please, do it to my face. Don't judge me behind my back with sympathetic whispers and pitying eyes. Not if you want to be a real friend to me. And believe me, I could do with a real friend right now. That's often the problem for women like us; no-one close to talk to when we need them most. That's certainly been my problem.

That's not entirely true. I did have a real friend, up until a few months ago. At least, I thought she was a real friend; my best friend, in fact. But it turns out I was wrong about her too. She did the one thing a best friend would never do.

I guess that's why I'm here talking to you right now; sharing my story - assuming you care about me. It's just that you might be able to help me. A problem shared and all that. I literally don't know who else to turn to.

Anyway, back to the question: why I put up with it.

The answer is - and you probably won't be too surprised to hear this - it's complicated. No, *complicated* isn't the right word. It doesn't even begin to describe what I've got myself into. It's a fucking mess, that's what it is. A fucking mess. And it's my fucking mess so I'm going to have to clean it up myself. As my dad would have said, if he'd still been around: *you've made your bed.*

So let me try to explain. Where should I start? The beginning, obviously. I promise I won't bore you with every tedious detail of my entire life from the day I was born, but there are a few things I should probably tell you about my childhood. That's where a psychologist, or is it a psychiatrist - I never know the difference - would start, wouldn't they? They'd assume it had something to do with my childhood.

I was born Katy Harrington. That's still my name, despite the marriage - but I'll explain about that later.

I am an only child.

There, I said it. It's not a big deal, at least not from my perspective. After I was born, my mother had three miscarriages and then just stopped trying. It might be nice to have a brother or sister, but I don't. There's really nothing I can do about it, is there?

I wasn't bullied at school or abused or anything like that. Definitely no traumatic childhood experiences to write in a journal and analyse to death. Basically, nothing controversial in terms of my nature or my nurture that I can think of. Obviously, the psychologists / psychiatrists would have a field day with the *only child* thing, but who cares what they think.

And I had loads of friends back then, and was even quite sporty; captain of the school swimming team no less - although there were only about two of us who could actually swim in a straight line. Oh, and I was good at maths; really good at maths. I don't normally like to brag about that last bit - for obvious reasons - but I needed to tell you. It's sort of important to my story. Not the actual maths, obviously.

Anyway, enough rambling. I'm sure you get the picture. Based on a random sample of one, I thought I was fairly normal as a child. I still do.

I should probably give my parents a quick mention at this point too. As far as I remember, they were reasonably happy with their lives and with each other. They both worked for the local council; something to do with planning, although what they were planning, I never really found out. I do remember mum worked in an office and dad didn't; he was always driving around the country. They weren't exactly rich, but I don't remember them arguing about money. I'm sure they did argue about money and other stuff - who doesn't? - but I can't think of any examples to give you right now.

The three of us talked constantly, usually right over each other. Dad told me off for talking with my mouth full, and then mum told him off for doing exactly the same. They supported most of my teenage decisions - apart from that dopey first boyfriend. By the way, I did eventually admit I was wrong about him, but could never quite bring myself to admit they were right.

I miss dad. He died almost ten years ago. It knocked most of the stuffing out of mum too. She's been on her own ever since. She says she's not interested in finding anyone else. It's probably the right decision. Anyway, it's her decision; nothing to do with me. I'm the last person to give advice on that subject, for God's sake.

So, there you have it. Nothing dark lurking in my childhood that pre-disposed me to screwing up my life. I managed to do that all by myself. That's kind of a lesson in itself: what happened to me could happen to anyone. Sounds like an excuse, doesn't it? It's not meant to be. It's just an observation. Maybe a warning too.

As you can see, rather inconveniently, I don't fit into any particularly obvious stereotype. That's why I hate it so much when people make lazy judgements without knowing the first thing about me. Hopefully, you won't fall into that trap, will you?

And when did my life start to fall apart? That's an easy one to answer. It was exactly three months after I'd moved to Oxford to start my new job. I was 27 going on 28. I hadn't had a serious boyfriend for nearly five years, but don't assume for one second that I was desperate. Honestly, I wasn't bothered either way. And it's not like my mother was putting me under any pressure about the ticking clock or anything. No, I was far too busy with my research work to worry about mundane things like boyfriends. That's what I was telling myself anyway.

I remember every detail of our first meeting. It was a typically grizzly grey Friday afternoon in late October. I was with a small group of my new colleagues in a café off St Giles. Not surprisingly, we were talking about work, or to be more precise, about other people at work - or to be even more precise, about other people at work who we found annoying for one reason or another. I'd had my fill of idle chatter and was about to set off home.

I happened to glance around the café, as I chewed the final large mouthful of the chocolate brownie that I'd bought in a moment of weakness. During this messy process, a couple of crumbs fell out of my mouth and tumbled onto my polo-neck jumper - which fortunately was also dark brown. As I desperately tried to brush them off, I noticed someone sitting at a small round table in the opposite corner of the café. He had a thick paperback book in front of him, but he wasn't reading it. He was looking at me; studying me. It was almost like he was reading *me*. Perhaps he was wondering how a nice girl like me ended up in a place like this - or words to that effect. More likely, he was wondering how a nice girl like me ended up being such a sloppy eater. My first thought - totally crazy, I know, but I remember it clearly - was that his hair looked extremely pleased with itself.

Instinctively - rather politely, I thought - I averted my gaze. For one thing, I'd always been told by my parents that it was rude to stare. For another, I didn't think he could genuinely be interested in me. It was a long time since anyone had looked at me that way, and I was seriously out of practice. Inevitably, my eyes were drawn back to him. I couldn't help myself. I assumed he would have lost interest by now, and returned to his book, but he was still watching me. He smiled at me. It seemed only natural and polite to smile back at him. I wasn't flirting, honestly. It's just what you do when someone smiles at you, isn't it? Smile back.

I've asked myself a thousand times since: what if I hadn't smiled back at him? What if I'd just ignored him and carried on chatting to my workmates? What if I'd gone home and had an early night? What if? What if? But I didn't do any of those boring sensible things. Instead, I smiled back at him. Life is all about those small decisions which have the big consequences.

I could suddenly feel the warmth in my cheeks and I knew I was blushing. I don't really know why. After all, he was looking at me just as much as I was looking at him. Why should I be the one who was embarrassed, while he just sat there with his engaging eyes and annoyingly thick black floppy hair, looking all charming and confident?

With the benefit of hindsight, I know exactly why.

I remember how special it felt to be singled out like that; to have someone take notice of me. Even today, despite everything that's happened since, I still feel a flutter in my stomach at that first memory; the same light-headedness. I also remember how disappointed I was when, after a few seconds of eye contact, he suddenly looked away. Maybe he wasn't interested in me after all. Maybe he was just messing with me; teasing me. Oh, well …

It felt like the moment had passed. There was no point hanging around any longer. I started putting on my coat and making my excuses, vaguely hoping that someone might ask if I wanted to do something together later. But everyone already had their own plans which, for one reason or another, didn't seem to include me.

As I reached for the handle and started to pull the door towards me, I sensed someone right behind me. Someone so close that I could feel their breath on my neck as I took a step back to open the door fully. Unable to move backwards or forwards now, I was quite literally trapped. For a split-second, I panicked. Caught between flight and fight, I felt a kind of instinctive fear. As I turned round, I was already preparing myself for conflict.

"Sorry, but I couldn't let you leave until I'd spoken to you," he said.

He was very direct; very confident. He seemed to be assuming it was up to him when I was allowed to leave. A bit arrogant, don't you think?

"Why not?"

My abrupt response sounded rather more aggressive than I'd intended, but even that didn't seem to put him off his stride.

"Well, for one thing, I like your smile,"

"And for another?"

The words were out of my mouth before I could think what I was saying. What on earth was I doing, fishing for compliments? That was absolutely not the sort of thing that Katy Harrington did … ever.

"I enjoyed watching you eat that cake."

"Ah, you saw that did you?"

"I'm afraid so."

"Well actually, it wasn't cake; it was brownie," I said, as if that made any difference to my dignity.

We were still blocking the doorway and a couple of the guys from my department were now trying to leave. They gave me a sideways glance as they squeezed out through the door. My plan for the evening didn't seem to include them now.

"Are you not going out with your friends tonight?" he asked.

"No, we just came here for a quick drink after work. I'm not doing anything tonight."

I regretted my response immediately; it sounded like such a pathetic hint. He didn't seem unduly daunted by the fact I was being abandoned by my friends. At this moment, it didn't bother me that much either.

"Oh right. So, do you have time for a chat then?"

"I suppose so."

"Should we just sit back down here?"

He pulled the chair out for me, and I dutifully sat down.

"Something to drink?" he asked.

"Yes please; a regular tea maybe."

"Another slice of brownie?"

"Perhaps better not."

"By the way, my name is Henry."

"I'm Katy."

While he was at the counter ordering, I took my coat off again and inspected my jumper for any stubborn crumbs still lurking in the chunky wool. I made sure he didn't catch me this time. As he walked back over towards me, *fit* was the word that came to mind. I quite liked the look of him - and I hoped that he quite liked the look of me.

"So, Katy … is that short for Katherine?" he said as he sat down beside me.

That's basically how it all started. Trust me, I've replayed that first encounter in my head countless times, but I still can't see any warning signs. Did I miss something obvious? A look? A word? He

was perhaps a bit too confident for my liking, but someone had to make the first move. I can't really blame him for that, can I? I know I would never have had the nerve to go over and talk to him. And it wasn't his fault I was relatively new in town and didn't have anywhere else to go that Friday evening.

Admittedly, I should perhaps have slowed things down a bit that first weekend. We ended up going out for dinner, and then spent most of Saturday and Sunday together. In my defence, we didn't sleep together until Sunday night.

It scares me now to realise how quickly I let another person - a stranger at that - become the centre of my world, almost to the exclusion of everyone else. I stupidly allowed my life to start revolving entirely around his. I became a dark moon to his bright star. Even when we were not together, I was thinking about him, so strong was the attraction. I never stopped to wonder if I might be having too much of a good thing. I hate to say it, but I even cancelled my regular Sunday lunch slot with mum. I told her I wasn't feeling well. Now I come to think about it, that little fib was Henry's idea. Anyway, even if it was, that doesn't excuse it. I was stupid to go along with it. Stupid, stupid, stupid.

Henry seemed to have loads of friends and always knew where there was something going on in Oxford. I think he'd lived there about five years when we met. It sounds pathetic, but it was just less hassle to let him decide what we should do, and simply follow in his slipstream. My own social life away from Henry was pretty much non-existent anyway. I didn't have anything to invite him to except the occasional work thing with a bunch of mathematicians. If I'd been on my own, I probably would have gone along and enjoyed myself. But Henry showed no enthusiasm for my work colleagues, and I couldn't afford to risk him getting bored with me.

Yes, I know; classic mistake. How stupid was I to cut myself off from my own circle of acquaintances like that? As I hear myself telling you now, my own stupidity makes me shudder. But I'm afraid that's what happens when you get swept along - especially when you don't have a close friend to press the alarm button for you. Before I knew what was happening, I was in way too deep. Of course, I wasn't the first, and I'm sure I won't be the last, to be that stupid. That sounds like another excuse, doesn't it?

I've often thought about all the things I should have done differently in those first few days and weeks. The list of dumb decisions I made back then is so disgustingly long that I'd rather not talk about it right now, if you don't mind. Suffice it to say, the thing I regret most is the way I brutally dropped the few friends I had. In some cases - I'm ashamed to say - their only crime was a mere suggestion from Henry that he didn't particularly like them. In others, it was just me screwing up my priorities. I was so desperate not to lose Henry that I was prepared to sacrifice my family and friends. What sort of person did that make me? Not a very nice one, that's for sure. I had changed. He had changed me - and not for the better. Believe me, I'm not proud of the way I treated the people around me. But most of all, I'm not proud of the way I treated my mother.

Back then, the only person I truly cared about was Henry. Within six months we were married. Everything happened so damn fast I didn't have time to think anything through. I scarcely had time to breathe. I hadn't planned any of it, but it happened anyway. I'd made my bed - to use my dad's phrase - and now I had to lie in it.

But I'm rushing ahead of myself.

I need to tell you about Isabella.

Chapter 2

In those first few months, I was bedazzled by Henry. He was always so attentive; surprising me with expensive presents and trips to interesting places. He completely overwhelmed me. He was constantly telling me how much he cared for me and wanted to be with me. I genuinely believed he loved me.

The fact that he was almost six years older than me, also gave me a sense of security. And no - just in case you were thinking it - *no*, I was *not* seeking a father figure. A psychologist would love that, wouldn't they? I can just picture them nodding sagely and writing in loopy letters on the first page of their pristine little notebook:

Katy Harrington
1. Only child.
2. Looking for father figure.

Please don't get me started!

Sorry - back to Henry. Of course, not everything about him was perfect. I couldn't expect that. He had his faults. But, don't we all? Rather than faults, let's just say there were a few things he was super-sensitive about.

Top of the touchy subject list was any reference, no matter how oblique, to his job status and/or salary. When Henry first discovered that I earned more than him, he was not a happy bunny. I soon realised that if I mentioned this topic, it was at my own peril. So, I didn't.

Sadly, other people occasionally did, and thereby unleashed Henry's wrath. Let me give you a typical example from early on in our relationship, so you can see what I mean.

Henry had reluctantly agreed to put in a brief appearance at the Mathematics Institute Christmas party, but only on the condition that we wouldn't stay very long. I had expected him to refuse completely, so was grateful for his generous offer to compromise. We were standing around making small talk. I saw him glance at his watch a couple of times, and sensed he was getting bored. It was time to leave. Unfortunately, I was just a bit too slow off the mark.

"So do you work at the university, like Katy?" one of my new colleagues asked Henry innocently.

Oh God, I wish he hadn't said *like Katy*.

"Yes, I'm the Director of Marketing at OUP," Henry replied.

Henry assumed everyone knew Oxford University Press was part of Oxford University. He was looking rather smug - especially with the word *Director*. And with the word *the* he inserted in front, even though he was actually only one of many with a similar title.

"Oh, I meant for the university proper; you know, part of the academic staff, like Katy."

I braced myself, knowing Henry would regard this as a serious affront to his ego. I could almost hear the bristles on his neck stiffening to attention, as he prepared his attack.

"No, I leave all that ivory tower stuff to Katherine. Some of us have to earn an honest living in the real world."

Henry may have been smiling, but his eyes narrowed like those of a killer. Fortunately, I managed to drag him away before things could escalate any further. On the way home though, he just wouldn't let it drop. He demanded to know why I would want to spend my time with such *dickheads* - his word - and vowed that he would never again set foot inside the Maths Institute. I was treated to - yet another - lecture on how, not only was OUP a bona fide department of the university, but it was actually older than many of the colleges. I felt he was rather over-reacting to the perceived slight, but didn't want to risk interrupting his rant and appearing to take sides with a *dickhead*.

Now that I'm telling you about this incident, I would just like to point out that it didn't dawn on me until much later, that Henry's defence of his own job had effectively been an attack on mine. After all, I was earning an honest living in the real world too. I know now, that to let his hurtful put-down go unchallenged, was a terrible mistake on my part. A mistake I came to regret more and more each day.

Oh yes, and one more thing, while I'm at it. You probably noticed that Henry called me *Katherine*. This was something he'd started doing, even though he knew perfectly well that the name on my birth certificate was *Katy*. Katy, pure and simple. Absolutely everyone else called me Katy - apart from Henry's mother and sister who followed his lead, probably because they knew it annoyed me. Initially, I thought it might be meant to be a sign of his affection, but I soon realised it wasn't that at all.

I said earlier that I was bedazzled by Henry. Perhaps a better word would have been *blinded*. I can only think it was because I simply couldn't believe how lucky I was to be with Henry. That's why I was always so ready and willing to forgive and forget his foibles. Too ready and willing; appeasement turned out to be a poor strategy where Henry was concerned. Anyway, inexperienced as I was with serious relationships, I convinced myself that I had made a good choice with Henry. Of course, in reality, it was Henry who had chosen me.

We were in Portugal over Easter when he asked me to marry him. He'd been playing golf during the afternoon - which was why we were on the Algarve in the first place - and then taken me out for a fancy seafood dinner in the evening. Neither of these two events was particularly unusual, so I had no reason to suspect he was planning anything. The excitement of his proposal took my breath away. The apparent suddenness didn't bother me in the slightest. I said yes immediately. I couldn't risk him changing his mind. I had become so dependent on Henry taking the lead in our relationship, that when he suggested we get married as soon as we were back home, I just went along with that too. Everything was decided before I had chance to do any dreaming about a big white wedding with all the trimmings.

I know what you're thinking: *yes*, I only have myself to blame. Why did I ignore the warning lights? Why the hell did I rush ahead and marry him? Marry in haste; repent at leisure - you might say. And you'd be dead right. As was mum.

I could tell straight away that she'd taken an instant dislike to Henry.

"He seems quite nice," she said, when I asked for her first impression.

Talk about damning with faint praise.

"But?"

"But there's something about him I don't like … no, that's not the word … something I don't … *trust*."

"Don't trust? Why would you say that, mum?"

"I don't know exactly. I can't quite put my finger on it."

"Thanks mum; that's really so incredibly helpful."

Being sarcastic to mum was new to my repertoire. Another *gift* from Henry?

"I'm sorry Katy, but you asked me what I think and I'm just telling you. If you don't want my opinion, I will keep it to myself."

"I do want your opinion but you've only just met him. You don't know him like I do. Why can't you give him the benefit of the doubt?"

"Look, it doesn't really matter what I think, does it? Do you like him?"

"I do … and I wish you would too."

Unfortunately, each time mum met Henry, her opinion of him sank to new depths. I would have preferred not to take sides, but I was forced to. It seemed like the best way to minimise conflict. The inevitable result was that I saw less of mum and more of Henry.

Mum tactfully never said anything directly to Henry that might jeopardise our relationship. Dad wouldn't have been able to stop himself. At the very least, he'd have given Henry a severe grilling as to whether his intentions were strictly honourable. But dad wasn't around anymore and, in any case, it probably wouldn't have made any difference. I would have been backed into a corner and forced to defend my decision, and by extension, to defend Henry. Digging my heels in harder would only have made the situation worse. And anyway, it was far too late now. I'd agreed to marry him. There was no going back.

Mum was absolutely horrified when I told her my exciting news.

"Did you know he was going to propose?" she asked.

"No, to be honest, it was a complete surprise."

"So … it's all very sudden then."

She looked at my waist.

"No, I'm not."

"So why the rush then?"

"It's not exactly a rush, mum. We've been together for six months."

"Your father and I were together for over three years before he proposed to me. It gave us time to really get to know each other."

"Well, Henry and I don't need three years to know *we* love each other."

Mum looked so incredibly hurt by my cruel words. I hated myself for saying them; it wasn't like me at all.

"Well, I suppose if it's what you both want."

"We do. He wants to marry me and I want to marry him. We don't really care what anyone else thinks."

See, that's exactly what I mean about digging my heels in.

Mum gave a resigned sigh. She must have realised her protestations were pointless; counter-productive even. She put on a brave face and pretended that she'd accepted my decision. I played along with her pretence, even though we both knew she hated the idea. At that precise moment when I most needed her advice, I stopped listening. I stopped behaving rationally. I made it impossible for anyone on the outside to get through to me. I was completely lost to all reason.

It was a modest wedding. Henry didn't want anything too extravagant - or expensive - and I suppose I kind of went along with his plan. He said that keeping it small, meant we would be able to enjoy it properly ourselves. I don't want to sound like I'm complaining now, but it might have been nice to … oh, well never mind.

There were just twelve of us: me and mum, Henry and his parents and sister, plus six friends we'd both been hanging around with in Oxford over the past few months. I was disappointed that Elena, my long-term friend from school and university, couldn't make it, but to be fair to her, the suddenness of the invite gave her very little notice. We were married at the registry office in the centre of Oxford and had our reception at a posh manor house hotel just north of Oxford. Henry knew the manager and made all the arrangements. The weather was absolutely perfect; a warm gentle breeze; beautifully clear blue sky. Money couldn't buy that, Henry said. He seemed happy, and I convinced myself that it was the wedding that I wanted too.

So, you might be wondering when I first began to suspect that something wasn't quite right. Not just the superficial stuff - like him calling me Katherine - but something deeper; something buried much deeper. I'd be the first to admit that I wasn't exactly looking for problems in those early days. I was far too busy enjoying myself with the man I loved - and who I believed loved me. So, to be honest, if there were any warning signs, I probably just missed them - or worse, ignored them.

But what about your mum, you might say? She warned you, didn't she? Well, yes she did, and maybe it should have made me stop and think. But she didn't come up with any specific reason, did she? She couldn't expect me to break up with him just because of her gut feeling. And anyway, even if I'd had one or two concerns back then, would that really have been enough to stop me marrying him? Probably not, is the honest answer. I would have convinced myself there was nothing to worry about. Or maybe - the biggest self-delusion of all - that I would be able to change him.

So, for better or worse, I married him. Only then did I begin to detect a subtle change in his behaviour. It was only slight at first. A hint of irritation; a brusque correction; a sharp glance. Just enough for me to notice, but not quite enough to start an argument. At first, I was reluctant to make a fuss in case these changes in Henry and in our relationship were somehow *my* fault; the result of something I had said or done - or not done. Or that it was because I had changed. So, I decided the best thing to do was to keep quiet. I resigned myself to what I assumed were the realities of married life, and threw myself into my work once again. Weren't all marriages like this anyway? A triumph of hope over experience. Was that the phrase? Or was that only for second marriages? I can't remember.

Even though the honeymoon period was beginning to lose its sparkle, I still loved Henry. I didn't want to lose him. I was determined not to fail. And there was absolutely no way I could admit to mum that I'd made a mistake. So, I would just have to keep my mouth shut and make the best of it.

And that's exactly what I was doing. But then the thing with Isabella changed everything. I really don't think I was over-reacting or being unreasonable or ridiculous or emotional or hormonal - or any of the other things that Henry accused me of. It wasn't me that did anything wrong. I wasn't the guilty party. Why should I apologise for anything? He was the one who …

Sorry about the rant. It makes me so mad to think about all the things he said back then. Anyway, I've calmed down now so let me tell you exactly what happened and then you can judge for yourself, rather than taking my word for it.

I'm hoping you will agree with me though.

Isabella's name first appeared on my radar not long after I met Henry. I was already falling under his spell and ingratiating myself into his social circle.

"I've been invited to a birthday party on Saturday," he said.

I was a bit confused. When he said *I've* been invited, did he mean that he wanted me to go with him? Or was he going to wait for me to ask if I could come too? Self-confidence wasn't exactly one of my strengths. I think Henry had already figured that out about me. Maybe he was toying with me, and wanted to make me ask.

"So, am I invited?"

"Sorry, yes, of course. I sort of assumed you would want to come with me. I already said yes for both of us."

I suppose I should have made a fuss about him saying yes without even asking me first, but what was the point? I couldn't have it both ways. Obviously, I wanted to go with him, so why make a fuss? It might have been nice if he'd asked me though …

"Oh right. Whose birthday is it?"

"Isabella. It's her thirtieth."

"Isabella?"

"Yes, you know: Isabella. She owns that art gallery in Woodstock. I'm sure I've mentioned her before."

No, he hadn't.

I've tortured myself a million times since with her name, and I'm still absolutely convinced that day was the first time he'd ever mentioned her. I think I would have known when I first heard her name. Anyway, it's a name I won't forget in a hurry now.

Of course, back then, the only thing that mattered to me was that Henry did want me to go with him. It didn't really bother me whether I'd heard Isabella's name before or not; at least, not enough to make an argument out of it.

"Oh right, yes, maybe you did."

"I'm sure you will like her. Everyone likes Isabella."

Henry was certainly right about that. Everyone liked Isabella; especially me. She was just one of those people. No-one could resist being drawn to her, and I was no different. I was seduced by her charms. It wasn't just her physical appearance - the first thing I noticed was her beautiful dark brown eyes. It was that when you were with her, she had that amazing ability to make you feel incredibly special. Her eyes and her smile captivated and entranced you. She was fun, alluring, slightly mysterious. Her mind was open, uninhibited, almost wild. She was intoxicating to be with. And when you didn't have her full attention, you desperately craved it. It's impossible to fully explain the effect that Isabella had on me - even that very first time I met her. This will probably sound ridiculous, but it would be no exaggeration to say that I think I fell in love with her.

I began to see a lot of Isabella over the coming days and weeks. Henry wasn't too keen on most of my friends, old or new. But he didn't object to me spending time with Isabella. In fact, I'd go so far as to say he actively encouraged my friendship with her. I never stopped to ask myself why. I enjoyed being with Isabella, so I didn't really care about Henry's motives All that mattered was that she was *my* friend now.

I couldn't keep any secrets from Isabella; I didn't want to. I told her absolutely everything - including what was going on between Henry and me. I wanted her to know everything about me. She was a good listener. It wasn't just one way either. Isabella shared her most private thoughts and fears with me. Just like so many other superficially confident and extrovert people, she had some truly dark secrets of her own. Eighteen months ago, after a particularly intense and passionate affair with a married man - one of her many artist friends - she tried to kill herself. Overdose. She told me some other things too; things about her past which she'd long kept buried in the deep recesses of her mind. Things which to this day, I have never - and would never - repeat to a living soul. Even after what she did to me.

In a perverse, perhaps rather selfish way, I was grateful for her private revelations. They made me feel more confident about myself, and more intimate with her. I have no idea if Henry already knew about Isabella's past, but I wasn't going to be the one to tell him. That's not what you do to a friend, is it? They were her secrets; not mine. And definitely not Henry's.

When I told you about my wedding, I forgot to mention what happened about my bridesmaids. I'd only ever wanted Elena as my bridesmaid; she was basically my oldest friend. However, on the spur of the moment, I had decided to ask Isabella too. So, then when Elena wasn't able to come, fortunately I still had Isabella as my sole bridesmaid. Henry suggested that if I still wanted two, I could ask his sister, Caroline. I'll tell you about her later, but for now, let's just say *over my dead body* was that ever going to happen.

When Henry and I first met, we were living on opposite sides of Oxford, each renting over-priced one-bedroom flats, badly neglected by their landlords. It wasn't long before we started looking for something to buy together. Isabella knew of a recently-renovated two-bedroom apartment which was coming onto the market shortly. She was a friend of the vendor and put in a good word for us. It was just off Walton Street in Jericho, only five minutes from both the OUP head office where Henry worked, and from my office in the Maths Institute. The central location meant we could easily walk into town or meet up with friends whenever we wanted. Also, rather conveniently, Isabella's own terrace house was just around the corner - did I mention her parents were absolutely loaded? She didn't really need to work at all.

So, there I was; new city, new job, new husband, new best friend, new apartment. What's not to like - as they say.

Admittedly, the gloss had started to peel off my relationship with Henry, but when I discovered I was pregnant, I dared to dream that everything would work itself out after all.

Then I found out about Henry and Isabella.

Chapter 3

Let's deal with the baby first. Forget the other thing for now; I'll get to that in a minute.

I decided to tell Isabella my news first. I knew I could count on her to be really excited for me. I wasn't so sure about Henry or mum. I say that, but I knew exactly what mum would think.

Isabella was often home early on a Friday afternoon. Come to think of it, the opening hours of her gallery were always something of a mystery. I wasn't convinced it was ever really open, except for private viewings. Anyway, when she came to the door and saw me standing there, she looked a bit startled. She was still fumbling with the final button on the long white shirt which she must have thrown over her skinny body. Even so, she looked gorgeous - as always. Why do some women just have it? It's not fair, is it?

"Sorry, are you busy?" I asked.

"No, no, come on in. Sorry, Katy, I just wasn't expecting you. I thought you would still be at work."

"Have I come at a bad time? Were you expecting someone else?"

If she was, she gave no clue.

"No, no, it's lovely to see you."

She quickly recovered herself, locked onto me with one of her trademark hugs, and dragged me into the kitchen with her. I plonked myself down in my usual spot: on the white wooden rocking chair by the window. I picked up one of her pastel-coloured cushions from the window seat and placed it across my lap.

"I'll get you a glass of something. Red?" Isabella said, grabbing an already-open bottle off the granite worktop.

"Actually, can I just have tea, thanks."

"Tea? It's Friday afternoon for fuck's sake."

"Sorry, it's just … well … I'm …"

Our eyes met on the pastel cushion. She guessed in a flash.

"Holy fuck. A baby. That's fantastic, Katy. Congratulations."

She smothered me in hugs and kisses and placed her hand gently on my stomach. She seemed a little disappointed when she couldn't feel any movement, until I told her that I'd literally only just found out at lunchtime. She wanted to know absolutely everything; every tiny detail. Once her questions were finally exhausted - as was I answering them - she suddenly looked serious.

"Does Henry know?"

"No, not yet; you're the first person I've told."

"Oh, that makes me feel really special, thank you."

I could see her getting quite emotional; close to tears. Then she said something quite strange.

"It is Henry's, I assume?"

I just laughed. After a few awkward seconds, she started to laugh too.

"Sorry, just wanted to check. You never know these days," she said, as if it didn't matter either way.

Henry still wasn't home when I arrived back two hours later, so I called mum.

"Mum, I've got some good news."

Given what she thought of Henry, I wasn't convinced she would agree it was good news.

"Oh, right, what is it, darling? What's happened?"

"I'm pregnant."

I waited for her reaction. I think she must have been slightly stunned because she didn't say anything for several seconds. It was rare for her to be speechless.

"Mum, are you still there?"

"Sorry, yes, I'm just … wow that's amazing … congratulations."

"Yes, I'm really excited."

"What did Henry say?"

"He doesn't know yet. I'm going to tell him when he gets home."

"Oh, right. Do you think he'll be pleased?"

"I hope so. Why wouldn't he be?"

"No reason. Yes, he should be very happy."

I decided not to tell mum that I'd already shared my news with Isabella. Although I think she quite liked Isabella, she found her a bit overwhelming; almost intimidating. Besides, it would be nice for mum to believe that she was the first to know.

Now that I was pregnant, I desperately needed mum. I told her I'd go and see her over the weekend and give her all the details. Once she got used to the idea that I was going to be a mother - and she was going to be a grandmother - she seemed to fully embrace it. It made me so sad and so ashamed to think how I'd been neglecting her recently.

Henry was back late. He started telling me about some marketing crisis at the office, but I wasn't listening. I was waiting for an opportunity to tell him my news; our news. I couldn't wait any longer. I had to interrupt him.

"Henry, I'm pregnant. We're going to have a baby."

He stopped mid-sentence and went pale.

"Right … wow … that's …"

"Amazing," I prompted.

"Yes, amazing. Come here you."

He pulled me towards him and gave me a long deep kiss.

"Are you absolutely sure?"

"Yes, I did a pregnancy test; it's definite."

"Oh, right. Well, that's great news. When did you find out?"

"Lunchtime."

"Have you told anyone else yet?"

"I phoned mum about half an hour ago, while I was waiting for you to come home."

He looked a bit miffed that he hadn't been the first to know. I decided not to mention that I'd also told Isabella. So, he was actually the third to know … fourth if you count me.

"Oh, right, and what did she say?"

"Yes, she's really pleased. She loves the idea of having a grandchild."

"I guess I should let my mother know too."

He picked up his mobile and called her. I was relieved to hear him talking enthusiastically about the baby. I hadn't known what reaction to expect; whether he'd even be happy. That doesn't say much for my confidence in our relationship, does it?

Henry secretly arranged a romantic weekend in the Cotswolds for us to celebrate our news. He still seemed genuinely excited. He told every single member of the hotel staff who was willing to listen. He was as passionate and attentive as ever, and for a short while, it was like the early days of our romance. The baby seemed to be working some magic, and bringing us closer together again.

But it didn't last.

About two weeks later, something drastically changed in Henry's behaviour. It was like a switch in his brain was suddenly flipped. He became very distant; secretive almost. Every little thing that didn't quite go his way, irritated him beyond belief. He started working late during the week, and spending more time at the golf course at the weekends. I tried to be understanding and rationalise this change in his behaviour; explain it away; make excuses. He had a lot on his plate at work and an emotional wife at home. He was dreading the additional financial pressure once I went on maternity leave. Stupidly, I didn't challenge him or ask him what the problem was. I suppose I was afraid that he might say it was *me* that was the problem.

When I talked to mum, I pretended everything was fine. She probably guessed that it wasn't, but didn't want us to fall out and push me closer to Henry.

The thing I found hardest to accept was that Henry just seemed to lose interest in our baby. He simply stopped asking me about my pregnancy. It was like a non-topic from his perspective. And whenever I tried to talk to him about it, he made only a half-hearted attempt to engage. I got really excited when I found out it was a baby girl we were expecting, but when I told Henry, he just looked disappointed. It sounded like he would have preferred a boy. The way he was talking, it was almost as if I had failed. It felt like he was losing interest in me too.

Wake up Katy! He's having an affair. It's so obvious. Why can't you recognise the signs? They're all there, staring you in the face. How can you be so blind?

If that's what you were thinking, I don't blame you. I don't know what to say in my defence. I feel so stupid that I couldn't see it. I told myself that I was obsessing about my pregnancy; that I was being far too needy; that it was unreasonable to expect Henry to be as emotionally engaged as me; that I should stop worrying about everything and get on with my life. After all, hundreds of babies are born every day, aren't they? So, why expect a big fuss about my baby? Was there really anything to worry about?

I didn't have to wait long to find out.
One Saturday afternoon, when Henry was out playing golf again, Isabella came round to see me. Strangely, for once, she didn't throw herself down theatrically on the sofa. She looked very subdued; not her usual self at all.
"Is something the matter?" I asked.
She was distracted; edgy.
"I'm fine," she said, adding a weak smile.
If Isabella had something to tell me, I knew she would get round to it in her own time. There was no point in pressing her. Instead, I started to pour my heart out about something Henry had said - or not said - about the baby. I don't remember exactly what. Suddenly I noticed she was crying.

"I can't do this anymore," she mumbled in a flood of tears.

Given what I knew of Isabella's past, I was afraid to ask the obvious question.

"Look, Isabella, you know that whatever it is, you can tell me about it," I said.

"No, you don't understand. I *have* to tell you about it. I don't … oh God, you are going to hate me for ever. What have I done?"

Now I was seriously worried.

"What have you done?"

She looked away and shook her head. Slowly she turned her face back towards me and locked me with her eyes full of tears.

"I slept with Henry."

Her voice was dull and flat, but the sharp pain those four words inflicted on my heart is as raw now as it was then. As her words sank in, I felt sick; numb. I slumped back in my chair and stared into the gulf between us. I couldn't bring myself to look into her eyes. When? Where? Why? So many questions began to rear their ugly heads, but I couldn't ask them. I couldn't speak to her. My head throbbed. I couldn't think.

"I am so sorry, Katy. I am so sorry."

She moved towards me, but I put my hand up as if to fend her away.

"I think you should leave," I heard myself say.

"No, please don't say that. Just let me try to explain …"

There was no point; there *was* no explanation. Nothing could make it right.

"I think you should leave," I repeated.

She didn't try to say anything else. I stood up to open the front door for her, and looked away. As she passed me, she flung her arms around me and pressed her face against mine. I could feel the wetness of her tears on my cheek.

But I did not react. I was stone cold to her.

"I am so sorry, Katy. I don't know how you can ever forgive me but please …"

I couldn't find any words to say to her. I knew there was no way I could ever forgive her. She had done the one thing a best friend would never do. The one thing there is no coming back from.

I closed the door on her and stood there shaking. After several minutes - I don't know how long - I went into the kitchen and poured myself a glass of water and took two paracetamol. I lay down on the bed in the spare room and hugged a pillow into my stomach. I cried and sobbed until it seemed like I had no tears left. Even then, I could not sleep. My skull was splitting; crushed by the weight of so many unanswered questions.

As I lay there utterly distraught, my anger, slowly and surely, began to turn against Henry. Deep down, something told me that this was *his* fault. Yes, of course, Isabella was a guilty party. But, no matter how close we were, she was just a friend. Whereas Henry was my husband and the father of my baby. He was supposed to love me. He was never supposed to do this to me. It was unforgivable. I hated him with every fibre of my body.

Did I already suspect something? That's the question you want to ask me, isn't it? Did I already have some doubts, or did I honestly have no idea? Was I really so stupid, or was I just hopelessly naïve? Those are exactly the questions I began tormenting myself with as I lay there. I didn't have the courage to answer them. How could I? Why should I? I wasn't the one with questions to answer. It was him.

Oddly, the only question I didn't ask myself, was whether the revelation that Isabella had just made, was true. Not for a single moment did I doubt that Henry was guilty as charged. I didn't wait to hear his side of the story. I didn't need to. I knew he had done it. That should have told me everything I needed to know about the state of our relationship.

"What the hell are you doing in here?" I heard Henry asking.

I sat up slowly but couldn't look him directly in the eye.

"I've been calling you. Why are you hiding here in the spare room?"

He put his hand on my cheek and turned my face towards him.

"Have you been crying?"

Still, I didn't answer him.

"What is it now? It's not about the baby again, is it?"

"Isabella told me," I said.

"What? Isabella told you what?"

I didn't want to have to say it. I couldn't say it. I wanted him to admit it. Why didn't he just admit it? Damn him!

"You mean about the job in London?" he said after a moment.

"What? No. Sorry, what job in London? What?"

"You're not making any sense, Katherine."

"Isabella told me about you and her," I said coldly.

"Me and her? Sorry? What? I don't know what you're talking about."

The cheating bastard was making me say it. I wanted to slap him; to punch him; to kick him.

"Isabella told me you slept with her."

"What?"

"Isabella told me *you slept with her*," I repeated, enunciating each word slowly and carefully so there was no confusion - and no escape for Henry.

"Slept with her! What? That's ridiculous," he said, making a sort of exasperated gasping noise through his mouth.

It almost sounded like he was laughing. Was he laughing at me? What a bloody nerve.

I leaned forward and slapped him across his smug face as hard as I could. He raised his hand. For a moment I thought he was going to hit me. But then he checked himself and put his arm down again, slowly. He just stared at me.

"Look, Katherine, I don't know what she's been telling you, but I did not sleep with her. Right?"

My mind was spinning. None of this made any sense. One second I was accusing him of cheating on me; the next, I couldn't even be sure it happened. The cross-examination I'd been planning was in tatters. I needed some time to think before I said anything else.

"You've got to believe me, Katherine."

Why would Isabella lie?

"If you didn't sleep with her, then why would she say that you did?"

"I honestly don't know. Your guess is as good as mine. What state was she in? Was she drunk?"

"No, she was stone cold sober."

"Has something happened to her, do you think? You know she's had a lot of mental health problems, don't you?"

What was happening? I was still wrestling with Henry's denial. Why were we talking about Isabella's problems? That's not what I wanted to be talking about right now. What was I supposed to do with my anger? I was ready to explode.

"So, you are telling me, absolutely categorically, that you did not sleep with her."

"Yes, that's right, absolutely. I did not sleep with Isabella."

I felt foolish; deflated; embarrassed. I'd automatically assumed he was guilty and launched straight into attack mode.

"I don't understand. Why would she make it up?"

"I already said; I don't know."

"Something must have happened to make her say what she did. Is she upset with me for some reason? Or you?"

"Not that I'm aware of."

I tried to think of other possible explanations for Isabella's strange behaviour. Just then, I remembered what she'd told me about her past, and immediately started to panic. What if she did something; something terrible. I would never forgive myself.

"Oh God, I threw her out. I need to go and see her," I said.

Henry suddenly looked agitated.

"Maybe it's better if I go round and see her tomorrow when she's calmed down."

"I just think …"

"I don't want you getting even more upset, especially in your current condition," he said.

I think, by *current condition*, he meant being pregnant - as if that was some sort of illness!

"Do you think Isabella will be alright on her own tonight?"

"Look, don't worry about Isabella. I'm sure she'll be fine."

"But shouldn't we at least check up on her?"

"You need to take care of yourself. You and the baby are the priority right now. How about if I go and run you a nice bath so you can relax?"

Relax! Was he fucking joking? How in God's name was I supposed to relax? There was not the remotest chance of that happening. My head was tight; my neck and shoulders ached; my mind was racing all over the place. The more I thought about what Isabella told me, the more I was confused.

If Isabella was telling the truth, then not only had Henry been unfaithful - which was bad enough in itself - but he had lied about it to my face too. The consequences of such a double betrayal were almost too awful to contemplate. Not only that, but I would also have lost Isabella as my closest friend. Although she had the decency to confess and apologise, that didn't mean I could forgive her for the deed itself.

On the other hand, if Henry was telling the truth, then I needed to know what had prompted Isabella to say the crazy thing that she just had. If there was some rational explanation - although I couldn't think of one - then I wanted to hear it. She had been my best friend, after all. Shouldn't I give her the benefit of the doubt? Maybe there was some way she could still be my friend.

Who should I believe? Who should I trust? Initially, I found myself coming down firmly on the side of Isabella - which didn't say a lot for my marriage. In the end though, I decided I didn't have enough evidence either way.

It also occurred to me that letting Henry talk to Isabella on his own, was a very bad idea. Of course, I would have to talk to her myself at some point, but I couldn't face that conversation right now. I couldn't talk to mum either. I knew exactly what she would say. Basically, I just wanted to make it all go away, but I didn't know how to.

As Henry came into the bathroom to check up on me, I remembered something else he'd said earlier. It would avoid the awkwardness of the other topic.

"What was that you said earlier about a job in London?" I asked.

"Oh, it's nothing really; a call from a head-hunter."

"You never mentioned it."

"I just forgot to tell you."

I was tempted say that he hadn't forgotten to tell *her*.

"Well, what's the job anyway?"

"VP of Marketing for a publishing company in central London. It actually sounds quite interesting. They're going to email me some details on Monday."

"I didn't realise you were looking for a new job."

"I'm not really."

"I thought you were happy at OUP. And you haven't exactly been there very long."

"I've been there long enough to know there isn't much opportunity for me in the near future. And the money with this job in London would be a lot better."

"Yes, but you'd have to travel into London every day."

"I do realise that, Katherine. Anyway, I haven't definitely decided to go for it, so there's no point interrogating me right now."

He was obviously getting defensive, so I decided to back off. I'd had more than enough stress for one day. I felt absolutely worn out, and although I knew I wouldn't be able to sleep if I went to bed, I couldn't face staying up and talking to Henry. I didn't want to listen to his bullshit anymore tonight. I didn't know if I could trust what he might say about Isabella - or anything else, for that matter.

I recalled how mum said there was something about Henry she didn't trust. And that was based purely on her first meeting. So how come I was only just sensing the same now? How did I completely miss all the signs? Realising that mum was probably right all along annoyed me even more.

"I'm going to bed, Henry. I'm feeling completely drained."

"Don't we need to talk about …?"

"Yes, we do, but I can't face it right now. I'm just too exhausted."

After a terrible night, I was up early on Sunday morning. I had no idea what time Henry came to bed, but he was fast asleep now. I knew Isabella was not an early morning person at the best of times, especially at weekends, but I called her mobile on the off chance. She didn't pick up. I didn't leave a message. What I needed to say was far too complicated for a voicemail, and I wanted to look into her eyes when I heard what she had to say. Anyway, she would see the missed call from me. She knew where to find me, if and when she wanted to talk.

Despite my protests, Henry insisted that he was going to see her straight after lunch. He was out for quite a while, so I assumed they were having a long and deep talk. However, when he returned, he said Isabella was not at home and there was no sign of her car either.

"So, what took you so long? What have you been doing?"

"I just needed to go for a walk along the river to clear my head."

That was exactly what I needed too. But I didn't want to go for a walk with Henry - or do anything else with him. I just wanted to be left alone. I *needed* to be left alone to think. I wasn't ready to make any decisions; at least not yet.

Over the next few days, Henry and I somehow managed to avoid the subject of Isabella or what she had said. I tried phoning her again a couple of times, but eventually gave up when she didn't answer or return any of my calls.

I literally didn't know what to do. What could I do? I still didn't know the truth about whether anything happened between Henry and Isabella. And even if I did, what options did I have? I was married to Henry; we owned the apartment together; I was pregnant with his child; I would be on maternity leave before too long. I was trapped.

What I needed was a real friend to talk things over with. But I didn't have one. Like I said at the start, that's often the problem for women like us. Never a real friend close by when you most need them. I felt like I literally had no-one that I could talk to.

So, I was trapped *and* I had no-one to talk to. Having a showdown with Henry was out of the question; there was no way I was strong enough for that. I would have to bide my time and wait for something to happen.

Chapter 4

And so, I waited. And waited. Henry assumed I had calmed down - to use his patronising phrase. But my anger had not subsided. I was a dormant volcano; not an extinct one. For the time being, we fell back into a sort of meaningless routine together, each stepping uncomfortably around the deep shell-hole in our relationship.

Henry took the job in London. He didn't bother to consult me and I didn't care. We left the centre of Oxford, and bought a non-descript house in a small rural village about twenty miles south of the city. Henry called it a fresh start. At least there was no chance of bumping into Isabella down there. He started working even longer hours in the office, and spending even more time playing golf at the weekends. Not seeing too much of him, helped keep my anger at bay. But it had absolutely not gone away.

My sole focus became the imminent arrival of our daughter - or as I increasingly thought of her, *my* daughter. Henry was totally disengaged from the whole pre-natal process; he never asked anything. I couldn't help wondering how much interest he would show if it was Isabella having his baby. Anyway, the truth is I just had to accept his lack of interest and involvement. In many ways, it made things easier for me.

For one thing, it left room for mum. She was only too willing to help in any way she could throughout my pregnancy. Nothing was too much trouble. I had totally misjudged her response. When I tried to tell her how sorry I was about the way I had treated her, she just said that she understood and that I shouldn't worry about it. I should have known she wouldn't blame me or hold a grudge. It just shows how much my frame of reference had been warped by Henry. Spending so much time with mum brought the two of us very close again, like we used to be. That was the silver lining to my exceedingly dark cloud.

I don't know what I was expecting from Henry when our baby girl was born. Would it change things between us? Would it change anything at all? I wasn't naïve enough to think everything would now be magical, but I did expect him to mellow a little.

I was completely wrong. Beth's arrival seemed, if anything, to make him colder, almost hostile, towards me. Of course, I'd read all about how fathers can sometimes become jealous of a new-born baby, but this was different. It was controlled and deliberate.

Let me give you an example: Mother's Day.

For some reason, Henry was adamant that we should spend it with *his* mother. Given that he hadn't bothered on either of the two previous occasions since I'd known him - and that his relationship with his mother was, at best, indifference, and at worst, intolerance - I knew he was just being difficult.

"You can see your mother any day you want, now that you aren't working," he said.

He was being deliberately provocative. He knew that describing looking after a new-born baby as *not working* made my blood boil. I didn't rise to the bait - which probably annoyed him. Instead, I tried reasoning.

"Yes, but this is Mother's Day; it not just *any* day. It's special."

"It's not that special. It's just a marketing creation."

I was sure I'd read something about Mothering Sunday being based on an old religious tradition, recently revived. But if I'd had the temerity to mention this little factoid, he would have accused me of being a know-it-all. He absolutely hated it when I knew something he didn't. For that reason alone, University Challenge was banned in our house.

Of course, his statement had now opened him up to another dose of reasoning.

"So, if it's not that special, why does it matter where we spend it?"

"It doesn't. I just think it's only fair we see my mother for once."

"What about me? What about what I want? I'm a mother too."

"Well, you're not *my* mother," he snapped.

Not for the first time, I simply gave up the fight. It wasn't worth the effort. I didn't have the same need to be right all the time like he did. Once I'd stopped fighting, he backed off. The compromise we eventually settled on was that first thing in the morning, Henry and I would take Beth for a walk on our own. Then Henry's parents and sister would drive over and join us for lunch at a local pub. Finally, in the late afternoon, we would call in for tea with my mum. I was also under the impression - misguided, as it turned out - that we'd agreed on a reasonably equal allocation of time for each activity.

The walk along the towpath was going peacefully enough until a passing dog jumped up at Henry and left muddy paw marks on his cotton chinos. To make matters worse, Henry sensed the faint hint of a claw mark at the top of his left thigh. A furious shouting and swearing match with the dog's owner ensued, which achieved little. By the end, Henry felt he had made his point and obtained a satisfactory apology from the *dickhead* - his favourite word again. Even so, he continued to mutter the phrase *bloody inconsiderate dickhead* under his breath throughout the rest of the day.

His trousers were still dirty though, and despite my advice to let the mud dry and then simply brush it off, he insisted on trying to clean it off with a baby wipe. Even a rudimentary knowledge of nappy changing, would have told him this was bound to end badly. The oily stain by his crotch in those chinos never came out. No reasonable person could possibly say that any of this was my fault, but that didn't stop Henry twisting the story. By the time he told it over lunch, he claimed to have sacrificed himself to prevent the dog from jumping up on me, and I had suggested using the baby wipes.

Lunch was a total disaster. Beth wouldn't settle in the busy, noisy pub. I spent most of the time holding her on my knee and soothing her, whilst simultaneously trying - and failing - to eat my lunch. It should have been blindingly obvious to Henry that I was hating every minute, but he continued drinking and chatting idly. The only help I received was unsolicited advice, most of which implied I was a bad mother. When Beth's crying became too much for the complaining couple at the table next to us, Henry encouraged me to leave them all in peace. I had no option but to take Beth outside, and push the pram up and down the dreary car park.

Despite the fact that Henry knew mum was preparing afternoon tea for us, he insisted on having a huge dessert with extra clotted cream. When we finally, finally, emerged from the pub, Henry's mother suggested we went for a short stroll to walk off the heavy lunch. By now, the light was fading and it was already well past the time we agreed to be at mum's house. I wanted to scream.

When we eventually got in the car, I was seething.

"What's the matter?" Henry said, as if he had no idea. "Cheer up; it is Mother's Day after all."

I was ready to explode but just gritted my teeth and stared straight ahead.

Henry made absolutely zero effort with mum. His contribution to the conversation was negligible. He said he was *too stuffed* to eat anything and spent most of the time playing with his phone. He did graciously accept a cup of tea, handed to him as he slouched in mum's favourite Parker Knoll chair - with the leather sole of one shoe perched on the edge of her mahogany coffee table. I can't tell you how much I wanted to kick it off.

Afterwards, as I was trying to enjoy a nice quiet chat with mum - who was holding a now-tranquil baby in her lap - I could see Henry constantly fidgeting and looking at the clock.

"We should be going soon, Katherine," he hinted.

"Yes, probably," I said, but didn't make any immediate effort to get up.

Why should I, after the way he'd behaved? However, a moment's reflection told me it was going to be better for me if we did make a move, sooner rather than later. It would reduce the acrimony and recrimination later.

"God, I thought we would never escape," Henry sighed as we drove off.

It was just as well that I was busy putting Beth to bed when we arrived home, and that Henry had something to do in his study before Monday morning. I simply couldn't have been in the same place as him right then.

And did I mention he hadn't even bothered to buy me a Mother's Day card on behalf of our daughter? What a total fucking shit.

So what, you might be thinking. Your life isn't *that* bad. What are you complaining about? At least you have a husband. Even if he is a total fucking shit and might have slept with your best friend. And you have a daughter. Even if Henry doesn't show any interest in her. And a good job. Even if Henry doesn't respect it. And somewhere nice to live. Even if it's not so convenient for getting into work now. But come on, it's not *that* bad. Not compared to the lives some people have to endure. So why don't you just put up with it?

Well, that's exactly what I am trying to do: put up with it. I suppose, all things considered, my life isn't *that* bad. I made my choices. I got what I deserved for rushing into marrying Henry and ditching my friends. Now, I have to lie in the bed I made for myself.

So yes, perhaps I should just *put up with it*.

Chapter 5

Everything has changed in the past 48 hours. *Everything.*

Put up with it is no longer an option. I need to *do* something about it. But what? What am I going to do about it?

Before I do anything, I need to slow down. Take a deep breath. And then another. I need to tell you exactly what happened.

Most of it is still a blur, but this is what I do remember.

Sunday

She must have come up behind me as I stepped out of the cold stone porch, immediately after the christening. I was momentarily dazzled by the bright sunlight outside and didn't see her approach, but I suddenly felt the gentlest of touches on my arm; no more than the brush of a butterfly's wing. Instinctively, I turned my head. I had no idea who she was. I didn't even know if she was in the church during the christening. Just then, I realised that she was earnestly pressing something - a note or a piece of paper or something - into my hand and wrapping my fingers over it. She put her mouth close to my ear. Her perfume was familiar. She whispered only a handful of words, and then, before I could react to her scarcely audible question, she suddenly dipped her head and scurried away. And that was it; it was over.

I had no time to register any details of the nervous face framed between the large-brimmed blue hat and the turned-up collar of her woollen coat. I could only gape after her as she rushed down the uneven flagstone path between the leaning gravestones, and disappeared out through the lychgate and along the road. It all happened so quickly; she was gone.

Despite the brevity of my encounter with the stranger, I already understood her haste. She was scared of something, of someone - and I thought I knew who. Her furtive behaviour compelled me to act with similar caution; to hide the envelope - it was a small white envelope that she put in my hand - until I could open it in private. I needed to be discreet and to suppress my curiosity until I could find a moment - a rare moment - away from prying eyes. If nothing else, my experiences over the past two years had taught me that.

35

The wait for a suitable opportunity was interminable; the nervous feeling in the pit of my stomach, unbearable. I couldn't concentrate on anything while endless baby photographs were taken, and the procession of assembled friends and relatives crawled back to the house. Eventually, I managed to escape and slip upstairs, seemingly unnoticed. Closing the bedroom door quietly, I retrieved the envelope from the baby changing bag where I'd concealed it.

I held it in front of me, and turned it back and forth slowly. There was no name or address; no clue at all. The identity of the woman was a complete mystery. And there was no way of knowing what I would find inside or what it might mean. For a few moments, I held back, afraid. But then my need to know overcame my fear. My hands were shaking and I could feel my temples throbbing.

I unsealed the flap cautiously and peered into the envelope. It looked empty. Was this some sort of cruel joke? Then I noticed the tiny newspaper cutting, creased and dog-eared, cowering in the corner. I pulled it out carefully so as not to rip it, and rotated it upright in front of me. My eyes opened wide as I read down the column of black words under the bleak heading.

LOCAL GIRL FEARED DROWNED
Annie Wilson, 22, from Lyme Regis is missing, feared drowned. Annie, a final year student at London University, was on study leave and home for the weekend visiting her mother. She was last seen late on the evening of Saturday 12 May, walking on top of The Cobb. Her car, a blue VW Polo, was later found abandoned nearby. Inspector Peter Collins, who is leading the inquiry, said: "There was a strong gale blowing on Saturday night, and we believe Annie may have been swept into the sea. However, at this stage, we cannot rule out other possible explanations for her disappearance. We would like to hear from anyone who has seen or spoken to Annie in the last few days." Police investigations are continuing.

I read the story again and again, each time with a growing sense of foreboding. The words became jumbled on the paper and in my head. I stared into space, eyes unfocused, mind floating. The story of the girl's drowning was tragic enough, but it was the mysterious woman's whispered words that consumed me now:

"Did your husband tell you what happened to Annie Wilson?"

Over the past few months, I had tried to rebuild my relationship with Henry. If not for my sake, then at least for Beth's. I kept telling myself that, rather than expecting Henry to change, I should just accept him for who he was, and make the best of it. But now, the woman in the churchyard had tossed a hand-grenade into my life, shattering any illusion that I knew him at all. Everything was broken.

As I slumped on the edge of the bed, attempting to make sense of something - of anything - I heard the rustle of the bedroom door handle behind me and knew it would be Henry. Foolishly, I had not locked myself in the bathroom this time, like I normally did when I needed to be alone. I frantically stuffed the clipping and envelope under the corner of the mattress and out of sight.

I sat up straight, rubbed my eyes and cheeks and took a deep breath, waiting for the criticism that was surely coming.

"Why the hell are you hiding in here? I've been looking everywhere for you."

For a moment, I was tempted to say something sarcastic about the massive effort that must have gone into finding me in our bedroom, but what was the point? I knew it was best to keep my thoughts to myself and my mouth firmly shut - and just be grateful that he hadn't actually caught me reading the newspaper cutting. I stood up with as much grace as I could muster and turned to face him, trying to look calm and collected, whilst my insides churned like boiling acid. I could see the muscles around his jaw set firm, so I prudently chose apologetic mode.

"Sorry, Henry, I just needed to get something from our room."

Fortunately, he didn't ask what I needed, nor did he seem to care. The sole purpose of his mission was to restore me to my rightful place by his side for today's social occasion. To him, appearance was everything, however deceptive it might be.

"Everyone is waiting for you. Mum thinks there's something the matter with you."

I wanted to shout at him. There *is* something the matter with me. *Annie Wilson.* Who the hell is Annie Wilson? What happened to her? What did you do to her? My whole body was trembling; my mind screaming. However, over the past two years, I'd learned to bury my emotions somewhere deep inside me. I had to stop him from knowing what was going on in my head right now. I barely knew myself. So, the best strategy was contrition - or at least the appearance of contrition. Fortunately, he didn't come close enough, nor was he attentive enough, to notice the slight redness of my eyes or anything else unusual in my demeanour.

"Sorry," I repeated.

"Could you hurry up then?" he said, hovering menacingly in the doorway.

How things had changed since that first romantic encounter in the doorway of the Oxford café. Dutifully I followed him back down the staircase and through the hallway into the living room. He was smiling now for the benefit of our guests. It always came so easily to him; the schmoozing. His confident and engaging manner could charm anyone when he felt like it. It certainly worked its magic on me when we first met.

By contrast, my social interactions seemed rather hesitant and angular. It hadn't always been like that, but these days, even an innocuous invitation to a drinks party, filled me with terror. Clutching a glass of wine in one hand, and making small-talk with strangers - while Henry closely supervised me - was not my idea of a good night out. This disparity in our need for an audience was part of the problem; one of the many schisms that had opened up between us like a yawning crevasse. Over the past few months, Henry had made it perfectly clear that he regarded this particular problem as *my* problem. He had actually called me antisocial on more than one occasion recently.

There was one person I was happy to socialise with though.

"Thanks for looking after Beth, mum. How is she?"

We had actually named our baby daughter *Elizabeth*. It was Henry's idea. I think he had some private delusions about a link to English royalty. I preferred a simple, single syllable, name that everyone could spell correctly and that wouldn't need to be shortened or corrupted. My favourite choice was Jane, mum's mother's name - and a name with fine literary associations. He rubbished my suggestion, adding sarcastically that he would have expected someone of my supposed intelligence to be able to handle more than one syllable. His mother was also dead set against using a name from my side of the family. In the end, his stubbornness prevailed and we named her Elizabeth. So that was the name written on her birth certificate, and the name Henry insisted we always use in full.

In private, mum and I called her Beth, the name of the poor young girl I loved most in *Little Women*.

"Sleeping like a baby. She was so good during the christening; she's such a darling."

"Yes, she didn't seem to mind the water at all."

"Perhaps it's a sign. She might be another duck, like you."

She was referring to all the hours I spent in the swimming pool as a child. These days, I felt more like an ugly duckling.

"I don't have much time for swimming at the moment."

"How things have changed. I only wish your dad could have been here today."

I smiled as I always did whenever she mentioned dad - which was quite frequently these days. I knew she missed him terribly. It was ten years since he died, but her grief was still intense. Every year she was on her own without him, only made her loneliness deeper.

"She looks so peaceful, doesn't she? I wish I had the knack like you," I said, aiming to refocus our thoughts on the future rather than the past.

"A lot of new mothers don't find it easy the first time around. You only have to read the books to know that. Don't worry, darling, it will come; it just takes a little time."

"Well, I hope so," I sighed.

"And I don't suppose you get much help from his lordship," she said, jerking her head in the direction of Henry and his entourage.

"Well, he's extremely busy with work at the moment. He's on the train into Paddington before seven, and doesn't get back until after seven most nights."

"And then plays golf most of the weekend. He seems to spend more time at that golf club than he does at home. It must cost a fortune too."

"It's his way of unwinding. He's always been a golf fanatic. I knew that when I met him. I can't expect him to stop playing now. It doesn't bother me really."

I don't know why I still tried to defend him to mum. Perhaps it helped me justify things to myself. She knew perfectly well what Henry was like, and we both knew that she knew. Thankfully, she didn't bother to argue with me.

"Let's forget Henry. How are *you,* Katy? How are you coping, darling?"

She called me Katy, and that was the name on my birth certificate. It was supposedly derived from the Greek word for pure - as I discovered when I was old enough to ask the question. Katy, pure and simple, no pretensions; that's how I liked to think of myself. But most people assumed it must be short for Katherine. Strangely, the only time it bothered me being called Katherine now, at the ripe old age of 30, was when it was *his lordship* doing it. To him perhaps it sounded more dignified, more regal, than Katy. To me, it felt as though he was lengthening my name the way parents do when telling off a naughty child. I think he also found it difficult to cope with the fact that I possessed only a single first name, whereas his family had plenty of names and liked to use them liberally. This was probably why after he'd got his own way with the name Elizabeth, he'd reluctantly agreed to add Jane as a second name.

"I'm fine mum, honestly; I have Beth now," I said trying to reassure her.

"Yes," she said, smiling at me as only a mother can.

"Do you want me to take her now, mum?"

"No, I'm fine darling. I've been on my feet all morning. I'm quite happy sitting here with my beautiful grand-daughter. You go and talk to your friends; enjoy yourself."

"OK, thanks," I said, scanning around the room anxiously for someone I might actually want to talk to.

For one crazy moment, I found myself missing Isabella. What? Yes, I know; how crazy is that? After what she did to me and everything. But I knew she would have absolutely loved being with me today, and I would have loved having her there. Sadly, it couldn't be. Would I ever forgive her? Would we ever be friends again? With every passing day - and especially with today's shock revelation - I wondered if my friendship with Isabella might in fact prove *more* important to me than my relationship with Henry. It seems weird to say such a thing, but that's honestly how I felt. Even worse, I desperately wanted the falling out with Isabella to turn out to be Henry's fault - is that even possible? - so that I could forgive her and we could be friends again. God, if Henry only knew what I was thinking …

Without Isabella at the christening, there were only a couple of other friends for me to choose from, as Henry said he wanted to keep it as an intimate family event. Curiously though, he managed to invite quite a few of his own acquaintances. I wondered which closed-up circle of backs to latch onto, and quickly eliminated the three clusters around Henry, his sister, and his mother. Henry's father, on the other hand, was fairly harmless. He acted as a kind of anti-dote to the dripping poison his wife and daughter spread about me. I knew where to find him. He was guaranteed to be keeping out of the way in the kitchen. I liked to think he was hiding from his wife and daughter, which was probably not far from the truth.

Just then, I sensed someone standing beside me.

"Doctor Harrington, I presume?"

I was not a medical doctor, but I did have a doctorate. Of course, I rarely used the title *Doctor* - and certainly never outside of the academic world. I remember overhearing Henry's mother once making a snide comment about how difficult it was to talk to people with PhDs. I don't know what evidence she based this hypothesis on, as she certainly never made any effort to talk to me.

Harrington was my maiden name, and I decided to continue to use it after my marriage, as all my prior research work was published in this name. It was therefore a key component of my professional reputation. Although this is fairly common practice for women in research and academia, Henry hated it. He expected me to drop my surname and take his. The other option of concatenating my maiden name with Henry's surname to form a double-barrel name was effectively excluded, because Henry already had a double-barrel surname. Of course, when Beth was born, he made a huge fuss about her taking his surname.

"Hi, Malkit. Are you stalking me?"

Someone at work once told me that she thought Malkit fancied me, but I never personally witnessed any evidence. As far as I was concerned, our relationship was friendly but always strictly professional; nothing more. He was generally regarded as a bit of a nerd, although this was probably because his thesis was on a subject so obscure that few mathematicians outside our specific research group even understood the title. However, he did have a great sense of humour and could laugh at himself - unlike someone I could think of.

"Of course I am," he said, moving closer to me. "Apparently some men find pregnant women irresistible."

"Yes, I heard that, but in case you haven't noticed, I'm not actually pregnant anymore."

I ran my hand down the front of my still-not-quite-back-to-shape body. We both laughed. At that moment, I noticed Henry was glaring in my direction with a face that spelled trouble for me later. I quickly put my hand back by my side and suppressed my smile.

"Ah, that explains where that baby over there came from. She is absolutely gorgeous, by the way. That is the correct thing to say about babies, is it not? Absolutely gorgeous."

"Yes, I think that's right. Anyway, thank you for the compliment."

"Are you feeling alright now? I noticed you disappear upstairs for a while, and you looked rather pale when you came back down with Henry."

He was very perceptive. It was nice to know someone was concerned about me and how I felt.

"Oh, yes, I was feeling a bit faint. I think it was all the standing still in the freezing church. But I'm alright now, thank you."

Why did I keep making excuses for Henry?

"Good, good. By the way, who was that woman?" he asked, stepping in even closer so as not to be heard by anyone else.

"What woman?" I whispered, suddenly on guard.

"You know, the one who came up to you outside the church."

I was horrified. Never for a moment had I suspected that anybody else spotted her. Oh God, did that mean Henry also saw her? Was he waiting to confront me about it when everyone else had gone home? I felt sick at the thought.

"I'm not actually sure," I said truthfully. "I don't even know if she was there during the service. I didn't see her until afterwards."

"Oh yes, she was in the church. She was sitting at the back, behind one of the pillars. It was almost as if she was hiding from someone."

"What did she look like?"

"Well, that is the strange thing. She was all dressed up in her hat and coat and everything - and I only got a quick glimpse of her - but … she looked just like you. I suppose that is why I noticed her in the first place."

"Really?"

"Yes, she had straw-coloured hair like yours. I noticed a curl of it poking out from under her hat. And she was about the same height as you."

I recalled the moment she stood beside me and whispered closely in my ear. Yes, he was right about her height.

"Oh, that's interesting, but it must be a coincidence. I think I'd know if I had a twin sister," I said. "In fact, I'm an only child."

I tried to laugh it off.

"It looked like you were the only person she spoke to before she left."

There was absolutely no way I could tell him what she said.

"I think she just wanted to give me her best wishes for the baby - for Beth - oh, and a card."

I added the final part to explain the envelope, in case he saw that too.

"Oh, right," he replied, not sounding totally convinced.

"Anyway, Malkit, I was on my way to find Henry's father," I said, keen to escape the interrogation, especially as Henry was watching me closely now.

"He was in the kitchen a couple of minutes ago."

"I must go and have a word with him. See you later."

Malkit looked a little disappointed and hesitant, probably wondering who else might want to talk to him. He could always try Henry's mother of course; that would certainly make for an interesting conversation, given Malkit's impressive list of academic qualifications, which went well beyond a simple PhD like mine.

"Hello, Katy. How are you?" Henry's father said, clutching my cold fingers between his generous hands.

He called me Katy; I liked him.

"I'm fine, thank you. Did you enjoy the service?"

"Yes, it was wonderful. You must have been very busy organising the food and everything."

"Actually, Mum did most of it."

"Well, she's done us proud. It will be a day to remember."

He was damn right about that, except that the main thing I would remember about the day would be the name Annie Wilson.

Just at that moment, a most unwelcome visitor joined us: Henry's older sister, Caroline.

"Oh dear, you look worn out, Katherine," she said as her opening shot. "Is Elizabeth still keeping you awake all night?"

This criticism was hard to take from someone who did not have a single maternal instinct in her body. She hardly ever looked at Beth, never mind held her.

"No, she's sleeping quite well now actually."

"Oh, right; Henry said you were still having a lot of trouble with her."

I bet he did. The only trouble I had with Beth now, was when Henry had to hold her for some reason. Fortunately, his lack of patience meant that these rare occasions were mercifully short. I decided to fill the awkward silence before she could reload.

"How's Jeremy?" I asked.

I enjoyed provoking her with the name of her soon-to-be-ex-husband. Henry's father obviously sensed things were going to kick off and beat a hasty retreat.

"Fine," she said in a clipped tone that conveyed utter loathing for him - and probably for me too.

Our verbal shoot-out continued until Henry came over and suggested it was time to prepare the glasses and champagne. At the mention of doing some actual work, Caroline made herself scarce and left me to get on with it. A few minutes later, Henry gathered everyone around him and made a toast.

"Katherine and I would like to thank you all for coming to Elizabeth's christening. We are delighted that you could join us for this very special day. For those of you who were at our wedding reception two years ago, you might remember me saying during my speech that I was the luckiest husband in the world, because I have Katherine. Well, now, I can add that I'm also the luckiest father in the world, because I have Elizabeth."

There were polite laughs all round. The elderly woman next to me - one of Henry's ancient aunts, several times removed, I believe - leaned over and congratulated me on being the luckiest wife and luckiest mother in the world too.

Henry was still talking but I was no longer listening. I felt too nauseous, and not just because of the well-worn wedding and christening clichés he was spouting, but because it was all a total pack of lies.

Even if he did genuinely believe himself to be the *luckiest husband* on the actual day of our wedding, his interest in me had now degenerated into barely disguised contempt. I could just about endure this charade, as I was the only real victim. But his *luckiest father* act was too much to stomach. He cared nothing at all for his daughter. Beth deserved so much better than that.

Eventually he finished his loathsome speech and invited us all to join him in a glass of champagne to honour his beautiful daughter. Predictably, there was no invitation for me, Beth's devoted mother, to add a few words of my own. It was probably just as well given my current frame of mind. I don't think I could have kept it together.

Chapter 6

One by one our guests began to depart, and I felt the tension rising in my body as the moment approached when I would be alone with Henry. I sensed the straining muscles in my chest; the dull ache deep down in my gut; the faint unsteadiness in my legs.

Finally, I waved goodbye to mum who had kindly stayed behind to help clear up, and closed the front door on the public face of our lives. I braced myself for what was to come in private.

"Thank God for that. I thought she was never going to leave," Henry said, retrieving his glass and sloshing in a generous helping of red wine. "Do you want a refill?"

"No thanks, I'm fine. I should go and sort Elizabeth out with some milk."

I decided to use her full name so as not to give Henry an easy excuse to start criticising me. That was bound to come later anyway.

"Oh, come on, join me," he urged, pouring a glassful for me anyway, and thrusting it in my face. "I'm sure she can wait five minutes. After all, she's been the centre of attention for the whole bloody day."

Being the centre of attention was, of course, the place he craved for himself. I took the glass and sat down opposite him, but did not venture to say anything.

"Well, everyone had a good time," he began. "All the champagne went, if that's anything to go by."

I was relieved that, so far, his mood seemed benign.

"Yes, they all seemed to enjoy themselves. Mum was ..."

I was not allowed to finish my sentence.

"It's a shame she doesn't join in a bit more. I can see where you get it from; being antisocial. It must be genetic."

"I think she was a bit tired after the past few days. She's been working non-stop on all the preparations. Anyway, she was quite happy sitting with Beth ..."

I saw that look on Henry's face.

"... with Elizabeth, and it gave me chance to circulate a little."

"A little!" he scoffed. "That reminds me. Who was that you were talking to earlier? They were so close up they were practically whispering in your ear."

I froze for a second and felt my face colouring. He must have seen the mysterious woman after all. Should I confess straight away or tell him the same story I gave Malkit? I was caught in two minds.

"And flirting with you," he added.

"Sorry, what?"

"You know, that guy; that guy in the turban," he said.

I was shocked by his rudeness. At the same time, I was extremely relieved that he wasn't alluding to the encounter in the churchyard. Maybe he was saving that for later. He seemed quite irritated by me talking to Malkit. No doubt he considered it an affront to his own ego.

"Oh, Malkit, he's just someone I work with."

47

"Well, I didn't like the way he was looking at you, or telling you that you were absolutely gorgeous. And you were all over him, laughing and joking."

"Don't be silly; he was talking about Elizabeth when he said that. Malkit's harmless. He's actually an amazing mathematician," I said, aiming to deflect the conversation.

"If he's that amazing, he'd be earning a fortune in the city."

"Possibly, but not all brilliant mathematicians want to work for hedge funds."

"What a waste," Henry said.

Presumably he was including my career in this waste bucket.

"Anyway, you don't need to worry about Malkit."

"I'm not *worried* about him, Katherine," Henry corrected me. "I just don't appreciate the way you were flirting with him, that's all."

His over-reaction was laughable, coming as it did, from a man who had systematically pawed his way around most of the young female guests at the christening. But I was in no state to laugh. I had other things on my mind, and top of the list was Annie Wilson.

"I had a good chat with your dad," I said, aiming to lead him in a different direction, but he didn't follow.

"How do you think it makes me look? And you, for that matter. You shouldn't encourage him."

"I wasn't encouraging him; we were chatting, that's all. Can we drop it now? Anyway, maybe if you spent a bit more time with me …" I said, deliberately leaving the suggestion open.

I regretted it immediately.

"Well, someone needed to make an effort with our guests, rather than disappearing upstairs like you. We did invite them after all. It's no wonder we don't get asked out in the village."

"Not that many of my friends were invited. Anyway, I chatted to quite a few people."

"Yes, your mother for most of the afternoon. Oh, and I nearly forgot: your secret admirer," he added.

"That's not fair. I talked to your father, and even your sister briefly."

"Yes, Caroline mentioned you were quite rude to her."

"What? I was not rude to her. It was her that started … oh, never mind."

"No, go on, do tell me, she started what?"

"She said I wasn't coping properly with Elizabeth. She tried to make me look stupid in front of your father."

"I think you might be over-reacting. Anyway, she's right, isn't she? You have had problems."

"Yes, when it was all new to me at first, but we're doing fine now. I think we're through the worst patch."

"That might be wishful thinking."

"Let's hope not."

"I'm sure it would help if you were a bit firmer with her routine, especially during the night, so we can all get some sleep. That's what my mother has been telling you for ages, but you don't seem to want to listen to her."

Here we go again, I thought: the Henry Edward Hunter-Watson guide to childcare - with a few helpful hints from his mother thrown in for good measure. As far as I was concerned, if Henry and Caroline were supposed to be poster children for the strict routine approach, then it didn't have much to recommend it. Anyway, I was a firm advocate of the Benjamin Spock trust-your-instincts-as-a-mother approach. That was how mum raised me, and we both firmly believed it was the best policy for Beth. I was not going to give in on this particular issue, especially as I was the one actually doing the baby care.

However, I knew that once Henry got started on this particular pet subject, it was pointless to argue the merits of our respective approaches rationally. I would end up saying something I would regret later. Besides, I'd had enough confrontation for one day.

I went and sat on the armrest of his leather Chesterfield chair and gently stroked his thick black floppy hair. I knew he liked that, and I could still remember how much I used to enjoy doing it - at least in the early days. Now, I felt nothing.

I was relieved to see the frown lines on his forehead begin to fade a little.

"Let's not argue about that now. Do you want to go to bed soon?" I asked.

I saw the twinkle in his eye; felt the quiver in his body.

"Yes, OK."

"But I need to go and give Elizabeth a feed first …"

He let out an exasperated sigh, and jerked his head sideways, away from my touch.

"How long are you going to be this time?" he asked, the frown lines now back like deep crevasses.

"Fifteen minutes, twenty at the most. I'll be as quick as I can. I can hear her rustling and she needs some milk to settle her, otherwise she'll only wake up as soon as we get into bed."

"Go on then. Don't be too long," he said, shaking his head.

It was nearly an hour and a half before I returned. The christening must have been quite disturbing for Beth. She was now rather crotchety and restless, and didn't want to be put down. Maybe Henry's philosophy was right after all. Maybe I was *spoiling the child* and *making a rod for my own back* - as his mother kept saying.

Eventually I managed to sooth her and, after waiting a few minutes to check she was settled in her cot, crept out of the nursery. Henry had already gone to bed without me. The champagne and wine had worked their magic, and he was fast asleep. At least for tonight, there would be no need for sex.

Chapter 7

With the coast clear, I crept quietly around to the corner of the bed. Keeping one owlish eye on Henry, I slipped one hand under the mattress and rescued the items I had hidden there earlier. With the other hand, I slid my silk nightie and dressing gown from the chair, and draped them over my arm as I tip-toed into the bathroom.

This time, I was going to take the precaution of locking the door behind me.

Throughout the day, my mind had been bombarded with innumerable questions about Annie Wilson. Even now as I sat on the linen basket, almost twelve hours later, it was difficult to keep my thoughts together. It had been an exceedingly long day and I was completely exhausted - not least, by the sparring with Henry.

The first question; the question the woman asked me; the question now flashing like a blinding light in my brain: 'Did your husband tell you what happened to Annie Wilson?' The answer to this question was a definitive no. He'd never even mentioned the name Annie Wilson. It reminded me how he'd never mentioned Isabella's name prior to her birthday party, even though he claimed that he had. This seemed to be a pattern for Henry; forgetting to mention other women in his life.

The obvious insinuation within the mysterious woman's question was that Henry *should* have told me what happened to Annie. That alone was deeply worrying; he had kept some dark secret from me. However, it was the subject of the newspaper article which sent shivers through my spine. Was Annie's disappearance somehow connected to Henry? My intuition told me that it was. To my mind, the mere fact that the woman had linked Henry with Annie so deliberately, confirmed it beyond all reasonable doubt. The implications were too awful to comprehend.

My emotions began to take over as my subconscious conjured up images of what might have gone on between Henry and Annie, and led to her disappearance. My brain tried to re-establish some sort of control, insisting that before jumping to any more wild conclusions, I should first analyse the facts of the story in some sort of logical order.

I closed my eyes and took a few deep breaths. For want of any better approach, I turned to my trusty *who-what-why-when-where-how* approach, which had served me well in the past when organising my thoughts.

In this particular case, the most obvious place to start was *who*. Who was Annie Wilson? There was also the equally intriguing question of the identity of the woman who had whispered to me in the churchyard - but that would have to wait. Besides, I could think of no way of tracking her down. So, for now, I would focus on Annie. In the process of solving that mystery, I might find a clue to the other woman's identity.

Something suddenly occurred to me. Could the woman who had accosted me in the churchyard actually *be* Annie? What if she hadn't disappeared? What if she was alive and well, and wanted to give me some sort of warning? Hopefully that question would resolve itself once I figured out who Annie actually was. For now, it was probably safer to assume that they were two distinct people.

The newspaper article contained some basic facts: her name, her age, where she was from, where she was studying, and so on. Unfortunately, there was no photograph of her, which might have been useful. With luck, even though this brief profile of Annie's life was a number of years old - judging by the ageing appearance of the paper - there should be enough keys to begin my search. As I combed through the existing fragments of information to make sure I hadn't missed anything, I began to wonder if I might be asking the wrong question. Instead of 'who *was* Annie Wilson?', perhaps I should be asking 'who *is* Annie Wilson', since there was nothing to indicate that she was subsequently confirmed as dead.

This led me onto my next set of questions. *What* happened to Annie, and *how* and *why*? Perhaps she did drown accidentally as the headline suggested, although the more I thought about it, the more I realised there were endless *other possible explanations for her disappearance* - to use the police inspector's phrase. And even if she did drown, it was not certain that it was simply an accident.

What was she doing walking on the top of The Cobb on a stormy night anyway? We had visited Lyme Regis a couple of times when I was a child, and I had been warned that the slippery causeway, frequently lashed by waves, was no place to wander at the best of times, never mind on a stormy night. I had also read *The French Lieutenant's Woman* and *Persuasion,* so The Cobb was already indelibly linked to tragedy in my mind.

There was nothing about the tone of the inspector's comments to suggest he knew more than he was saying. Young female students presumably went missing for all sorts of reasons: exam stress, boyfriend issues, girlfriend issues, problems at home, drug problems - to name but a few. Indeed, I could recall one or two of my own year at university who simply failed to turn up for lectures one day, and were never seen on campus again. No-one ever seemed to know definitively what happened to them. Their names were quickly forgotten and they became simply *the disappeared*. I could also remember how distraught I was when my own father died in terrible pain from lung cancer during my second year; how I had wanted to throw it all in, and disappear into my own black hole of despair.

Perhaps the inspector already knew of some possible motive for Annie Wilson's apparently strange behaviour. He would, no doubt, have interviewed her mother, who might have been able to shed some light on her daughter's state of mind leading up to that weekend. And another thing, there was no mention of her father. Was that significant?

In terms of *when* and *where*, the where was easy - Lyme Regis - but the when was trickier. There were a few clues. The ageing of the newspaper clipping suggested this all took place several years ago, but presumably not so long ago that Henry could not have known the girl. Perhaps within the past twenty years or so? The main clue was the date and day combination in the article. There could only be a handful of days during this period in which 12 May had fallen on a Saturday. I didn't have my phone with me to look them up on an app, and right now my brain couldn't cope with trying to figure them all out.

Even though I had barely scratched the surface of the most obvious questions, I felt utterly drained. I desperately needed a few hours sleep. The issue of how I was going to investigate and pursue Annie Wilson's story further would have to wait until morning.

Suddenly the bathroom door handle rattled and I jumped, dropping the newspaper cutting, and nearly falling off the linen basket in the process.

"Katherine, is that you in there?"

Stupid question! Who else could it be?

"Hang on, I'll be out in a second."

I scooped up the clipping and rammed it and the envelope deep down inside the linen basket. This was a place where I could be sure Henry would never venture. Then I gathered the clothes I had changed out of, and opened the door, attempting not to look too flushed.

"Why did you lock the door?" he asked, standing in front of me, almost barring the way.

"I didn't realise I had," I replied, not daring to look him directly in the eye.

"Well, you did."

Why did he feel it was always necessary to have the last word?

"Sorry, I must have done it without thinking."

I don't know why I was apologising - yet again. Surely, I could lock the bathroom door if I wanted to. Maybe I just wanted some privacy. It wasn't exactly a crime.

"What have you been doing?"

"Elizabeth was a bit cranky after today. It took me ages to settle her."

"You should have left her to cry for a bit. I'm sure she would have calmed down eventually."

"I was worried she would wake you."

Not even Henry could argue with such altruism. Or so I thought.

"Anyway, I meant what have you been doing in the bathroom?"

"Oh, nothing; getting into my nightie and brushing my teeth."

"You've been in there for ages."

"Have I? Sorry. Anyway, I'm coming to bed now," I said, walking past him as quickly as possible and climbing into my side of the bed by the wall.

Mention of the word *bed* seemed to mollify him. I think it was because in his head, the word bed was subconsciously linked to the word *sex*. But not in my head. For me, the word bed was subconsciously - and consciously - linked to the word *sleep*.

I switched my light off immediately and lay still on my side, facing away from him, and praying he would leave me in peace. I could sense his irritation with me from his exasperated tugging of the duvet. But to my relief, after a minute or so, he put his own bed-side light off too, and rolled over, facing away from me. I was safe for now.

Chapter 8

Even though I was totally exhausted, my over-active mind refused to let me sleep. Henry's rustling and snoring didn't help much either. Random untamed hypotheses jostled for pole position in my head. It was pointless to continue thrashing around like this. I needed to focus on something specific and constructive. After wrestling with my pillows yet again in a vain attempt to find a comfortable position, I started trying to think about the actions I could take if I wanted to begin an investigation into Annie Wilson's disappearance.

I wondered how someone would go about tracing a missing person. Suppose she was my daughter, what would I do? My first port of call would be the police. But how much time would they really devote to a case which was several years old now? Alternatively, I might be able to find some charity support group that could help. The problem with both of these options was that Annie was not *my* daughter. I would be asked what was my specific relationship to her, and why was I looking for her. How could I explain, without being suspected of some ulterior motive? I didn't want to become personally tangled up in her disappearance - not unless I absolutely had to. So rather than seeking help from potentially inquisitive professionals, I realised that I would need to use a more indirect and anonymous approach.

The inevitable starting point would be the internet, but typing *Annie Wilson* into Google would be bound to throw up thousands of links, which would lead me precisely nowhere. And what if there happened to be a famous Annie Wilson? No, I couldn't search solely on her name; I would have to do something smarter. There were a few references in the newspaper article that might help narrow down the search - like studying at London University and disappearing in Lyme, for example. It would also help if I could figure out the year in which the article was written. Otherwise, I would be shooting in the dark.

There was always the option of going to Lyme Regis and attempting to track down Annie's mother, assuming she still lived there. If I couldn't find her, I could ask around. Maybe someone else there would know something. After all, the suspected drowning would have been big news at the time in the local area. Such a trip would, of course, take very careful planning, and - here was the problem - I would have to do it without Henry's knowledge. How on earth could I do that?

The next logical place to start my search was the local newspapers around Lyme. I needed to identify the right publication, but that shouldn't be too difficult. How many local papers could there be in that part of Dorset? Would they be available online? Would this particular local paper still even exist?

I was desperate to get started on my search, but it was far too risky to go down to the study and switch on my laptop in the early hours of the morning. Henry had already discovered me, first hiding in the bedroom, and then locked in the bathroom. So far, he didn't seem to suspect anything, but even so, that was enough clandestine activity for one day. And anyway, since I was still on maternity leave, I'd be able to wait until he left for work the following morning, and then have the house to myself all day.

Chapter 9

Monday

Just as I was starting to drift off, I heard the unmistakable rustlings of a baby about to need feeding. I forced back the duvet and struggled out of bed. As I sat there nursing her, I witnessed the darkness of the night giving way to the first greyness of dawn.

Unfortunately, the tranquility was soon shattered by Henry clattering about in the bathroom. He seemed to be making a lot more noise than usual during his early morning routine. A few minutes later, he came padding towards the nursery, still in his T-shirt and pants. Was he, by some miracle, going to offer to take over from me? I thought it most unlikely.

"God, I've got a splitting headache," he groaned.

"I wonder what brought that on," I said in my most sympathetic voice.

"I didn't get much sleep last night, what with all the interruptions," he replied.

He was clearly implying it was my fault, whereas in my humble opinion, it was the vast quantity of champagne and red wine that he'd drunk which was the more likely culprit.

"Have you taken anything for it?" I suggested.

"I couldn't find the paracetamol anywhere."

"I'm sure we have some in the kitchen drawer."

"Do you know exactly where you put them last?"

In other words: could I go and get them? I knew this would be easier than trying to explain to him where they were, only for him to say he still couldn't find them. And no doubt, he would then accuse me of *hiding* them.

"Just let me finish with Elizabeth and then I'll get them."

"Do you want me to hold her while you go downstairs?"

He had that impatient look on his face, but I preferred not to hand Beth over. I didn't want him upsetting her.

"No, it's fine, I'll be putting her back down in a minute."

"I think I might have the day off," he said. "I feel really rough."

Oh fuck! That totally screwed my plan for the day. There was no way I could start my private investigation with Henry on the prowl.

"Oh right. I thought you said …"

"Is there a problem with me being at home for just one day? It's alright for you to be on maternity leave for weeks on end."

"No, there's no problem, but I thought you said you had an important marketing strategy meeting this morning."

"I do, but they'll just have to manage without me, won't they?"

"I guess so."

"I'm going back to bed for a bit. Could you do me a favour and let the office know I won't be in today? Tell them I've come down with something over the weekend."

It wasn't the first time I'd been asked to carry out this particular *wifely* duty - as Henry called it. His commitment to his new job in London had long since evaporated.

"OK. I'll phone around eight o'clock. There's usually someone in by then."

"Thanks. By the way, have you had any breakfast?" he hinted.

"Not yet, but I'm going to make it now. You go back to bed and I'll bring you some tea."

"Thanks. Would you mind bringing me a large glass of orange juice too? I'm so dehydrated."

All morning, I couldn't concentrate on anything. I was going out of my head. I needed some answers. But my mind was made up on one thing. Under no circumstances, was I going to ask Henry directly about Annie Wilson. I didn't trust what he might say. I didn't trust how he might react. This was something I was going to do on my own. I would make it my personal mission. I quite liked the idea of having my own secret. Why should he be the only one with secrets?

Shortly before lunchtime, Henry made a miraculous recovery and announced he was off to play golf. Quelle surprise! For obvious reasons, I didn't dissuade him. I suggested the fresh air might do him good and even ironed his favourite shirt. Anything to get rid of him. As soon as I heard his BMW crunching along the gravel drive, I opened up my laptop and grabbed my trusty notepad and pencil.

First things first, I wanted to establish when the newspaper article might have been written. I pulled it out of the envelope to check the date and suddenly felt cold: *Saturday 12 May.*

Henry's birthday was 12 May. Why hadn't I noticed this before? Could it really be a coincidence that the date Annie disappeared was Henry's birthday? I doubted it. I quickly established that 12 May had occurred on a Saturday five times since Henry was born. He would have been a child during the two earlier dates, but that still left three possible years. I flipped over the clipping to see if there were any clues on the other side. Yes, there was a brief reference to the Fossil Festival which had just taken place in Lyme Regis. That got me started, and with a little more web surfing, I soon figured out the year of Annie's disappearance. It was eight years ago. So that would have been Henry's 28th birthday; five and a half years before I first came to Oxford and met him. I was already feeling quite pleased with my first bit of detective work.

As a follow-up, I wanted to know what Henry would have been doing then. Although I had a vague idea of his career - admittedly based on what he'd previously told me, which might not be totally reliable - an actual copy of his CV would help pin down where he was working at that time.

There was something else intriguing about this date. It was the same year I graduated, so Annie and I were both in our final years of university at the same time; both aged 22. This strange coincidence of dates and ages made me wonder if there might be some link between us. I couldn't rule out the possibility that our paths had crossed at some point during our student days.

What I needed to do next was find out which local paper the article had appeared in, and then check whether there were any later reports, and in particular whether Annie had subsequently turned up - either dead or alive. Given the date of her disappearance - almost eight years ago - she might well have been declared dead *in absentia* if she hadn't been seen since.

After a few minutes, I had my starting point. There were a number of possible papers for the area around Lyme, but the most likely candidate appeared to be the *Dorset Echo* which was published daily in Weymouth. Unfortunately, after about half an hour on the *Dorset Echo* website, I could find nothing at all about this story, or any other mention of Annie Wilson for that matter.

Out of curiosity, I searched their online archive for references to the police inspector quoted in the article. His name came up on a number of recent cases so it looked like he was still working the patch around the Dorset coast. But how could I possibly get any information from him without explaining my interest, which would inevitably mean introducing Henry into the picture? For all I knew, Inspector Collins might never even have heard of Henry. The more I considered the idea, the more complicated and problematic it became. It confirmed my previous conclusion that all enquiries should remain anonymous, at least for the present.

My final session of internet browsing for the afternoon - looking for some reference to Annie Wilson on the University of London website - turned out to be a complete waste of time. To obtain any useful information about her, I would have to contact the University of London. And I was pretty sure they wouldn't tell me anything.

Chapter 10

The afternoon had flown by, and it was already time to give Beth her daily bath. This was one activity I always looked forward to. Everything seemed rosy when it was just the two of us having fun together. Over the past three months, bath time had become a rare safe haven for us; a brief lull between the grumbling storms.

Before logging off, I deleted all my browsing history in case Henry decided to have a sneaky look at my laptop - something he did from time to time - and stumbled across the pages I'd visited. If he knew I'd been on the *Dorset Echo* and London University websites, it could lead to some tricky questions, for which there would be no easy answers.

Once Beth was bathed, changed and fed, she was soon fast asleep. That gave me ample time to prepare a meal for Henry's imminent return from the golf-course. But by six o'clock, he was still not back. It would be starting to get dark soon. Surely, he couldn't still be out playing? What was he doing? Had he forgotten to mention yet another woman in his life?

Just then I heard the familiar sound of the car on the drive, and saw Henry's personalised number plate illuminated under the security light by the garage. I'd always thought the '3' as a backward capital 'E' was pathetic. However, given his aggressive reaction the one time I did poke fun at it, I didn't dare mention it again.

Chameleon-like, I prepared to adapt myself to his mood. I always felt as if I was walking on egg-shells when he was around. When he entered the kitchen, however, he looked relaxed and even smiled at me. I was surprised when he came over and hugged me, pecking my cheek like he used to. He was almost like the man I'd fallen in love with two and a half years ago. I tried to preserve his cheery disposition by indulging in a subject I knew was still close to his heart - even if I no longer was.

"Did you have a good round?" I asked.

"Yes, thanks, not bad at all. I feel a lot better for being outside in the fresh air all afternoon," he said. "And thanks for covering for me with the office this afternoon; much appreciated."

I smiled to acknowledge his appreciation, but in truth, since I'd phoned his office that morning, there was no covering to do, since no-one wanted to speak to him. They were obviously able to decide marketing strategy without him - which was a bit worrying since he was supposed to be the Marketing VP. By contrast, even after many weeks of maternity leave, I was still getting calls from my office on an almost daily basis. I'd had two calls this afternoon, although admittedly one of them was from Malkit just phoning to see how I was after Sunday - which was kind of him.

"Are you ready for something to eat, or do you want to get changed first?" I asked Henry.

"Well, I am quite hungry, but can I have a quick shower first? Do I have time?"

"Yes, sure."

"Dinner smells great. I'll be as fast as I can; ten minutes."

This was praise indeed from someone who regarded himself as a Michelin star chef - although admittedly, it was some time since he'd graced the kitchen with one of his prima-donna performances. Of course, this never included clearing up after himself, which he always kindly left to me. I generally found it less painful if I took care of the cooking, and just left him to critique my efforts. One dish that was guaranteed to spark conflict though, was spaghetti bolognaise. Unless I served up exactly the same reddy-brown gunge as his mother, Henry pretty much deemed it unfit for human consumption.

Anyway, I prayed that tonight his good mood would last longer than his shower. When he returned a few minutes later, I was relieved to see that he still looked happy.

"I've got something for you," he said, handing me a small box, neatly wrapped in gold paper, with a matching bow.

It was a beautiful diamond-set eternity ring. He slipped it on my finger and it fitted perfectly, as I knew it would. Henry's attention to detail on such matters was meticulous. I put my arms around his neck and kissed him firmly on the mouth. As I did so, I felt ashamed. Ashamed of my affection being bought so easily? Ashamed of my doubting and suspecting of him? Ashamed of not sticking up for myself more? I didn't know what I felt ashamed of, but I did anyway.

"Thank you, Henry; it's lovely," I said admiring the sparkling of the diamonds under the light in the dining room.

"I wanted to give it to you on Sunday before the christening. It was supposed to be ready for the weekend, but there was some delay in sizing it. I went to collect it tonight before the shop closed. Anyway, I'm glad you like it."

"I do. It's beautiful and I love the setting of the diamonds," I said.

There was a large part of me that couldn't help worrying that somewhere there was a catch. Was this a guilt purchase? About Isabella perhaps? Would he want something in return?

"I'm sorry I've been a bit grumpy over the past few months. I think it's all the commuting in and out of London. It's been getting to me over the winter; leaving for work in the dark and coming home in the dark. The season ticket costs a bloody fortune and I don't even get a seat. Can you imagine what it's like having to stand up all the way to Paddington on a packed train?"

"I'm sure I would hate it. I think it would get to anybody. At least it's getting lighter in the mornings when you leave now," I said, aiming to sound supportive.

"And, it's not just the train. I have to travel to and from Holborn every day. We're all rammed in on the Tube like sardines; it's so disgusting."

I knew this is exactly what would happen when Henry threw in his previous job in Oxford, seduced by the lure of money in the City - and, no doubt, flattered by the female executive head-hunter that he said called him about the job. I remember how pleased he looked with himself when he told me his new salary was now higher than mine. Well, he didn't look quite so pleased with himself now, did he? I had absolutely no sympathy. He should have thought more about the commuting when he took the job. He didn't ask for my advice and, even if he had, I wouldn't have tried to persuade him either way, because any poor decision he made would somehow become my fault. It was best to *keep my beak out* - to use one of Henry's other favourite phrases.

"What about looking for something nearer to home?"

"You know there aren't any big publishing companies out here that could afford to pay me a half-decent salary. There's really only OUP, and I'm not going back there."

The truth is, they wouldn't have taken him back anyway. That bridge had been well and truly burned by Henry.

"What about other industries outside of publishing? There are so many high-tech companies around Oxford."

"It's not that easy. All my experience is in publishing. It's like me suggesting you change subject from maths to geography."

"OK, maybe it's not that easy, but if the travelling is really getting to you … and you could save the cost of the season ticket if you didn't need to go into London. Anyway, it's your decision. It's up to you. It's just a question of getting the right balance."

I was trying to beat a tactful retreat. I knew precisely where this conversation was heading.

"You don't need to tell me that, Katherine. Believe me, I know. But what alternative do I have? Someone has to pay the mortgage, and with a baby to look after, and you on maternity leave, I don't have any choice, do I?"

We had purchased the house in joint names. He paid the mortgage; that was true. But I paid for just about everything else. Each month, he went through my credit card statement with a fine toothcomb, constantly criticising me for spending too much on food and clothes and petrol - basically everything. Unsurprisingly, he never gave me a similar opportunity to review his credit card purchases or question his expenditure. Once Henry got started on the subject of money, it was almost impossible to stop him. Tonight, I didn't want the gathering clouds to obscure this rare glimpse of sunlight in our relationship.

"Can we talk about this later, Henry?"

"I suppose one option would be for us to move nearer to London," he said.

I was horrified. His suggestion was like a thunderbolt from nowhere. I loved the quietness of the small village in the countryside where we now lived. There was also mum to consider. When I first moved to Oxford, she had - not without some sadness - sold our long-term family home near Northampton to be closer to me. After all the upheaval she'd gone through, I couldn't very well turn round now and tell her I was moving away.

And another thing, although getting into Oxford city centre from where we now lived wasn't ideal, the commute was manageable. I had no intention of moving further away, and there was no way I was going to give up my research position. The competition for this much-coveted post was brutal. It was for this dream job that I'd left all my friends and colleagues behind in Cambridge.

No-one, not even Henry, was going to persuade me to move closer to London. Somehow, I had to defuse this alarming new idea of his, but if there was one thing I knew about him, it was that if I dug my heels in, he would dig his in deeper. He would force the issue, almost for the sake of making a point.

"Anyway, can we have dinner now," I suggested. "It's all ready."

For the rest of the evening, I worked hard to steer the conversation away from this, or any other, sensitive subject. Believe me, that was no easy task. I also had to keep thoughts of Annie Wilson at the back of my mind during this short cessation of hostilities.

As Henry began to relax, I found myself reminiscing about what I had seen in him during those early days of our relationship. He had - to use a well-worn cliché - swept me off my feet. Before I arrived in Oxford, I'd led a relatively sheltered life. I faced the constant pressure of being a successful young female in a world dominated by middle-aged men. I had to work hard to build my academic reputation, which didn't leave much time for socialising or other interests.

So, at the time I met Henry, I was feeling strangely lost and lonely. Then miraculously, he had rescued me and taken me under his wing. He really seemed to care about me back then. Sadly, it was a side of him I rarely witnessed now when we were alone. I had even begun to wonder if all the attention and affection in those early days was not quite what it seemed. Maybe it was just an act. I'd read a magazine article recently about what psychologists called *love bombing*. Rather worryingly, Henry's behaviour seemed to fit the description perfectly. Maybe psychologists did know what they were talking about after all.

Even more upsetting, however, was the fact that this charming side of Henry still very much existed. Indeed, it was the face visible to everyone who knew him - except me. It was his public image, but it was reserved exclusively for others. Not only was this intensely hurtful to me, but it made it impossible to talk to anyone about the problem, because the Henry that I would be describing, would be unrecognisable to them. They would think I was exaggerating or imagining things.

To compound matters, the friends I had made before moving out to Oxford, seemed to have faded from view. I would never have described myself as the life and soul of the party, but I did have a small circle of what I thought were solid friends. Now, one by one, they had all retreated or dropped out of my life - and most of the reasons were connected with Henry. He ruthlessly targeted, analysed and criticised each character in turn, until I became uncomfortable even mentioning their names, never mind keeping their company. Of course, this condemnation was always delivered behind their backs to me - or rather, at me. They themselves had no way of knowing that the charming Henry they'd recently met was their cold-blooded assassin.

In the end, I stopped contacting them, and I guess they assumed I wanted them to stop contacting me. Maybe they were simply too busy with their own complicated lives to make the effort to come over to Oxford. However, I couldn't help feeling that Henry had systematically frozen them out of my life - and me out of theirs - as part of some sinister plan to make me more dependent on him. Maybe I was imagining things, but I didn't think so.

Of course, he had also tried this insidious tactic on my relationship with mum - and to my eternal shame, it had worked initially. But not now. The newly reformed bond between mum and me was now so strong that it could withstand whatever sticks and stones Henry might throw at it. In fact, the more he isolated me from my friends, the closer I became to mum. Whatever happened, she would always understand me; believe in me; take my side.

I didn't know how I would manage without her.

Chapter 11

Tuesday

The sound of my phone ringing woke me with a start. I was up with Beth most of the night, and went back to bed for a short nap after Henry left for work. I assumed it was him, calling to moan about some tedious train-rage incident during his commute into the office that particular morning. Perhaps yet another rant about the guy who always blocked the aisle while he *farted around* - Henry's words - with his heavily-velcroed waterproofs and fold-away bike. I'd heard so much about *velcro-man* recently that he was almost part of the family.

"Hello, is that Katy?" a woman's voice asked.

"Yes?" I said, not quite being able to place the voice, although I did vaguely recognise it.

"It's June ... June Williams."

I'd met mum's neighbour several times and could picture her rosy face. She was a cheery, helpful sort of person, always popping in to see mum and generally keeping an eye on her. Although I lived only about fifteen minutes away from mum, it was comforting to know she had such a caring and reliable friend right next door.

"Oh ... hi ... hello. Is everything alright?"

There was a tell-tale moment of hesitation before she answered.

"Katy, I'm afraid it's about your mum," she said.

I felt the dull blow of her words as if I'd been kicked in the stomach.

"Why? What is it?" I asked in dread.

"She took a bit of a tumble this morning."

"Oh, God. What's happened? Is she alright?"

"The paramedics were just here. They think it might have been a small stroke, so they've taken her in an ambulance to the JR. I said I would call you."

"Right," was all I could mumble in my confusion.

I was desperately trying to think straight. My head was spinning. The worst part was the not knowing. What had happened to her? What was happening to her now? The fact that they'd taken her to the John Radcliffe - Oxfordshire's main accident and emergency hospital - meant it must be serious. I assumed the worst.

"Is there anything I can do to help? Anybody else you want me to call?" she continued.

My immediate and only thought was to drop everything and go straight to the JR. There was nothing else to be done; no-one else to call. There was no point wasting valuable time trying to persuade Henry to come home to look after Beth, and then wasting yet more time having to wait for him. I would rather take her with me. I wanted her with me. She was my life now.

"No, it's alright thanks. I need to get to the hospital as soon as possible. Thank you so much for letting me know."

I was very familiar with the route to the JR as Beth was born there, and I'd driven myself to several pre- and post-natal appointments. Nevertheless, by the time I'd struggled through the sluggish Oxford traffic and found somewhere to park - always a nightmare at the JR - I was frantic. My nose was streaming, my eyes stinging, my vision blurred from the uncontrollable bouts of crying. My body and brain no longer seemed connected to each other.

In a rush to go and find mum, I grabbed my handbag from the front of the car, and then struggled frantically with Beth's baby seat at the back. Henry had over-ruled my choice of a simple practical seat, in favour of an upmarket designer-label one he preferred, and with which I was now fighting. With great difficulty, I extricated the fiddly clips from the rear seatbelt, breaking off most of a fingernail in the process. Then, as I dragged the heavy seat out through the car door, the clumsy frame snagged on something, slipped from my grasp and toppled sideways onto the tarmac with a sickening thud. I threw my handbag back in the car and stooped down to free Beth's twisted body from the car seat. As I turned her over, I noticed the huge purple bump swelling up on her forehead. Within a few seconds, it was the size of a small egg. I felt physically sick and sensed that I was going to faint. Just in time, I slumped back into the car, clutching Beth tightly. I closed my eyes and forced myself to breathe deeply. Tears were streaming down my face. I was quite literally at the end of my tether; at breaking point.

"Do you need some help, love?" a kind female voice said.

I looked up to see a middle-aged woman in a blue uniform, smiling sympathetically at me. It must have been my guardian angel, come to rescue me. Or more likely, Beth's guardian angel, come to save her from further harm at the hands of her mother.

"Yes please," I whispered, and instantly dissolved into tears again.

She helped me out of the car and picked up the rest of my things, leaving me free to focus my attention on Beth. In between the deep sobs, I poured out a jumbled explanation of why I was at the hospital. I then let the nurse take control. Without concentrating on where we were going, I followed her through a labyrinth of corridors, and then waited while she disappeared for a couple of minutes before returning with a doctor. The doctor assured me the bump on Beth's forehead did not appear to be serious; there was only a slight graze which she cleaned carefully. The swelling was already coming down, but I was told to keep a close eye on her for the next 24 hours. I was amazed that throughout the whole episode, Beth didn't cry once - unlike her useless mother.

I was then pointed in the direction of the ward where mum would be. One of the ward nurses took me into a small private side room and sat me down. I could feel myself shaking, too distraught to frame any questions. She came straight to the point.

"Your mother has had a stroke," she said in a very matter-of-fact way.

I would never forget those words for the rest of my life. It felt like the end of something. Or at least, the beginning of the end of something. The acronym FAST came to mind, but in my current state I couldn't think what the letters stood for.

"A stroke ... how serious is it?" I stuttered.

"Your mother is stable now. The paramedics got there in good time, thanks to the call from her neighbour."

Yes, that was it: the letter '*T*' in FAST stood for Time. I remembered that was very important. Thank God for June Williams.

"Do you know … when will?" I began, but quickly trailed off, not knowing what I was asking.

"Your mother is still under assessment. Right now we are carrying out some routine tests. When anyone has a stroke, it's important that we find out what caused it as soon as possible, so we can minimise the risk of any complications."

I didn't like the sound of that word *complications*.

"Is she … will she be alright?"

"We need to wait for the results before we can say what the prognosis is."

"Will I at least be able to see her soon and talk to her?"

"Yes, she should be back on the ward before too long, so you will be able to see her."

"Oh, good," I said.

My optimism was short-lived.

"However, it might still be a little too early for you to have a conversation with her," she added.

Now I remembered what the letter '*S*' in FAST stood for: Speech. The thought of not being able to chat with mum was too much. I collapsed in a heap of tears.

That's basically all I remember of the 48 hours between Beth's christening and mum's stroke. Two days of absolute hell.

So many things to do; so little time to do any of them. So many questions to think about; so few answers. Is it any wonder I'm losing my mind? The only thing I *am* sure of right now, is that mum has to be my number one priority. Forget Henry; forget Isabella; forget Annie Wilson even. They will all have to wait for a while.

I remember how down and lonely I felt when dad died, but this is worse. If mum … no, I can't think like that. I need to stay positive. I'm going to sit by the side of her hospital bed and talk to her - even if she can't hear me or talk to me. On Sunday evening after the christening, the last thing we were talking about was her generous offer to spend more time with Beth once I went back to work. So, that's where I'm going to restart our conversation; exactly where we left off, as if nothing has happened.

One immediate action I took was to extend my maternity leave for another four months until the end of September, just before the start of the new academic year. It felt like the right thing to do. I needed this extra time for whatever support mum might need. Henry wasn't too keen on the idea - especially on the resulting income reduction - but I think he realised that my mind was made up, and this was one argument he was never going to win.

Being in the Acute Stroke Unit, day after day, seeing the other patients and their distraught families, and reading all about strokes, brought home to me the fragility of life. And I was totally in awe of the staff in the NHS. If ever there was an example of dedicated people with different backgrounds, nationalities and cultures, working together for a common cause, this was it. I was so grateful to all the consultants, doctors, nurses, and support staff who looked after mum during those first few critical days. Their commitment and kindness quite literally saved her life - and kept me going too.

I was worried that the stroke might be the result of mum wearing herself out with all the preparations for the christening, but the nurses assured me that was most unlikely. These things just happened, they said; under no circumstances should I start blaming myself. It wouldn't help mum.

The biggest surprise to me during those first few days, was Henry's apparent patience. He couldn't cope with my delicate emotional state, but he did provide some practical support, working from home for a couple of days to help look after Beth. He didn't quite stretch to doing any shopping or cooking though; that was still left to me. Also, to my huge relief, he made no further mention of moving nearer to London.

Perhaps most surprising of all was that, after I told him about my struggle with the car seat, instead of criticising me for dropping

Beth and scratching the frame, he went online and ordered the unpretentious model I originally wanted. He also managed to sell the fancy one on eBay a couple of days later for a slight profit, which definitely helped him get over it.

I was beginning to wonder if I'd been too hard on Henry recently; had I perhaps misjudged him. Maybe it was, just like he said, the commuting getting to him. Maybe I was being over-sensitive and he wasn't so bad after all. Maybe there was even a perfectly innocent explanation about his connection with Annie Wilson. Should I perhaps give him another chance?

Any such thoughts were banished instantly by what he did at the end of the week.

Chapter 12

On Sunday morning, we went to mum's house to collect some clean clothes and a few personal items; things that would make her life a little more bearable; things like the silver-handled hairbrush that dad bought for her. I left Henry downstairs while I went up to mum's bedroom. I felt so dejected knowing that, at that exact moment, she was lying in a hospital bed on a large public ward, and however much the staff tried to make her comfortable, it was not her home. I hoped and prayed she would soon be well enough to return.

As I came back down, I heard Henry rustling about in the living room. To my disgust, I found him nosing through my mother's writing desk. It was the battered oak antique bureau that had been my father's pride and joy. I could still remember sitting on his knee as a child, fascinated, watching him write and sign cheques. It was where mum now kept all her important financial documents, and did all her paperwork. I knew it brought back many happy memories for her too. It was sacrosanct.

"What on earth are you doing?" I demanded to know.

"Nothing; just killing time while I wait for you."

"That's mum's private stuff in there."

"Calm down; I wasn't doing anything."

"I am calm. It's you who shouldn't be poking about in her things."

"OK, Katherine, don't overreact."

I knew perfectly well that telling me to calm down and not to overreact was his way of winding me up, and thereby deflecting the argument from his own suspect behaviour. I still couldn't help myself though.

"I am not overreacting," I shouted. "Right now, mum is lying in a hospital bed and I have no way of knowing when - or even if - she will ever recover. When I'm with her, I have no idea what I should say or do. I feel so completely helpless and useless. So, I am allowed to be upset. Deal with it."

"OK, OK, I get it. Look, I know we both have a lot on our plates at the moment, but you need to make sure you don't overdo it. You need to stay on top of things. You need to make some time for your own family too."

By that, I assumed he meant himself. I was too tired to argue with him about what exactly was on his plate - apart from the meals I cooked for him. All I wanted to do was take mum's things to her, have a chat, and then come home for a well-deserved soak in the bath.

"Right, I've got everything I came for. Can we head to the hospital now, please?"

"Should we check the post to see if there's anything that needs dealing with, you know, like bills to pay?"

"If there are, I'm sure they can wait a few days. Anyway, Mrs Williams has a key and she comes in every day to check on everything. I already asked her to keep an eye out for any post that looks important."

"Yes, it's probably all junk mail that your mother gets anyway," he said.

God, he was so irritating.

"No, it isn't all junk mail. She's had a lot of *Get Well* cards from her friends."

"Well, it might be nice if a few of them also made the effort to visit her in hospital. It would take the pressure off you a bit."

My head was throbbing. I closed my eyes and did my best to ignore this latest infuriating comment from Henry, as we drove back to the JR.

Later that evening, after I'd put Beth to bed and was squatting on the edge of the bath, staring at the water flowing from the hot tap, Henry cornered me.

"I was wondering … you know how we talked about your mother having to deal with her financial stuff while she's in hospital."

"How *you* talked about it, you mean. Well?" I said, irritated that he'd brought it up again when I was trying to unwind.

"Do you think there's anything we need to do?"

"No, not really. She's always pretty organised and up to date with her admin. I wouldn't have thought anything particularly urgent would have come up in the last week."

"Yes, but what if this goes on for a while? What if she's stuck in hospital for a few months? We'll have to sort something out then."

"I can help her with anything she needs to do."

"Do you know all her usernames, passwords, PINs, things like that?"

"I know some of them … not everything … but she can give me the details when she needs help with something specific."

"And what if she isn't well enough to explain things?"

"Well, I suppose we'll have to cross that bridge when we come to it. Look, Henry, I'm not going to start bothering her about that sort of thing now. She just needs to rest and recover; that's the priority."

"I think it's worth considering; we shouldn't leave it too long."

Henry had now completely ruined any chance of me relaxing in the bath. All I could think about was how I would cope if mum's illness dragged on indefinitely. Annoyingly, he was right; it *was* something - yet another thing - for me to start thinking about, or rather, start worrying about.

Fortunately, after that first week, mum's condition began to improve steadily, if rather slowly. She was still easily fatigued and prone to bouts of anxiety and frustration. She was also having some problems with her speech and with swallowing. Nevertheless, her consultant suggested that, with the help of the Early Supported Discharge service, her recovery and rehabilitation might proceed more smoothly at home. Without asking Henry, I made her the offer of coming to live with us. But as I suspected, she was adamant that she wanted to be in her own home, with her own things, surrounded by her own network of neighbours and friends.

Once mum was back home, I tried to visit as often as possible, and always took Beth with me. I wanted to make sure mum had an opportunity to hold her each time, even if only for a few minutes. I had no intention of depriving either of them of these special intimate moments. Henry rarely joined me, and even when he did, he found it difficult to deal with mum's slow and slightly impaired speech, getting impatient with her all too easily. He preferred to fade into the background, absorbed in his phone screen or a newspaper.

On one visit, I took the opportunity to speak to mum about an issue that was troubling me, ever since my interrupted bath.

"Mum, do you mind if we talk about something? I don't know how to bring this up; it's a bit touchy."

"What if I have another stroke?"

"Sort of. I know I shouldn't be stressing about it, but I can't stop myself."

"Don't worry, darling. I know it might happen again."

"I just wanted to say that if anything does happen, you know you can always stay with us, whenever you want, for as long as you want."

"Thank you. Did Henry agree to that? Does he even know?"

"I'm sure he won't mind."

I wasn't so sure.

"Talking of Henry, there's something I need to tell you, Katy. It's about what will happen to my money and the house if I have another stroke."

I now wished I hadn't started this awful topic.

"Oh, mum, please, let's not do this now. Can't we just wait and see what happens?"

"Everything is arranged in your dad's old bureau. A few months ago, I made a list of everything … accounts … passwords … that sort of thing … everything you might need. It's in a large sealed brown envelope with your name on it."

Did she have some kind of premonition?

"Oh right, that's very organised of you."

"And Katy, promise me, you won't show it to *anyone*."

We both knew who she was talking about.

"I promise."

"And I've made a will."

"We don't need to talk about that now, mum, please."

"I don't want Henry to get anything," she persisted.

"It's your will; it's up to you, mum. Obviously, I know you don't like Henry."

"And more to the point, I don't *trust* him either, darling, not with my money. I want to do what's best for you and Beth."

"That's fine, honestly, mum, I understand."

I did understand. I completely understood. I didn't trust Henry either. The way he behaved around money made me nervous. I was relieved that he'd never suggested opening a joint bank account or putting any of our meagre savings into joint names. Having to account for my monthly household expenditure was one thing; giving him actual control over my money was quite another.

"Also - and this is very important - you need to go and see Helen Franklin at McGrew's. It's a bit complicated, but she will explain everything."

I'd met Helen Franklin a couple of times. She'd always done mum and dad's legal stuff.

"Yes, I'll go and see her as soon as I can."

"There's one more thing. You know if I do have another stroke, it might affect my … well, you know, my mind."

"Oh, mum, don't say that."

A runaway tear rolled down my cheek.

"I know it's difficult, darling, but we need to talk about things like this. I've arranged with Helen to give you power of attorney over my finances and healthcare decisions. You understand … just in case."

"Yes, I understand."

A couple of days later, I went to McGrew's office in Oxford, and Helen Franklin walked me through the arrangements in my mother's will. Basically everything - apart from a few personal items mum wanted to leave directly to me - was to be put in trust for Beth. The will had been structured to include possible future children, which I found oddly amusing, since I wasn't planning to have any more - at least not with Henry. Helen and I would be the trustees of Beth's trust, with the power to make investment decisions. Mum's house was to be included in the trust. I had the option to live there with Beth, or sell it and put the proceeds into the trust. Helen said that my mother was a bit concerned I might feel bypassed by these arrangements, but I told her I totally understood the reasons. I was sure Henry wouldn't.

Mum appreciated fresh reading material, so I tried to take a magazine or book with me on each of my visits. One day, short of inspiration, I wondered if there might be anything interesting in Henry's study. My eyes were drawn to a dark blue leather-bound hardback copy of *Northanger Abbey* on his bookshelf. He had quite a collection of the classics and liked to impress people with his superficial knowledge of them. I knew mum had enjoyed the more popular Jane Austen novels, but I didn't think she'd read this one.

I took it down off the shelf and opened it somewhere in the middle. The font and typeface were large and clear, which would make it easier for mum. Out of curiosity I flicked open the front cover to see how old the edition was.

I suddenly felt short of breath. There, on the inside page, handwritten in pencil, were the initials: AW.

I blinked and took another look: AW.

Annie Wilson.

Her name had been lurking at the back of my mind - mostly undisturbed - for the past three weeks. I felt incredibly guilty for abandoning my nascent investigation into her disappearance, but in my defence, I had been totally preoccupied with mum's condition.

But now Annie's initials were right there staring me in the face. The two letters were drawn simply, with straight line segments and without flourish. So simply, in fact, that they gave no clue as to the age or sex of the person who wrote them. I flicked through the rest of the front few pages, but couldn't find any other annotations. I decided to take a photo of the initials for future reference - just in case the book or the initials disappeared.

On my next visit to mum, I handed her the book.

"I thought you might like this."

"Thank you, darling. I haven't read this one."

"Oh good."

She opened it exactly as I had done.

"Is this Alan's book?"

"Alan?"

"Yes, look at these initials: AW. Alan Watson. Did Henry borrow it from his father?"

I felt such a fool. When I first met Henry's father, he explained to me how their family name was simply Watson, but Henry had taken it upon himself to unofficially join his third forename to this family name. So instead of Henry Edward Hunter Watson, he became Henry Edward Hunter-Watson. I could scarcely believe that anyone would go to so much trouble for a single dash. Mind you, he did have a personalised number plate. His father had been even more offended when Henry subsequently changed his surname by deed poll, and the Hunter-Watson became official.

What a *dickhead* - to use Henry's own word.

Chapter 13

Just over two weeks after mum was discharged from hospital, Henry arrived back home quite late on the Friday evening. I could tell from the expression on his face that he was in a foul mood, and duly braced myself for the onslaught.

"Bloody trains …" he began, launching into yet another commuter rant.

I did my best to look sympathetic, but I'd been subjected to so many of these rants since he started commuting into London, that it was difficult to be genuine. Frankly, I couldn't care less if the 17.49 - or whatever time it was supposed to leave Paddington - had been cancelled, delayed, re-routed, or even abducted by aliens. What did he expect me to do about it? It made no difference what I said; he would still be bad-tempered. The last thing I wanted was to accidentally say something that would suck me into his angry vortex and make everything my fault.

"I'll make you a cup of tea. Why don't you have a shower and get changed, and then you can relax?"

"Relax! Easier said than done after the day I've had. You should be thankful you don't have to slog into London."

"I am."

"It's fine for you being at home all day."

He made it sound like I'd spent the entire day sitting on the sofa with my feet up, rather than running around after mum and *our* child.

"I've been at mum's this afternoon. I haven't been home that long either."

"Has the hot water been on?"

He'd stopped bothering to ask how mum's recovery was going. He seemed to assume that because she'd been discharged from hospital, she couldn't really be that ill.

"Yes, I put it on as soon as I came in."

"It was freezing this morning when I had a shave."

I knew that wasn't true because I'd managed to have a perfectly comfortable shower after he'd gone to work.

"Well, it should be fine now."

"You need to make sure it goes on every day."

"I do."

"Well, you obviously didn't yesterday."

He wouldn't let it go. His snarling continued and grew increasingly petulant with each exchange.

"I'm out at work all day, so the least you could do is to make sure the water is hot when I get home."

I stayed silent.

"It's not asking much, is it?"

Still, I said nothing.

"Well, is it?"

"No."

"OK, then."

This argument, like so many before it, had finally ground to a close. I'd been dragged down this rutted road so many times before that my resistance was broken. Once again, it appeared that he was the winner of the argument, which always seemed important to him. For my part, I no longer cared who won the arguments. I felt drained by them and empty.

He went upstairs for a shower, and I carried on sorting out the kitchen. When he returned, he started at me again.

"I thought you were making me a cup of tea."

"Do you still want one?"

"No, it doesn't matter now; we may as well have our dinner."

"What do you fancy?"

"You mean you haven't prepared anything yet."

"Not yet, I haven't had time."

"What have you been doing all day?"

"Well, as I said, I've been at mum's all afternoon. Then I had to give Beth a bath, feed her and put her to bed."

"Right, so there isn't anything to eat either?"

The *either* suggested he was adding this to the charge sheet on which he had already written *no hot water*. I wondered how many other minor misdemeanours I might have racked up.

"I've done a full shop on the way home, so there's plenty of food in the house. There are various things we could have."

"Like what?"

And so it continued, on and on and on. It felt like psychological warfare. In response, I'd developed my own version of *The Art of War*. My techniques included: avoid conflict, adapt to his moods, bend like a straw before the wind, keep my feelings bottled up. With this approach, I managed to survive, but survival was no longer good enough. I probably deserved better; Beth certainly did.

I didn't know what had caused his foul mood - probably nothing - but it only hardened as the evening progressed. I was tired. I didn't have the energy to fight endlessly over trivial things. But he obviously did. About nine-thirty, I told him I had a bad headache and went to bed.

Next morning, I heard him moving about downstairs, and then the front door slammed. When I came down for breakfast half an hour later, there was a one-word scribbled note which said simply: *GOLF.*

I wasn't annoyed or even bothered; I was relieved. In fact, I was *glad* he'd gone out, particularly after the previous stormy evening. I gave mum a quick call. She sounded quite despondent, but no more than usual of late. She had a couple of friends coming over later who were going to take her out for some gentle retail therapy, so she was looking forward to that. I told her I would come over on Sunday, probably around lunchtime.

When Henry returned from the golf course, the thick dark clouds over his head seemed to have been blown away. He even came bearing gifts - a bunch of my favourite freesia flowers - and sounded quite chipper. He was particularly pleased with his birdie on the 15th hole, which he talked me through in minute detail; apparently it was almost an eagle. I knew the difference but wasn't sufficiently interested to ask any follow-up questions. The fact that I'd put together a nice lunch also seemed to appease him.

However, midway through our surprisingly harmonious meal, he dropped into the conversation that his parents had invited us over for Sunday lunch.

"Oh, I told mum I might go over to see her at lunchtime tomorrow."

"Couldn't you go earlier or maybe later in the day?"

"Well yes, I suppose so. I'll need to check what she's doing. It would have been nice if you'd told me earlier about the invite from your parents."

"Well, it would have been nice if you'd told me earlier about your arrangement with your mother. You visit her almost every day, and we hardly ever see my parents."

He'd obviously forgotten about Mother's Day.

"That's because she hasn't been well recently, in case you hadn't noticed."

"Don't worry, I am *fully* aware of that. It's pretty much all I hear about these days. And it conveniently killed off any idea of us moving closer to London to reduce my commute."

Conveniently? There was nothing *convenient* about having a stroke.

"She had a stroke. I'm not going to abandon her, am I? You wouldn't abandon your mother in the same situation."

I wasn't convinced that last statement was true.

"Anyway, I thought your mother was getting better."

"Well, she has improved, but she's still a long way from her normal self. I doubt she will ever fully recover."

"Anyway, you're going off on a tangent as usual. Let's focus on the plan for tomorrow. Can't you change the time you go over to your mother's so we can go to my parents for lunch?"

"Let me check with her."

"The thing is, I already told my mother we would be coming. She will have bought the food and started preparing things by now."

"When exactly did she make the invitation?"

"Friday evening. She phoned after you went off to bed sulking."

"I wasn't sulking; I had a headache."

"OK, well after you went to bed with a headache then."

Yet another conversation had been turned into a confrontation in the space of a minute. Before I'd even had chance to put the flowers in a vase.

On Sunday, Henry's mother and sister pitched a few barbed insults in my direction, aided and abetted by Henry. He started telling them how I dropped the car seat with Beth in it, and then *guilted him* - his words - into exchanging it for a simpler one that I was actually capable of operating.

"I would have thought that someone with a brain the size of a planet could have managed a few simple clips and catches," Caroline said. "Don't you have a PhD in physics or something?"

I wished I had a PhD in smacking her in the face. I could think of several verbal ripostes, most of them including the word *fuck*, but none of them remotely suitable for Sunday lunch with the in-laws.

Not for the first time, I ended up chatting to Henry's father in the kitchen, while he was clearing up and I was giving Beth a feed.

"Oh, by the way, I hope you don't mind, I lent your copy of *Northanger Abbey* to my mother. I was looking for something for her to read and found it amongst Henry's books."

"*Northanger Abbey*? I didn't know I had a copy," he said, shaking his head slowly.

"It has your initials in it: AW."

"Does it? Oh, right, I suppose it might be mine then. Henry must have had it so long I've forgotten all about it."

"Anyway, you will be pleased to know mum is enjoying it."

"Good. Feel free to have a look on my bookshelves to see if there's anything else you think she might like."

That was about the only kind word I received all day.

Chapter 14

Once Henry had gone off to work on Monday morning, I started thinking about how I could re-start my investigation into Annie Wilson's disappearance. So far, all I have discovered is a date and a couple of initials in a book. No, sorry, forget the initials; they probably belong to Henry's father. So, all I have is a date. Well done, Katy; pretty feeble effort, wouldn't you say?

I was struggling to think what else I could do, when during Monday lunchtime, Henry called about his latest office drama and unwittingly presented me with a perfect opportunity.

"You will never guess what," he said.

Experience told me not to try. Anyway, he didn't wait for my guess.

"The new VP of Marketing started today, and she's planning to reorganise us again. There was one reorganisation just after I joined; now there's another one. It's absolutely ludicrous."

Hang on! Didn't Henry tell me *he* was the new VP of Marketing? I was confused, but if I'm honest, not totally surprised.

"Do you think it will affect you?"

"How should I know? I guess it's bound to."

"A change could be a good thing. Maybe you will end up better off."

"Why would I?"

That would teach me to be optimistic.

"I don't know. I was just trying to look on the bright side."

There was a long pause, but I decided not to say anything else.

"Anyway, the main reason I'm calling is to tell you we're having a stupid two-day off-site meeting in a couple of weeks' time. It's going to be at some fancy hotel in London, and we have to stay overnight. I think she's going to announce the new marketing structure then."

Rather than worrying me about what he might get up to in a hotel, his news triggered an idea in my head; an idea I'd previously had to abandon. While he was away - doing whatever he was doing in London - I would go to Lyme Regis.

I don't know what I hoped to achieve there - apart from maybe visiting the *Dorset Echo* office nearby - but I didn't have any better ideas, did I? Besides, a couple of days away from everything might be just what I needed to recharge my batteries. Mum had a lot of friends and neighbours visiting her now, and June Williams was right next door, so I didn't need to feel too guilty about leaving her for a short break. Obviously, it would take a lot of careful planning - not least, to conceal the trip from Henry - but hell, why not? It was the only opportunity I was likely to have in the near future to do something proactive.

Henry's call reminded me that I still wanted to check his CV to see where he was working around the date of Annie's disappearance. It was too risky to search his computer - I might leave an electronic trail - so I wandered into his study to see if I could find a hard copy. I thought he might have printed his CV for his most recent job application. I wasn't particularly comfortable snooping around, but after the way he'd shamelessly rummaged through mum's writing bureau, I only felt I was getting even.

It didn't take me long to find what I was looking for. As I read through his CV, it dawned on me that this was the very first time I'd seen the whole picture of his life set out in front of me. Some of the specific details I was already quite familiar with: the Oxfordshire private boarding school he attended; his third-class degree in Geography from Exeter; his first marketing job, also in Exeter. What I hadn't realised though, was that he'd worked for seven different companies, including the current one, in just under 13 years. I didn't need to be a mathematician to figure out that was under two years per job on average. Was this really normal in the marketing world or was it just that Henry found it difficult to settle anywhere? And he didn't seem particularly enthused about his current job either, so it might soon be eight companies.

From Henry's employment history, I could see that around the time Annie disappeared, he was working as a marketing manager for a large publishing company in central London. Nothing too controversial about that, except that Annie was a student at London University. So, it was possible they met in London - but London is so vast that it was equally possible that they didn't. Interestingly, his CV revealed that it was in the July of that same year that Henry made the move away from London to Oxford. Was that somehow significant?

Whilst I was at it, I couldn't resist a quick peek at the rest of his job file. I found the offer letter from his current employer; his official job title was: Senior Marketing Manager - Marketing Communications. So, *not* the Marketing VP, as he liked to refer to himself. Nothing like, in fact. Just how many levels below the new VP was he, I wondered. I also noticed that the starting salary he'd bragged about included a 20% bonus - which was far from guaranteed - and his basic salary was still lower than mine. Obviously, I wasn't planning to challenge him on this point, but at least I knew the truth now. I also found his application letter and some emails, which suggested that he'd actually applied for the job in response to an advert, rather than being personally headhunted as he claimed. The weird thing is that none of his half-truths and lies surprised me. I already knew he was a fraud.

As I replaced everything in the folder, and put it back exactly as I found it, something else occurred to me. It could only be about 30 or 40 miles from Exeter to Lyme Regis, so Henry probably visited this part of the Dorset coast when he was a student or soon after he graduated. Of course, by the date of Annie's disappearance, Henry hadn't lived in Exeter for several years, but he would still have been familiar with the surrounding area - including The Cobb.

This little bit of detective work further convinced me that a visit to Lyme Regis was the next step. I had just two weeks to come up with a watertight plan for my trip. First thing I needed, was an alibi.

Chapter 15

By the Wednesday night before Henry's marketing meeting in London, everything was in place for my trip - including the alibi.

I first considered telling him that I was going to stay with mum while he was away, but that would mean entangling her in my web of deceit. And there was a risk that he might phone her and ask to speak to me. Given mum's current fragile state - not to mention how tricky it would be to explain to her what I was actually doing in Lyme Regis - I quickly discounted that idea.

In the end, I settled on the cover story that I was visiting my old friend Elena in Cambridge. She was very happy to give me an alibi without asking too many questions - although a little hurt that I wasn't actually visiting her. I promised to bring Beth over very soon and explain everything. Henry said he couldn't understand why I was so eager to visit her, given that she hadn't made it to either the wedding or the christening. This was totally unfair; she was given zero notice of the wedding, and it was Henry who talked me out of inviting her to the christening because she hadn't come to the wedding! He insisted on having Elena's phone number in case there was a problem with my mobile. After some initial reluctance, I finally gave it to him - although I believe I may have *accidentally* mixed up two of the digits. I figured it was unlikely he would call, and if he did, well I would just have to apologise for giving him the wrong number - or even better, blame him for writing them down in the wrong order.

I have to be honest; I didn't feel the slightest bit guilty about all this subterfuge. I was actually quite proud of myself. For the first time in a long time, I felt in control. This was *my* mission.

Henry wanted to leave early for the train station. His department and his job were up for discussion, so he needed to be there on time for once. That suited me fine. My bags were already packed. The sooner he left, the sooner I could set off for Lyme Regis. Through the window, I could see him looking at one of the tyres on his BMW and pushing it with his foot. The next second he gave it an angry kick.

"Damn it, I've got a flat tyre," he snorted, flouncing back into the kitchen.

I tried not to say anything that could make it my fault.

"Oh, dear."

"I thought something didn't sound quite right on the way back from the station yesterday."

"Did you check it?"

"Of course I fucking checked it. It looked fine when I parked it last night."

"What about the spare?"

"For God's sake, I don't have time to change a tyre now," he barked. "Anyway, I'm in my best suit. Look, Katherine, I need to go. I'm going to miss my train. I need to take your car."

He grabbed my car keys from the kitchen worktop, crushing my own plans without a second thought. He had turned his problem into my problem. What a selfish bastard.

"Don't forget, I'm supposed to be going to Cambridge this morning."

"I know, but what am I supposed to do then?"

He was still holding my keys. I could see he was getting angrier, trembling slightly. He started kicking the leg of the kitchen table. I felt quite frightened, but I was also desperate to rescue my trip to Lyme Regis.

"Give me a minute to grab Beth. I can drive you to the station."

"Oh, OK …," he said, releasing the keys from his tight grasp into my outstretched hand.

We drove to the station in stony silence, and I dropped him right outside the ticket office.

"Look, sorry, I'm just so stressed about this reorganisation," he said.

He pushed the car door fully open with his foot, leaving a dirty mark on the interior. God help me if I'd done that in his beloved BMW. Without looking, he ran across the station forecourt, narrowly missing a sleek grey Mercedes taxi which came racing in.

A large part of me wished it had hit him.

Did I really just say that about my own husband? What a terrible thing to say. Does it make me sound horrible? I'm sorry if it does. Actually, I'm not sorry at all. Why should I apologise? He made me like this. This dark side; it came from him. It's his fault. If I don't do something soon, it will consume me completely.

It was still only a few minutes after seven o'clock in the morning, but I was already so tense I couldn't think straight. I started to ask myself whether I had the mental energy to go to Dorset. I could just visit Elena instead and enjoy myself for a couple of days in Cambridge. On the other hand, if I didn't go to Lyme Regis today, when would I go? I was unlikely to get another opportunity any time soon. On the other, other hand …

Just do it, Katy.

Earlier in the week, I'd spoken to a helpful man at the *Dorset Echo* office in Weymouth - about 30 miles from Lyme Regis - who said he'd be happy to help me track down some old articles relating to The Cobb. For obvious reasons, I hadn't told him precisely what I was looking for, but had given him the approximate date range I wanted to search. He was expecting me at 1pm, so that gave me plenty of time to drive down to Weymouth - under 3 hours according to Google maps - find somewhere for a snack, and take care of changing and feeding Beth.

After over two hours trawling through past issues of the *Dorset Echo*, there was nothing to suggest that the mystery of Annie Wilson's disappearance had been solved. I found one short follow-up article saying the police investigation was continuing, but there was nothing about Annie having turned up again. Nor was there any notice of her death. The trail seemed to have gone stone cold.

I sat there with my knuckles under my chin, contemplating what to do next. I pulled out the original newspaper article from the envelope the woman had given me, and put it on the desk for inspiration.

"I remember that poor girl; such a tragedy."

I looked up. An elderly gentleman was straining his eyes to read the clipping.

"The Cobb can be a dangerous place," I said, not wanting to appear too interested in the girl.

"She lived with her mother over in Lyme Regis."

"Yes, that's right. Did you know her?"

I was having a hard time concealing my eagerness for information.

"Not the daughter. My wife knew her mother though; they both worked in town. We used to live in Lyme Regis back then, before my wife … er … well, you know."

"Oh, right, sorry."

"How do you know Annie Wilson?" he asked.

This was the question I'd been afraid of.

"Oh, no, I just saw the article and realised she is … was … the same age as me. We must have been at university at exactly the same time. It's so sad."

"Boyfriend trouble."

"Sorry?"

"Boyfriend trouble, at least that's what Maggie said."

I assumed Maggie must have been his wife.

"What happened?"

"The word was she met some chap in London, a few years older than her; bit of a rotter. He sent her completely off the rails. She was all over the place when she came home, she was."

"That's such a shame."

"I don't think they ever found her. No-one seemed to know what happened."

"Does her mother still live in Lyme Regis?"

"Alison? Yes, as far as I know. Up the hill, just off the Charmouth Road. Not too far from where Maggie and I used to live, in fact. Fantastic view of the bay from up there. Beautiful spot."

I could hear the memories of his wife creeping into his voice. A feeling of guilt washed over me. He'd already given me far more information than I deserved, and I hadn't even been honest with him. I thanked the old gentleman warmly, and made my way back to the car. Beth was starting to get a bit grisly, and we still had the drive to Lyme Regis ahead of us.

As I left Weymouth, I realised that no amount of web surfing could possibly have unearthed the information I now had in my possession. It just proved that there really was no substitute for talking face to face.

Chapter 16

When I arrived in Lyme Regis, the sun was out and there was a pleasant afternoon breeze. The small car park by the memorial clock was full, but just as I was about to try my luck elsewhere, I noticed someone reversing out of a small space. I sneaked in quickly before anyone else spotted it. There was a large-scale map of the town on the side of the building above, which I studied for a couple of minutes to get my bearings. It all looked very different from how I remembered it as a child. Everything seemed so much bigger then.

I took Beth for a walk in her pram along the Cart Road - the old name for what is now a level strip of concrete between Marine Parade and the beach. Above us was an interesting selection of properties of wildly differing architecture. I smiled to myself at the names of two of them: Harville and Benwick Cottages - someone was clearly milking the *Persuasion* connection.

We passed the coloured beach huts and reached the curving wall of The Cobb. There were a couple of dire warning signs on the access steps:

Strictly no access to the public in high winds
Danger - unguarded drop

I climbed up the first couple of steps. I could see there was a camber on the top, sloping down towards the sea on the right. It didn't look like a wise choice for a pushchair, so I continued along the lower paved quay on the left of the wall, looking at the boats in the small harbour, and doing my best not to trip on the uneven stones. Further along, next to a flight of stone steps leading onto the top of the wall, was a square white sign with yet another warning, this one from West Dorset District Council:

Warning - this wall is slippery particularly when wet - users are advised to take special care - all persons using this wall do so at their own risk

I walked as far as I could to the end of the quay, past the little beach on the left, and then headed back the way I had come. Walking in this direction, I could now appreciate the spectacular fossil-filled dark grey cliffs to the west of Lyme. Back at the town end of The Cobb, I found an excellent selection of wooden benches nestled under the high wall, each with its own small brass remembrance plaque. I chose one with a good view and sat there for nearly an hour, watching people come and go, and chatting to anyone who stopped to admire my *oh, what a gorgeous baby*.

It was good to be away from Henry. To have some time to think. There were so many things I needed to think about, but right now, it was Annie Wilson who occupied my thoughts.

Was Henry the *boyfriend trouble*, the *chap in London*, the *bit of a rotter*? My heart said yes, even if my head told me I didn't have a shred of conclusive evidence. On the question of what happened to Annie on that fateful Saturday night, I could still only speculate. How could I ever possibly really know what happened to a 22 year-old final year student with serious boyfriend issues. The possibilities were endless.

But I did need to know. I needed to know how Henry was involved. He was my husband and the father of my child. I needed to know what sort of person Beth and I were living with. The woman in the churchyard, whoever she was, must have wanted me to follow up on her intervention. I had to find some answers.

I knew what I had to do next. I had to try and find Annie's mother. I knew her first name - Alison - and roughly where she lived. With a bit of luck, I might be able to find her and talk to her.

No, that was a stupid idea. Why would her mother want to talk to me? That's the last thing she would want; to talk to a nosy stranger and reopen all the old wounds. She would tell me it was none of my business, and she would be absolutely right. The best thing - the right thing - would be to leave her in peace.

But hang on; if Henry was involved, then I *was* involved. That did make it my business. And the woman at the christening had made it my business too. Maybe I should try to contact Annie's mother after all.

I kept going backwards and forwards in my head. Eventually, I made a decision - or rather, a non-decision. I would leave it to fate. I would take a drive up the Charmouth Road and just see what happened.

I checked the sat-nav and realised I'd already come down Charmouth Road on the way over from Weymouth. How did I miss that? I would drive back up slowly and be more observant this time. There wasn't anybody directly behind me, so I crawled up the hill like a learner driver. Ahead of me, on the other side of the road, I noticed a car waiting to turn right. I wasn't in a hurry so I flashed my lights to let it turn in. As I passed the junction a few seconds later, I happened to glance after the car and noticed that it was a blue VW Polo.

A blue VW Polo! I had memorised every word of the newspaper article off by heart. Surely it couldn't be the same blue VW Polo after all these years.

I turned round as soon as I could, and followed where the car had gone, looking about for any sign of it. The wide road curved round and up with an amazing view out over the sea. This definitely fitted the description I'd been given by the old gentleman.

Out of the corner of my eye, I caught sight of a blue car parked on a sloping driveway. A thin lady with grey hair was unloading some bags of food shopping from the back of her car and taking them into the house. As I cruised by, I noted the registration number; it was definitely old enough. I parked about 50 yards further along the road, just out of sight. Then I put Beth into her pushchair and took her for an innocent little stroll back towards the house.

As I approached, the lady lifted out the last shopping bag and locked the car. She glanced over and smiled; just a sort of instinctive reaction to seeing a young woman walking along with a baby in a pushchair. A little brown springer spaniel was fussing around her heels. She looked away, but then looked straight back at me and froze. It was as if she recognised me. I realised that I'd frozen too. I knew that if I carried on walking past, I would never pluck up the courage to come back. It was imperative that I said something, and right now. There were so many things I wanted to say, but I couldn't find the right first word.

After a few seconds of this silent awkwardness, the woman put down her shopping bag and came over towards me. Her dog was now sniffing around my legs and the pram, but thankfully didn't jump up or bark at us. The woman had a strained look on her face as she studied us.

"Hello, I'm sorry, but do we know each other?" she asked.

There was a slight harshness to her voice.

"No, but …"

I knew it was her; it had to be. I took a deep breath.

"Sorry, but are you by any chance Mrs Wilson; Alison Wilson?"

Not surprisingly, her face tensed a little. Did she already sense this would be something about Annie?

"Yes, I am. How do you know my name?"

"It's quite complicated. I'm not sure where … sorry, my name is Katy Harrington … this is my daughter Beth, and we … look, I don't know quite … I was hoping …"

I burst into tears. Her expression suddenly changed. She put her hand gently on my arm.

"Right, Katy, well there's no sense in us talking out here in the road, is there? I could do with a cup of tea, and you look like you could do with one too. Why don't you come in for a few minutes?"

I think the fact that I had a young baby with me made her less suspicious, and more sympathetic towards me, than she might otherwise have been.

"Thank you, that's so kind of you. It's been a very long day."

She ushered me into her house and helped me fold up the pushchair in the hallway. She opened the door of her front room, and her spaniel settled himself down on an old dark brown blanket in the corner.

"So, Katy, why don't you and Beth make yourselves at home in here. Rusty won't bother you. I'll go and put the kettle on."

When I'd set off up Charmouth Road, I had never seriously expected to meet Annie Wilson's mother. Now, less than ten minutes later, I was sitting in her living room watched over by her dog. Fate had responded to my call.

While she was busy in the kitchen, I tried to organise my muddled thoughts. How was I going to explain to her what I was doing here? Surely, it would be far too upsetting to listen to me - a woman she literally just met in the road - talking about the precious daughter she lost eight years ago. But there was no way to protect her. The only way was to tell her my story. There simply was no other way.

"Mrs Wilson," I began.

"Alison; please call me Alison."

I told her everything: what happened at the christening; everything I knew about Annie - which wasn't much; about my relationship with Henry; about mum and her recent stroke. It all came gushing out, chaotic and emotional. I hardly drew breath for the best part of an hour. It felt good to have someone to talk to.

Alison listened carefully, never interrupting me, and as far as I could tell, never judging me. I could sense the emotion rising in her as I talked about Annie - especially when I slid the newspaper clipping from its envelope - but somehow she managed to hold it together. When I'd finished my tale of woe, she took a deep breath and smiled.

"Well, Katy, I am pleased you found me."

It was such a relief to hear her say that. I think I even managed a little smile.

"Me too."

"I want to show you something," she said.

She retrieved a large and rather battered photo album from the shelf under the coffee table. I looked at it with anticipation. I knew she was going to show me photographs of Annie.

"If you have time, that is. Are you heading back home tonight?"

"Yes, I definitely have time. I'm staying in Lyme Regis tonight. Oh, no …"

"What's the matter?"

"I've totally forgotten about booking a room. I didn't want to do it in advance, in case Henry found out. I even brought cash to pay for the room, so it wouldn't appear on my credit card statement. How ridiculous is that?"

It was ridiculous, but essential. Fortunately, I still had my own bank account, so it was possible to conceal a cash withdrawal.

"No, I can understand why you had to do that."

"Can you recommend anywhere local? A simple B&B would be fine. I could give them a call now and get it sorted."

Alison didn't reply immediately. I assumed she was thinking of somewhere to recommend.

"Why not stay here with me?"

"No, no, I couldn't possibly impose like that."

"Don't worry, you aren't imposing. We still have a lot to talk about, and you don't want to be dragging your baby around Lyme Regis late at night, do you?"

I felt guilty that I'd somehow trapped her, but the offer to stay with her was extremely tempting.

"That's so kind of you. Are you sure you don't mind?"

"I absolutely insist. There are four bedrooms and only one of me."

I heard the tremor in her voice. It was clear she wanted company.

"In that case, thank you so much. I would love to stay."

I moved my car onto her drive and brought our things in. Alison helped me take them up to one of the bedrooms, and erect Beth's travel cot in the corner.

"This is a beautiful room. I can't begin to thank you enough for letting me stay here tonight."

"You are very welcome."

As we started back down the stairs, I spotted a closed bedroom door with brightly coloured wooden letters stuck onto it. The letters spelt the name ANNIE.

So, after all this time, Annie still had her own room. I tried to imagine what it would be like inside. Had it been kept just as Annie had left it on that fateful day - to preserve the memories? Or had it been cleared out - to eliminate the memories? I felt sure that Annie's room would be exactly as she had left it; Alison would not have changed anything. If it was my daughter that had gone missing, that's what I would do. I would never give up hope. I would still be waiting for her to return.

Chapter 17

Alison opened the photo album. There were two almost identical baby photos, side by side. The only difference was that the cute face on the right had a hint of a smile. I assumed they were two photos of Annie.

"Annie was a pretty baby, wasn't she?" I said.

"Yes, and Amy too."

"Amy?"

"Sorry, yes of course, you wouldn't know. Why would you? Annie and Amy are twins. That's Annie on the left and Amy on the right. It's Amy's old bedroom that you are staying in."

So, Annie had a twin. I'd been so focused on Annie that it hadn't occurred to me to ask Alison if she had any other children. I was even more surprised when I saw the date neatly written on the little card below the photos. Incredibly, it was just a few days after my own birthday. We were all basically the same age. I was dying to ask about Amy, but decided to let Alison reveal her family's story in her own good time.

The album contained all the usual types of photos: baby, toddler, primary school, dressing up, holidays, senior school, parties, exam results, home. They looked like a happy family. There was just one photo of a man; he was with the two girls when they were in their early teens.

"That is … that was their father," was all Alison said by way of explanation.

I avoided the obvious question. She would tell me if and when she was ready. As we progressed through the photos, I began to wonder how far they would go. Would there be any photos of Amy after Annie had disappeared, or would there be only blank pages? I would totally understand if Alison had lost the will after that.

A strange sense of recognition had been building up in me as we worked our way through, page by page. Then it dawned on me what was happening. The two young girls I was watching grow up through their photographs were beginning to resemble someone I knew.

And that someone was me.

Suddenly it clicked. I remembered what Malkit had said about the woman outside the church: *she looked just like you.* It made perfect sense now. That woman must have been Amy. Now I also understood why Alison had stared at me when she first saw me.

She thought I was Annie.

Alison continued turning the pages, but more pensively now.

"This is a few days before they both went off to university. Annie loved books; she read all the time; she wanted to study English; she had offers from everywhere and picked London in the end."

Where she met Henry?

"Amy wasn't so academic; she wanted to do something more practical and chose marine biology; she went to Portsmouth."

Alison turned over the final page. There was a single graduation photo. She collapsed in tears. I didn't know what to say or do; I was in tears too. The idea of a young life with so much promise, being taken away so cruelly, was too much to bear for anyone.

After a long while, Alison wiped her eyes with a tissue.

"Sorry about that." she said.

"No, no, don't apologise, I can't begin to imagine …"

My words trailed off. I genuinely couldn't begin to imagine.

"Things were very complicated at the time. My husband was very difficult to live with. I managed to hide it from the girls when they were young, but once they left for university, it got so much worse. I was at the point where I couldn't put up with him any longer. I was going to leave him."

No wonder she had a strained look on her face.

"Oh dear, I am so sorry to hear that."

"Anyway, suddenly, he became seriously ill; heart problem. I ended up looking after him until he died. That was the summer before the girls went back to university for their final year. They were devastated. They still didn't know what he was really like, of course. Fortunately, Amy had started going out with Jake the year before. He's in the Navy … based in Portsmouth … nice boy. He was very supportive … really helped her. Actually they've just got engaged and bought a house together. She's doing fine now."

I was waiting for the *but*.

"But Annie, she couldn't cope. She was completely traumatised. She wouldn't come out of her room for days. She didn't want to return to university; she wanted to stay at home. I made her go back. I physically put her on the train at the start of term. Why did I? … why did I do that? … it's all my fault … it's all my fault."

Alison couldn't carry on talking, she just breathed and sighed.

"Can I make you some tea?" I suggested.

She nodded.

"Do you mind if I sort Beth out for bed first?"

"Is there anything I can do to help?"

"Not really, thanks."

"Are you sure? I'd be happy to."

"Well, if you like …"

She made it all seem so effortless. Perhaps it wasn't surprising, given all the practice she'd had with twins. I couldn't imagine what it would be like having to do everything twice - and without any help from Henry. As we worked together, it occurred to me that - under very different circumstances - Alison might have been helping Annie with her own baby by now, rather than helping me with Beth. I wondered if she was thinking the same thing.

"You have a lovely little girl there. She's so well behaved. Reminds me of my Annie when she was that age. Amy was always a bit of a handful, but Annie was so easy, so placid. I loved them both equally of course."

I suspected that she added those final few words because secretly, deep down - never to be admitted to anyone - she had loved Annie a little more. Perhaps, in a way, she still did. Or maybe it was because Annie's time had been so cruelly cut short that Alison needed to love her more.

After we put Beth to bed, Alison picked up the story again and eventually reached the point where Annie's life story and mine became inextricably linked.

"… and it was in her final year that she met this guy. She told me his name was Henry."

I had known this moment was coming, but as she said his name, I felt my stomach tense. There could be no doubt about it now. This Henry that Annie had met was the same lying cheating scumbag Henry that I was now married to. It sickened and appalled me that he was the connection between our two families.

"I don't know what happened, but Annie changed completely. I rarely saw her, and when I did, she was on her own. He always had some excuse for not being there. Do you know, I never once met him? She dropped her friends; hardly spoke to Amy; was very secretive, and defensive about him."

This all sounded horribly familiar to me.

"That must have been very difficult for you and Amy."

"Extremely. And then, that weekend she came home. She turned up out of the blue, deeply upset about something. I tried to ask her what was the matter, but she said she needed to think first.

100

She asked if she could borrow my car to drive down into town, as it was so windy and wet that evening. She said: *I need to get out and clear my head.* Those were her exact words: *I need to get out and clear my head.*"

Alison stopped talking. She stared at the wall like she was in a trance. I realised immediately that these must have been the last words that Annie ever said to her. She had memorised them. They were engraved into her head; carved into her heart; burnt into her body.

When her strength finally returned, Alison started to tell me about the police investigation. Apparently, they talked to Annie's friends and tracked down her boyfriend. His name was Henry Watson. They established that he'd had a big argument with Annie on Friday evening, the day before she disappeared. He claimed it was about what they were going to do for his birthday on the Saturday. He wanted to have a big party with all his friends, but she just wanted a quiet night for the two of them. When he refused to back down, she decided to come home on her own.

After my recent experience with Henry over Mother's Day, I could understand exactly how Annie felt.

Her friends said she'd been acting a bit strangely for a couple of weeks or so, but they didn't know why. The police confirmed Henry was in London on the Saturday; several of his friends testified that he was with them at a party. There appeared to be no way he could have been in Lyme Regis - not unless he drove all the way there, and then back in the early hours of the morning, which didn't really seem possible. It sounded like Alison had been forced reluctantly to accept Henry's alibi. What else could she do?

After hours, then days, then weeks, then months, there was still no trace of Annie. No evidence of foul play; no evidence of suicide; no evidence of anything. Nothing. She had simply and inexplicably disappeared. Eventually there were no leads left for the police to investigate. The most likely explanation they came up with was that she must have had an accident, either falling into the sea or being swept into the sea. No body was ever found. Now, eight years later, Alison still knew no more than that.

With no proof of Annie being alive for over seven years, Alison was advised to apply to the Court for her to be declared *presumed dead*. One or two of her close friends said this would help her get closure - as they called it. But Alison didn't want this type of closure. It was too final. Whatever the evidence showed - or didn't show - and whatever the police thought, Alison would never ever give up hope.

And neither would I, if it was my daughter.

Chapter 18

My phone started ringing and I glanced at the screen. It was an unwelcome intrusion into our intimate discussion.

"It's Henry; I'd better take this," I said.

I got up, but Alison indicated I could stay where I was. She wandered off into the kitchen to give me some privacy.

Henry sounded like he'd had a few drinks, and there were some noisy people in the background, so the conversation was rather disjointed. From what I could make out, his part of the marketing team was staying more or less as it was. However, they were planning to promote someone to head it up, and would be interviewing internal candidates - Henry included - next week. His meeting in London should be finishing early on Friday afternoon, so I could expect him about five o'clock. He didn't ask how my trip was going - which was a relief for obvious reasons. Neither of us really made much attempt to prolong the call. It felt like he had somewhere else he'd rather be - as did I.

I went to find Alison.

"Sorry about that. He didn't ask me anything; he just talked about himself."

We picked up our conversation exactly where we left off and talked into the early hours. Eventually we called it a night. Most unusually for me these days, as soon as my head touched the pillow, I was gone. Thankfully Beth also stayed asleep until a civilised hour. Around seven o'clock, after I started moving about, there was a gentle knock on the door and Alison brought me a mug of tea.

Alison was in no hurry for me to leave - and neither was I - so we chatted for ages over a leisurely breakfast. She hadn't known anything about Amy coming to the christening - assuming it was Amy - but said she would call her daughter later to find out. We both agreed that it was best if I didn't confront Henry. We had no idea what he would say - or do - if he discovered I'd been digging into his past behind his back. I realised, perhaps not for the first time, but all too starkly now, that I was genuinely frightened of him. I could think of several times recently when I'd been distinctly uncomfortable being alone with him. That was no way to live.

When it was time to leave, I went upstairs to collect my things and Alison came with me.

"Would you like to see Annie's room?" she asked.

"Well … only if you're sure. I don't want to intrude."

"Yes, it's fine."

She opened the door slowly. It looked like the room of a third-year student, except perhaps tidier - although that may have been her mother's work. My eyes scanned the room. I tried to take in all the items and build a picture of the girl who had lived there. Alison looked fragile. She sat on the bed to steady herself.

Not surprisingly for a serious English student like Annie, there were rows and rows of books, neatly arranged in a large white sturdy-looking bookcase. I walked over to have a closer look at some of the titles. That was when I saw the line of dark blue leather-bound hardbacks. I knew instantly that one would be missing. I checked off the titles. *Northanger Abbey* was not there.

"Do you mind?" I asked, reaching for Annie's copy of *Pride and Prejudice*.

"No, please go ahead. Annie loved those novels. She'd had them in paperback for ages, but we bought that special set when she got her offer from London."

I carefully extricated the book and opened the front cover. Handwritten, pencil: AW.

I didn't need to, but I pulled up the photo on my phone anyway. The writing was identical. I carefully explained the significance to Alison, who sat shaking her head in disbelief and growing paler by the second. It made me sick to the core to know that Henry had kept Annie's book for all these years. It didn't matter whether she had loaned it to him or given it to him. He had absolutely no right to keep it. He should have found a way to return it - anonymously if necessary. It was special and it belonged with all Annie's other books. I promised to post it back to Alison without delay, so that she could return it to its rightful place.

We agreed to keep in touch - obviously only when Henry was not around. I stored her number under the name of an old friend I was no longer in contact with, just in case Henry saw my phone. It seemed ridiculous that I needed to behave like a secret agent with my own husband.

After lunch, as I drove away from the Jurassic Coast and back up through the Dorset countryside, my mind replayed all the events and revelations of the past 24 hours. Just knowing that there was someone else out there who understood, was important to me. I hoped Alison felt the same. I was strangely excited about my short adventure in Lyme Regis, and thankful for the new friend and ally I'd made there. After such a long period of relative isolation since the start of my pregnancy, it was reassuring to know that I still had the social skills to make a new friend - albeit under slightly bizarre circumstances.

Beth looked like she was enjoying herself too; she was happily chewing her fingers and gurgling in her car seat.

Chapter 19

When I saw Henry's car on the drive, my heart sank. My all too brief feeling of euphoria evaporated in an instant. It was back to reality and everything that meant. Wasn't absence supposed to make the heart grow fonder?

"Where the hell have you been?" was his opening greeting.

Clearly my absence hadn't made his heart grow fonder. Had he tried to call Elena in Cambridge? Did he suspect something? Was this a test to see if I would confess, before he extracted the truth from me?

"You know where I've been," I replied, not committing one way or the other.

"I meant, why are you back so late? I've been trying to call you all afternoon to get a lift. I gave up in the end and had to get a taxi home from the station. Cost me a bloody fortune."

I'd totally forgotten about his puncture. To be fair, rather a lot had happened since yesterday morning - but I couldn't tell him that.

"Sorry, I didn't realise you were expecting me to give you a lift from the station. You should have said something when you called me last night."

"I would have thought it was bloody obvious. How did you think I was going to get home? Walk? I've been here since four o'clock. The water was stone cold again. I had to wait ages for a shower."

"I was planning to be home earlier, but I've been stuck in traffic for nearly two hours. You know what the roads are like on a Friday afternoon."

I quickly reminded myself that I was supposed to have been in Cambridge, just in case he asked any specific details of my supposed nightmare journey.

"Yes, Katherine, I am well aware it's Friday, and thank God it *is* Friday. I really need some peace and quiet this weekend. It's been absolutely manic for the past two days."

Considering Henry must have left London around two o'clock at the latest - presumably after a lavish lunch - I wondered how he could possibly describe it as *manic*? It sounded more like a day in the life of a retired Victorian vicar.

"Anyway, let me bring my things in, and then we can have a chat."

He didn't offer to help. As I carried Beth into the light of the hallway, Henry bent down and stared at her face.

"What have you done to Elizabeth?"

"What do you mean?"

"Look at her! Her cheeks are bright red and she's covered in dribble down her chin and all over her clothes. How long has she been like this?"

"I'm not sure … I didn't …"

"Haven't you even noticed? What have you done to her, Katherine?"

I put the baby carrier down on the living room floor and inspected Beth myself. He was right; she looked awful. A huge bolt of guilt shot right through me. I'd obviously been far too preoccupied with my own thoughts to notice. It hurt me so much to think I'd neglected her.

"I don't know. She was fine earlier."

"Well, she isn't fine now. Where did you take her today? Did you leave her out in the sun? Did you give her plenty to drink?"

Why did he automatically assume it was all my fault?

"We were outside for a bit, but she was under the sun canopy, and she's been fine eating and drinking today. I don't know what the problem is. It must have just started."

"Well, we can't ignore it. We need to get her checked over right away by a doctor."

"I'm not suggesting we ignore it. Let me phone mum to see if she has any ideas."

"That's a complete waste of time. And anyway, your mother isn't going to be able to diagnose anything over the phone. I'm going to phone the surgery."

"There won't be anybody there now. Just give me a minute to call mum."

"What about the minor injuries unit? I think we should take her down there right now."

I ignored him as I was already dialling mum. Trying not to panic, I described the symptoms to her.

"Right, it sounds to me like she's started teething. It would be about the right time, maybe a little early, but all babies are different. I know it's distressing - for her and for you - but it's nothing to worry about. It's perfectly normal."

"What should I do?"

"Rub her gums gently with your finger. Wash your finger under cold water first, so it's clean and cold. Also, clean up the dribble so she doesn't get any sort of rash. And it might be worth buying a teething ring when you get the chance."

I told Henry what mum said, but he insisted on driving Beth straight to the West Berkshire Community Hospital near Newbury. I sat in the back of the car, attempting to soothe her, just as mum suggested. It seemed to be working. Fortunately, the clinic was fairly quiet - the Friday night pub fights hadn't started yet. And they gave Beth priority because she was a baby, so we were seen before too long.

"She's started teething," the doctor said.

Her advice was basically identical to mum's. So, it wasn't my fault at all. In fact, there was no fault. It was a perfectly normal stage in the development of our healthy baby daughter: her first tooth. It should have been a cause for celebration, not conflict. Henry didn't apologise for criticising me, or for dismissing mum's assistance. I was sorely tempted to say *I told you so* - and that *not* taking mum's advice had turned out to be the *complete waste of time* - but I couldn't face the flare-up this would cause. Grudgingly, I let the moment go, and we drove back in stubborn silence.

I was starving by now, but simply didn't have the energy to start cooking. Besides, I needed to spend time comforting Beth. I told Henry I was just going to have something simple - tea and toast. Of course, that wasn't good enough for him, but instead of offering to cook something for both of us, he said he was off to the pub to get a *proper* meal.

Beth didn't have a good night. She wouldn't settle and wasn't interested in feeding either. As I sat nursing her on my knee, I started to examine various aspects of my life with Henry.

When Beth was first born, of course I had felt anxious to start with. I could still remember bringing her home from hospital, putting her carrycot on the sofa, and bursting into tears. Inevitably, there had been issues - like the current teething - but overall, I thought I'd coped reasonably well. My world had been turned upside down when Beth was born, but in return, she had brightened every single day.

Henry, on the other hand, was totally indifferent. His routine remained almost entirely unaltered by her. The most annoying aspect of his behaviour was that, although he rarely offered to help, he was quick to criticise me for any perceived shortcomings. His reaction to Beth's teething, for example, was more about finding fault with my childcare, than genuine concern for her welfare.

Did he resent the time I was spending with her? Did he think I was neglecting him? Did I need to make more time for our own relationship? I guessed these were common problems for couples with a new-born baby. But were they really sufficient to account for Henry's antagonism towards me?

Or was it something else. Something to do with our respective careers, perhaps? The contrast in our situations was quite stark.

I couldn't have been happier with my job. It was genuinely my vocation. I loved the research; I loved the teaching. My colleagues and students constantly challenged and supported me. I found it incredibly rewarding. And having worked so hard to achieve this position, I wouldn't change it for the world.

Whereas Henry's career seemed to be all about his talents not being fully appreciated - or so he claimed. The fact that his CV was completely devoid of any internal promotions, suggested that a more rational explanation was that he didn't actually possess the required talents in the first place. And he was already dissatisfied with his latest role and ready for yet another change.

It occurred to me that what I really needed to do, was sit down and have a rational discussion with Henry about these two prickly issues: firstly, our daughter and secondly, our careers. Sorry, did I just say rational discussion with Henry? What was I thinking?

Chapter 20

Towards first light, Beth finally calmed down and went to sleep. I felt completely worn-out. I lay on my back listening to the woodpigeons rustling and cooing in the pine tree outside the bedroom window. My head and shoulders felt tight and my eyes refused to open. I consoled myself with the thought that while Henry was playing golf later in the morning, I would be relaxing at mum's house. With a bit of luck, I might even be able to grab a much-needed nap, while she kept an eye on Beth. I wasn't sure how I would get through the day otherwise.

Before setting off on the short drive to mum's, I gave Alison a quick call.

"Hi, it's Katy. I can't thank you enough for everything. It was so kind of you to let me stay with you."

"You're very welcome. I really enjoyed having you and Beth here."

"When I was driving home yesterday, I was thinking what a terrible shock it must have been, me turning up out of the blue like that. I hope you didn't mind talking to me about Annie."

"It's fine, don't worry. It's all been bottled up for so long and I don't ever want to forget about Annie."

I could detect a slight crack in her voice.

"No, I'm sure. She must be very special to you."

"Yes, she is. By the way, I tried to call Amy last night, but she was out with Jake. I think there was a Navy dinner at the base. I'm sure we'll speak later today though."

"OK, well I can't wait to hear what she says. I'm off to mum's in a few minutes. I'll make sure I pick up Annie's book."

"How is your mum?"

"I never know really. She has her good days, but … you know."

When I arrived, mum seemed rather subdued and pre-occupied. She didn't rush to take Beth from me, which was most unusual.

"How are you feeling, mum?"

"Oh, you know … up and down. Actually Katy, I've been a bit dizzy this morning."

This was obviously why she wasn't so keen to hold Beth. She didn't quite trust herself.

"What have you been up to?" I asked.

"Nothing much; just reading. I've finally finished *Northanger Abbey*. You can take it back with you, if you like. It's a bit strange, but I enjoyed it."

She passed me the book and I slid it down inside my handbag. I would need to keep it hidden until I had chance to post it back to Lyme Regis.

"By the way mum, you will be pleased to hear the doctor fully endorsed your advice about Beth's teething," I said, trying to cheer her up.

She didn't respond to this. I assumed she was still irked by Henry's lack of faith in her.

"That reminds me. I heard from Helen Franklin. Everything is fully set up now … you know … my will; the trust for Beth; the power of attorney for you. It's all sorted."

"That's good. And are you still happy with the way it's all been done?"

"Yes, it's what I want for you and Beth. You two are my family; the two most precious people in the world to me. It gives me real peace of mind to know you will both be taken care of, if anything happens to me."

For sure, her face did look relaxed, as if a heavy burden had been lifted from her. She seemed very calm in herself for the first time in quite a while.

I made us each a mug of tea and we sat down again for a chat. I was wondering if I should tell mum about Annie Wilson. Maybe I should save it for when she was stronger.

"Mum, you're spilling your tea."

She didn't seem to hear me.

"Mum, your tea," I repeated, louder this time.

She slumped over slightly and her right arm dropped down in front of her. The mug slipped from her grasp and fell onto the floor, spilling tea all over the chair and carpet. Her face was a strange grey colour and devoid of expression.

"Mum, can you hear me?" I said, as I gently touched her cheek and then, more firmly, her shoulder.

There was no response.

I knew instantly.

I dialled 999 and asked for the Ambulance Service. The call handler asked me a few questions. He grasped the situation immediately and said he would send an ambulance straight away. He asked me if I knew how to put mum in the recovery position. I'd done a first aid course not so long ago, but looking at diagrams and practising on dummies was one thing; doing it for real on my own mother was quite another. Mum looked so helpless; so frail; so vulnerable. It felt surreal arranging her crumpled body on the floor. I was completely distraught.

Now all I could do was wait by mum's side for the ambulance to arrive. How long was it going to take? I made a note of the time: 10.44am.

I thought of calling Henry, but he would be on the golf course at least half an hour away, probably with his phone switched off. I was desperate for some moral support right now. Beth was sound asleep so I left her and ran round to next door. June Williams didn't hesitate for a split-second. She dropped everything and came straight back with me. She told me to stay with mum, while she kept an eye out for the paramedics.

I sat on the floor next to mum, holding her hand. She needed my strength, but I had none to give. My mind was thrashing with questions, but there was only one question; the one terrible question which overshadowed them all.

Is she going to die?

I knew the outcome of a stroke - especially a second stroke - was far more complicated than that, but still, it was *the* question.

Is she going to die?

I tried to check her breathing and pulse, but she was so still it was difficult to tell. My whole body was shaking. I thought I could detect a shallow movement of her chest, but I couldn't be 100% sure. I searched frantically for a pulse, but to no avail.

Is she dying already?

I didn't seem to know what I was doing anymore. The throbbing in my head drowned out everything else. I knew, in my soul, she was slipping away.

Is she dying right here, right now, in front of me?

I'd been sitting cross-legged on the floor next to mum for what seemed like ages. I was feeling faint and kept trying to force myself to breathe deeply. I was starting to panic.

After an eternity, I finally heard June shouting at the top of her voice from the front door.

"The ambulance is here. The ambulance is here."

"The ambulance is here," I repeated, as much for my own benefit as for mum's.

I glanced at my watch again: 11.12am. I was so frantic that I couldn't even calculate how long the ambulance had taken. I jumped up out of the way to let the paramedics get to mum.

Suddenly I felt strange.

That was the last thing I remember from the morning of mum's second stroke.

Chapter 21

Where am I?

There's a bright light, somewhere above me. Why is it so bright? It's hurting my eyes.

Please stop the bright light.

What's happening?

I can hear someone talking. What is the voice saying? Is it talking to me? Is it talking about me? I can't tell. I don't care.

Please stop the voice.

I'm lying on something flat. I open my eyes a little, slowly. I am on a flat black bed. The bed is so hard. I can see a white blanket over me. I feel warm and comfortable.
Please leave me alone.
Please let me sleep.

What am I doing here?
My mind is empty of thoughts, except for the light and the voice and the bed.

The side of my head doesn't feel right. My mouth wants to open, but my lips are dry. I can smell something familiar. A chemical smell. I swallow, but my throat is sore.
I don't want to sit up or move from the bed. I want to stay where I am. Warm and safe.
Please leave me alone.

I want to close my eyes again and sleep. I need to sleep. I close my eyes.
The light is not so bright now.
The voice is not so loud.
The bed is not so hard.
I am alone now again.

Chapter 22

I remember waking up on a firm black bed with a bright light right above me. Had I woken up briefly before or had I been dreaming? Either way, there was no voice this time, but the side of my skull felt like someone was standing on it wearing steel boots.
I could just make out Henry's figure at the side of the bed. I recognised his familiar pose: slouched in a chair, staring at his phone. I must have made some sort of sound, because he suddenly

looked up and saw my eyes were open. He leaned forward, still clutching his phone like a comforter.

"Welcome back; you've been out for hours."

My eyes scanned around. There were curtains. There were beds on wheels. There were important-looking people with clipboards. There were other people sitting in chairs talking to other people in beds.

"Where am I?"

"The JR."

"How long have I been here?"

"Quite a while. It's after four now."

"What day is it?"

"Still Saturday."

"What happened? How did I get here?"

"Apparently you fainted. Maybe you stood up too quickly or something. Anyway, the paramedics said you bashed your head pretty hard on your mother's coffee table when you fell. You were knocked out."

"How did I get here?"

"They brought you in the ambulance with your mother."

I began to remember something, but couldn't quite follow my thoughts through.

"Yes, mum … what happened to mum?"

"I'm not sure exactly; they're still doing tests. I think she's already had a scan though."

"Have they told you anything?"

"Not in detail, but it sounds like another stroke. Unfortunately, it's much more serious this time."

"Oh God, is she going to be alright?"

"They don't know yet. It's too early to tell, especially about any long-term effects."

"Have you seen her?"

"No, I've been here for the past few hours, waiting for you to come round."

"Do you know where she is? I need to see her."

"You will be able to soon, but we need to wait until they've finished all the tests and she's back on the ward. One of the nurses looking after your mother knows you're here. She's going to come and take you to your mother as soon as the time is right."

"When will that be?"

"I don't know; probably sometime this evening."

"I need to see her."

"Yes, you will … you will."

Suddenly I noticed that I couldn't see the carrycot anywhere.

"Where's Beth? Who's looking after her?"

"I picked her up from your mother's house. The neighbour, Mrs what's-her-name called me."

"Mrs Williams."

"Yes, Mrs Williams. Anyway, she must have found my phone number on your mobile. It's a good job you don't have a PIN code on it. It was with your handbag at your mother's house. I brought them with me … here you go."

He reached over me with the handbag and put in on my bedside locker.

"God, that's heavy. What have you got in there?"

I remembered Annie's book.

"Women's things," I said quickly, which I guess was kind of true.

Fortunately, he didn't choose this moment to empty out all the contents onto the bed and critique each item - something he'd been known to do in the past.

"Mrs Williams told me what happened to your mother, and then to you. She said Elizabeth could stay with her, but I thought she'd be better off with my mother, rather than a complete stranger. I asked my parents to come over."

"So where is she now?"

"Like I said, she's with my mother … at our house."

Why couldn't Henry have brought Beth with him? I hated the idea of Beth being away from me - and even worse, being with his mother. I detested her ideas on childcare.

"I can't stay here. I need to see mum; I need to see Beth."

115

"Right now, you need to stay here. You had a serious bang on your head. You were out cold for several hours. You almost certainly have concussion. They want to keep you in overnight for observation, just to be safe."

"But what about mum? What about Beth?"

"Don't worry, they're both in good hands. Anyway, you can't be here with your mother *and* at home with Elizabeth at the same time, can you?"

I didn't want to abandon either of them, but what was the alternative? I couldn't think straight.

"Would you be able to bring Beth here?"

"What, now? Bring her to the hospital? You mean drive all the way home and back on a Saturday afternoon? The A34 will be a nightmare. I'll be gone for ages."

"I'd go myself, but ..."

"Well obviously you're in no fit state to drive."

"I want to see her, Henry."

"Look, we don't need to drag her to the hospital tonight. Let's leave her at home with my parents for now. I'm sure she's perfectly fine. You will see her first thing tomorrow morning; I promise."

This quarrelling was straining my sanity. I could feel the pressure in my head growing and spreading behind my eyes.

"I can't deal with this. I need to close my eyes for a few minutes."

"That's probably a good idea. You're just getting yourself stressed, when you should be trying to take it easy."

He was the one getting me stressed. I just wanted him to stop talking.

Later that evening, a nurse came to tell me I could go and see mum. She brought a wheelchair for me to sit in, so there was no risk of me fainting and falling again.

"It's probably best if you go without me," Henry suggested. "We don't want to overwhelm her, do we?"

116

I knew he wasn't being altruistic. He just didn't give a damn about mum. He wanted to get back to his beloved phone. Well, fuck him!

As the nurse wheeled me round to the ward, she tried to prepare me, but as soon as I caught sight of mum, I gasped. She was lying flat on her back, motionless, eyes closed. Her face had aged ten years in the ten hours since I'd last seen her. She was an old woman. I'd never thought of her like that before. The awful thought flashed through my mind that she was actually dead. It was the tube inserted into her nostril that shocked me most. It made her seem distant; connected to the hospital - belonging to the hospital - rather than to me. She was a patient now; she was not mum. These instinctive thoughts sickened me. I needed to banish them. She *was* mum, she *is* mum, I reminded myself.

"Thank you for bringing me over to see my mother," I said to the nurse.

"You're welcome. Let me know when you want to go back, and I'll collect you so you don't get lost. It's like a rabbit warren round here."

I wheeled myself the final two feet to the edge of mum's bed. It was hard to look at her face. It was so tranquil, yet who knew what was going on underneath. Was she in pain? Was she aware of anything? Would she be able to hear me?

"I'm here mum," I whispered softly. "It's Katy."

I looked for any sign of acknowledgement in her face, or movement in her body, but there was nothing.

"Mum, it's me."

Still nothing. I was overwhelmed with tears. A young woman, sitting by another frozen patient, looked up and smiled. My mind was cluttered with disjointed, incomplete, almost random thoughts. What had happened; what was happening; what was going to happen? Nothing was clear.

I stayed with mum for I don't know how long, until my neck muscles were like iron and my eyes like lead. The nurse came up beside me.

"Are you ready to go? You look worn out, dear."

I nodded.

"Bye mum. I'll be back first thing in the morning."

I turned to the nurse and smiled, looking for some kind of encouragement.

"Yes, you should definitely keep talking to her. It's amazing how many patients say they were aware of voices and other sounds, even though they were unconscious. It would be comforting for her to hear your voice."

Chapter 23

When I returned, Henry had disappeared from the blue chair beside the bed. I glanced around and saw him in the corridor talking on his phone. He was leaning back against the wall, with the sole of one foot tucked up on the wall behind him. And he was laughing. Yes, you heard me, laughing. What the hell was he laughing about? I had no idea, but I despised him for it all the same. It felt like he was laughing at me. From where I was sat in my wheelchair, there was absolutely nothing to laugh about. Mum was dying, I had severe concussion and, to cap it all, Beth was in the clutches of his evil mother. What was he laughing at, the insensitive bastard?

I prised myself out of the wheelchair and tottered onto the edge of the bed, and then gently lowered myself down onto the pillow.

"How is your mother?" Henry asked, when he returned.

He actually sounded concerned for once. The sudden contrast with his fit of laughing caught me off guard.

"She's still unconscious. They don't know how quickly she will recover … or whether she's going to recover at all."

"I suppose we'll just have to wait and hope."

"I need to be with her as much as possible over the next few days, in case she …"

"Yes, I understand."

"Have you asked your parents how Beth is?"

"Yes, I was just on the phone to dad. Elizabeth is absolutely fine, like I said she would be. Apparently, she's been making some strange giggling noises. Dad was trying to do an impression of her over the phone. He's useless. It sounded slightly Welsh - although I don't know how that's even possible. It's a shame we weren't there to hear her. It sounded hilarious."

A weak smile struggled towards the surface of my face, but it was repelled back inside by my firmly clamped mouth.

"What's your plan now?" Henry asked.

"I still don't feel quite right. I think the best thing would be for me to get some sleep, and then visit mum again later on to see if there's any change."

"In that case, if it's alright with you, I think I might take off now, so I can sort Elizabeth out and let my parents get off home."

"Yes, good idea. What time will you be back tomorrow?"

"I think visiting starts at ten."

Henry leaned over and kissed me gently on the cheek.

"Don't overdo it. Remember you've had more than enough stress for one day," he whispered.

He smiled and I closed my eyes, slightly warmed by this fleeting reminder of his prior affection.

When I saw mum later that evening, I was dismayed to find there was no change whatsoever in her condition. She was still lying in exactly the same position, lifeless. I sat with her and talked quietly for a few minutes, relaying Henry's story about Beth's giggling. There was no flicker of recognition or response. Could she really hear my voice? Was she even aware I was there? It was hard not to doubt it. To see mum like this was heart-breaking.

Before getting back into bed for the night, I phoned June Williams to thank her for all her help, and gave her an update on mum's progress - or lack of it. Despite my rather gloomy report, she was still keen to visit mum. She said she'd cleared everything up at the house, and promised to keep an eye on it over the next few days. I understood why mum valued her friendship so much.

I decided to call Alison. I needed someone to talk to.

"Sorry to bother you so late," I began.

"It's fine, Katy, I'm not doing anything."

She listened patiently and tried to console me.

"Anyway, at least I have Annie's book," I said, when I finished. "I'll try to post it back to you as soon as I can."

"Don't worry about that, I'm sure you have far more important things on your mind right now."

"That's important to me too."

"By the way, I did manage to get hold of Amy briefly this afternoon. She was rushing off somewhere as usual, but when I told her about meeting you, she got so excited. And you were right; it was her at the church. She's going to drive over tomorrow and tell me all about it."

"I'd really like to hear what she has to say. I'll call you tomorrow when Henry has gone, so we can talk privately."

Talking of privacy, I finally decided to put a PIN code on my phone. Henry had ridiculed me many times for not having one, but in the past, I had nothing to hide. Now, I did. Avoiding anything too obvious like my date of birth, I chose 1827. It looked like a year, but was constructed simply from the first three cubed numbers: 1, 8, 27. I was quite pleased with myself because I knew Henry wouldn't recognise a cubed number if it punched him on the nose - which is something I frequently wanted to do to him these days.

Chapter 24

A combination of complete exhaustion and strong painkillers helped me sleep soundly that night. I don't even remember dreaming, although I'm sure I must have done.

On Sunday, although far from refreshed, I did feel slightly more in control of my faculties. My mind was still simmering with questions though.

To his credit, Henry was the first visitor onto the ward that morning. I was so excited to see Beth. I realised it was almost 24 hours since I'd last held her, which was by far the longest period we'd been separated since her birth. Henry placed her in my arms and I snuggled back down with her. To the people around us, we must have looked like a normal happy family - if there is such a thing. But what is normal? What is happy?

It reminded me of that famous opening line: *happy families are all alike; every unhappy family is unhappy in its own way.*

For some time now, I'd definitely felt we were in the latter category.

Once the doctor had seen me, I was given the all-clear to leave hospital. I went to take another look at mum before we left and Henry came with me this time - probably to hurry me along. There was still no improvement. She was now lying slightly over on her right side, but nothing else had changed. The nurse had no news for me either. I could only interpret no news as bad news. I consoled myself with the thought that at least her condition didn't seem to be getting worse. I whispered to mum that we were going home, and that Beth and I would be back later.

When we arrived home, it looked like Henry had made a bit of an effort. The house was tidy; the dishwasher empty; the table set for lunch. He'd even collected a few flowers from the garden, and put them in my precious cut glass vase - one of the many impulsive presents he'd given me in those romantic early days of our relationship.

"I love the flowers," I said.

"Yes, nice aren't they. Mum picked them yesterday when she was inspecting the garden. She said it looked a bit neglected and needed a good tidy."

The flowers suddenly lost their bloom.

"Oh, right."

"And I dug out that old vase of your mother's to put them in."

So, he didn't even remember. The vase now lost its sparkle too.

While Henry prepared lunch - or to be more accurate, unwrapped lunch - I sorted out the dirty clothes and put the washing machine on. That had obviously been a step too far for Henry.

After lunch, I took Beth upstairs to the nursery, and was irritated to discover that all the baby changing paraphernalia had been moved. After six months, I had a well-established routine, and could literally change a nappy with my eyes shut - especially during the *wee small hours*, as I liked to call them. I put Beth down on the carpet and started moving everything back to its rightful place. After a few minutes, Henry poked his head through the door to see what was taking me so long. He saw Beth on the floor.

"Are you having problems with Elizabeth?" he asked, without offering any actual help.

"Someone has moved all Beth's stuff around," I said.

"Oh, yes, that was my mother. She was on nappy changing duty. She said it was all the wrong way round because it was set up for a left-handed person."

"That's because I *am* left-handed."

"Well, yes obviously, but don't forget it was her that was here looking after Elizabeth for most of yesterday, while you were in the hospital."

He made it sound like I'd spent the day being pampered at a health spa.

"And I'm very grateful to her, but it would have been nice if she'd put everything back where she found it."

"She was only trying to help you."

I couldn't recall the last time Henry had taken my side in a debate about his mother. Or about anything else, come to think of it. These days, we were always on opposite sides in the courtroom.

"Help *me*! I think you mean, help *us*. Beth's *your* daughter too."

"I'm well aware of that. Oh, and that reminds me; I didn't want to make a fuss in the hospital in front of a load of random strangers, but could we please use our daughter's full name, *Elizabeth*."

My head was full to bursting with frustration and anger and tiredness and worry. My mind was lurching from one thought to another and I couldn't focus on anything. I shut my eyes. I was so close to letting go. I wanted to stand and shout and scream until it all went away.

Suddenly everything started tilting; angled lines; blurred edges; ringing sounds; descending mist. All in slow motion. My thoughts emptied away. I was aware I was leaning and collapsing and falling. There was no strength in my body to keep me up.

I vaguely remember Henry launching himself across the nursery to grab hold of me before I hit the floor, but he was too late. He put his arms around me and lifted me into a sitting position on the carpet. When I was steady enough to sit up by myself, he moved back until he was leaning against the cot.

Neither of us said anything for two or three minutes. I wondered what he was thinking. Why was he constantly criticising and picking on me? Did he even realise he was doing it? Did he think it was for my benefit - to help me to improve in some way? Whatever the reason, it was driving me crazy.

"It's a good job I was here to catch you; otherwise you might have bashed your head again," he said.

It would have been nice if he *had* actually caught me.

"I don't know what happened there. I suddenly felt faint and knew I was going to fall, but I couldn't stop myself."

"It must be the concussion. The after-effects could last for weeks. You definitely aren't quite right yet. I keep telling you not to overdo it, but you don't take any notice."

"I do, but it's not easy with mum being back in hospital."

"I know you want to visit her, but you can't spend all your time there."

"No, but I do want to make sure I visit her every day, at least until I have a better idea of what's happening. I don't know when I'll be ready to drive again though. That reminds me, we need to collect my car from mum's house at some point. When can we go and get it?"

One of the drawbacks of living in a small village with no public transport, was that, without a car, I would effectively be isolated. I would have to rely on Henry if I wanted to go anywhere. I was already anticipating the next skirmish with him.

"I'd completely forgotten about your car. You don't really need it yet, do you? I suppose it all depends on when you're fit to drive. It might be a few days yet."

"I can't wait a few days. Can we get it tomorrow if possible?"

"Let's see how you feel. You can't afford to risk driving with concussion, can you?"

I continued reorganising the nursery while he went downstairs to make some tea. When he returned with a mug in his left hand, I was horrified to see that in his right hand, he was holding the blue hardcover book. He put the mug down carefully on a coaster. I held my breath and waited for the cross-examination to begin.

"What's this doing in your handbag?"

He held it up like a prosecutor with a piece of incriminating evidence.

"Oh yes, I lent it to mum a couple of weeks ago. She'd finished reading it, so I picked it up yesterday. Obviously, with her stroke and everything, I totally forgot about it."

"It would have been nice if you'd asked before you borrowed it."

"Yes, sorry, but it's not as if you were in the middle of reading it."

"I'd rather you didn't just go into my study and take my stuff."

When we bought the house, *the* study had automatically become *his* study. I don't remember there being any discussion about who would benefit the most from it. Henry just presumed, and told the removal men to put his stuff in there. Perhaps, in his head, the nursery, kitchen and utility room were all mine, so the study was his. And even though I'd now been working at home for months, and he did most of his work in London, it had remained *his* study. To add insult to injury, he now seemed to be saying I needed his permission even to enter it.

I was furious, but sadly had no fight left in me.

"Your dad said he didn't mind."

"My dad? What's it got to do with him?"

"It's his book."

"It's not his book; it's my book."

"Well, it has his initials inside the front cover."

"Where?"

He flipped the front cover open and stared at the two letters. AW. His face was stone. I watched him like a hawk, trying to detect any betrayal of emotion; any tiny clue. There was nothing. But the crucial thing now, was what he would choose to say next? This was the moment. Truth or lie. He took a couple of seconds to make his decision.

"Oh, right, yes, well maybe it is his book then. I suppose it must have been on the shelf for so long I'd forgotten I had it. I've got so many books like that … the classics … you can't expect me to remember where every single one of them came from originally."

He had chosen the lie. I knew exactly where that book had come from. And so did he. I could picture it right now: the third row of the bookshelf in Annie's bedroom. What a fucking liar he was.

"Anyway, why were you looking through my handbag?"

"I wasn't looking through your handbag. I was moving it off the work-surface to make the tea, when I noticed the book poking out. Let's just forget about it now. I'll go and put it back where it belongs."

As I sipped my tea, nursing my outrage at his cavalier attitude to the truth, I wondered why he hadn't simply admitted that he was given the book by an old girlfriend. He could have just left it at that. It might have been a bit awkward - as any mention of an *ex* always is - but keeping a present like that is hardly a crime. It was clear that he'd made a conscious decision to cover up his relationship with Annie.

Those words Amy had whispered into my ear came back to me: *Did your husband tell you what happened to Annie Wilson?* The answer to that question was still no, but something had fundamentally changed. His failure to mention Annie was no longer simply an accidental omission; it was a calculated and deliberate act. I was now certain that he had something to hide.

By the time I went back down, Henry was busy in his study. He must have heard me on the stairs.

"I've got to prepare for my interview next week. You know, for the promotion thingy," he called through the door.

This was something else that had completely slipped my mind. I stood in the doorway, trying to sound interested - although I was not. I was sure he didn't deserve the promotion. I almost hoped he wouldn't get it. It would serve him right.

"Oh, when is it?"

"Tuesday afternoon with the new VP, and some random person from HR."

As he said *HR*, he screwed up his face as if to spit.

"Do you know if anyone else is applying?"

"I wouldn't have thought so. I have by far the most relevant experience."

"What do you have to do for the interview?"

"Oh, you know, the usual sort of boring stuff. Put together a presentation with a marketing plan, priorities, headcount, budget; that sort of crap."

His use of the word *crap* didn't inspire much confidence that he was taking this interview process seriously. He was obviously irritated about having to be interviewed for a promotion that he regarded as his by right. I needed to make myself scarce before he went off on another rant about office politics.

"I'll leave you to it then," I said, backing away from the door.

By about six o'clock, I was getting concerned that he was still in his study, and hadn't said anything yet about taking me back to the hospital.

"What time do you want to have dinner?" I asked, trying to engage him and see if it might jog his memory.

"Oh, I don't know; maybe around seven, seven thirty. I still have quite a lot to do."

"I hate to mention this, but are you going to be able to take me up to the JR tonight to see mum?"

I braced myself for the onslaught.

"What? Tonight? We've only been home a few hours for God's sake."

"I know, but I did promise her."

"It's not as if she could hear you. I'm sure there won't be any change."

I desperately wished I had my own car and was fit to drive. I had no alternative but to keep pressing Henry.

"I would go on my own if I could, but I don't have my car and it's probably not safe for me to drive anyway."

"Look, I really don't have time, I'm afraid. I've got to finish this presentation tonight, and then I need an early night. We're having marketing catch-ups first thing every Monday morning now with the new VP, and I need to be there on time. Do you want me to get this promotion or don't you?"

"Of course I do. We don't need to stay long. I only want to look in on her."

"Do we really have to drive all the way up to the JR and back? Can't you just phone the ward for an update? It would take two minutes instead of two hours."

"Well, I could, but …"

I was so exasperated with him that I couldn't focus on my words. I knew it was hopeless. I was completely worn out. He was probably right; it was unlikely mum's condition would have changed since this morning. I gave up the struggle.

"Right, I guess I'll just have to phone then."

He ignored me.

"But can we definitely go tomorrow?"

"OK, fine. Anything else?" he snapped, turning back to his laptop without waiting for a reply.

I felt as if I'd just been dismissed from his office. I stood there for a few seconds, debating whether to scream at him or throw something. Instead, I went back into the kitchen, calmed myself down, and called the ward.

"No change; she's doing as well as can be expected," was the basic message from the nurse on duty.

Annoyingly, Henry was right. That didn't change the fact that I hated him so much right now.

Chapter 25

June Williams rang the next morning while I was having breakfast. During our chat about mum, I mentioned that I hadn't been able to visit her last night.

"How about if you and I go together today? I would love to see your mum. She's been such a good friend to me. Obviously, if that's not convenient …"

"Actually, that would be fantastic. Are you sure it's not too much trouble? Henry did offer to take me when he gets home from work."

I wasn't sure the word *offer* quite captured his reluctance.

"Plus, I could drop you off at your mum's house on the way back, so you can collect your car. That's assuming you're feeling up to driving."

"Yes, that would be great, thank you. I'm a bit stuck at the moment without my car."

When my trusty - and rusty - old Volvo estate, which had originally belonged to dad, finally gave up the ghost about six months into our relationship, Henry had insisted on taking control of the purchase of a new car for me. He thought he knew more about what I needed than I did, and was convinced that he would be able to negotiate a better deal than I could. That's how I ended up with a BMW - obviously a smaller model than his - for basically the recommended retail price.

When he floated the idea of me having a personalised number plate, I said I would think about it, to avoid an argument, but never actually got round to doing so. I still miss my dad's old Volvo and the memories it invokes - like when he used to take me to the swimming pool at some ungodly hour each morning.

Of course, Henry's chosen car was totally unsuitable for what I actually needed now - which was basically ferrying around tons of baby gear. Getting the pram in and out of the back was a total nightmare, as was trying to remove baby vomit from the sporty black seat material. Anyway, Henry was happy with the purchase, so that was all that mattered really, wasn't it?

A little after one o'clock, June's little white Hyundai appeared in the driveway. Her perfect reversing manoeuvre was straight from the textbook. As we drove up to the JR, she told me how her late husband had suffered a number of strokes. It was good to have someone to talk to who understood what mum was going through. She was a very pragmatic, no-nonsense sort of person. The more I got to know June, the more I liked her. Mum was lucky to have her as a neighbour.

When we arrived, the nurse told us that mum had opened her eyes briefly an hour or so ago. I seized on this tiny morsel of encouragement like a hungry chick. June and I took it in turns talking to mum, eagerly hoping for another sign.

"Look, Katy, your mum's eyelids are flickering," she said suddenly.

I moved closer and saw that she was right; there was a slight but definite tremor. We waited in anticipation for her eyes to open, but a few seconds later, the movement died down as quickly as it had begun.

"Don't be too disappointed," she said. "The recovery process can take a very long time."

I knew she was talking from experience.

Back at her house, June invited me in for tea and cake.

"That husband of yours is an interesting character," she said, once we were sat comfortably in her kitchen.

I assumed mum had painted a not-too favourable picture of him.

"Yes, he is. He's very stressed about work at the moment. There's some big reorganisation going on, so it's all a bit tense, to say the least."

"He seemed quite agitated when he came over to collect Beth on Saturday."

"I hope he wasn't rude to you."

"No, nothing like that; he was perfectly civil. Just rather agitated."

"I suppose I can understand why, with both mum and me suddenly in hospital. He must have been worried sick."

"Well, yes, that's the funny thing. I would have expected him to rush straight over to the hospital to see you both, so I don't understand why he stayed in your mum's house for so long before he left."

"Oh, right, yes, that does sound odd. How long was he in there then?"

"I don't know exactly, but around an hour, give or take."

I was shocked, but tried my best to conceal it from June.

"Maybe he was checking the house … windows closed … lights off … that sort of thing."

"I told him I'd already done all that. And he didn't need to do any tidying up or anything, because your mum's house is always so spick and span."

I knew that, never in a million years, would Henry have deigned to do anything like that for mum anyway. So, what was he doing all that time? My mind jumped back to when I'd caught him rifling through mum's writing bureau. What was he looking for then? What was he looking for now? With a sickening feeling, it dawned on me. He wanted to know about her money. I could just picture him looking through her paperwork - bank statements, savings certificates, everything - trying to figure out what she was worth. And then it struck me what he was looking for.

He was looking for her will.

I wanted to launch into a venomous tirade against all things Henry, but I sensed the blood pressure rising in my head and began to worry about fainting again. I would shortly be driving home with Beth in the car, and I couldn't take any risks.

Henry was late home. He didn't offer an excuse, let alone a reason. I suspected he'd done it deliberately to miss visiting hours at the hospital. His reluctant promise from Sunday evening clearly meant nothing to him.

"How did you manage to get your car back?" he asked, as he walked in through the front door.

"June Williams took me to see mum, and then brought me back via her house."

"Oh right, so you've been out driving. Do you think that's really wise given all the fainting fits you've had recently?"

Two, actually.

"I feel fine. Don't worry, I took it easy."

"You might feel fine, but don't forget you probably still have concussion. You need to be more careful, especially with Elizabeth in the car."

"The good news is, I've already seen mum today, so we don't need to go later tonight."

"Oh, right, yes that is good because I've got to do some more work on my interview presentation. I couldn't really focus on it properly over the weekend, what with all the interruptions."

I ignored his offensive use of the word *interruptions* to refer to everything that had happened to mum and me. Clearly, he'd never had any intention of taking me to see mum tonight. He didn't even ask about her. I wasn't surprised; I wasn't even disappointed. I was getting to the point where I literally didn't care about him either.

"By the way, it sounds like half the department are applying for this promotion. It's so ridiculous. Most of them have absolutely no chance. This whole interview process is such a bloody waste of my time. I'm tempted to tell them to shove it."

After dinner, he disappeared back into his study and I kept out of his way. I didn't want to be accused of being yet another *interruption*.

Chapter 26

The next day, it was my turn to take June to the hospital. On the way, we called in at the post office with Annie's book. I'd made a promise to return it to its rightful owner, and was prepared to risk Henry's wrath if he noticed it missing. I would tell him I'd given it back to his father and hope he didn't check. I also popped into the bank to return the cash I'd withdrawn for the night's accommodation in Lyme Regis - which obviously I hadn't needed thanks to Alison.

We spent a couple of hours at the hospital, during which time mum opened her eyes just once, and then, only for the briefest of moments. Although there was no sign of recognition behind them, we continued to talk to her as if we were sitting together around the kitchen table. June tried to comfort me by saying that even a little eye movement was a step in the right direction. However, I think we both knew in our hearts that it was an almost imperceptible step on a possibly endless road.

"How did your interview go?" I asked Henry that evening, once he'd poured himself a large pre-dinner drink.

"Don't know; hard to tell. I think it went alright. They didn't ask me anything particularly tricky. One of the women that applied said she had loads of difficult questions on her presentation."

Henry obviously thought that meant his interview went relatively well. Based on my, admittedly limited, knowledge of buying-signals, I wasn't so sure. To my mind, no questions asked, meant no interest in what he was saying. I could still remember the bruising questions I'd been subjected to in my interview, before I was successfully awarded my research post.

It turned out I was right.

When I arrived back from the hospital in the middle of Friday afternoon, Henry's car was already on the drive. The muscles in my neck tightened. He came to the front door and I saw the thundercloud drawn across his face. I didn't dare ask why he was home so early, although I had a pretty good idea. As I walked into the kitchen with Beth still in her car seat, he launched into his diatribe.

"I've had it with that fucking company. Can you believe they gave the promotion to that woman; the one who told me she'd been given a hard time in the interview? I bet it's because the new VP is a woman. Fucking typical."

In my opinion, it was his comment about women that was *fucking typical*. I really didn't know what to say, but I had to say something. I knew it was risky. There was a severe danger of tipping him over the edge.

"That must be very frustrating. Did they give you any feedback?"

"Feedback? What a fucking waste of time. It was just some bullshit from HR about having so many strong candidates that it was difficult to choose. Well, it wasn't that difficult was it, because they made their choice? They chose the woman. Apparently, she's a better *fit*, whatever that's supposed to mean. Well, I've made my choice too, and I didn't have any difficulty making it. I'm not working for that bloody woman."

"So, what are you going to do?"

"It's not what I'm *going* to do; it's what I *have* done. I've told them where they can stick their job."

There were so many questions racing around in my head.

"So, you mean, what, you've resigned?"

"Yep, that's right, I'm out of there."

"Have you actually formally resigned in writing?"

"I sent an email to HR at lunchtime. I get two months paid notice, so that should be plenty of time for me to find something better."

I wondered why he'd ignored the more obvious - not to mention, more mature - strategy of finding something better *before* resigning. This was a lot for me to take in. He'd just made an impulsive decision that would have a huge impact on us as a family - including financially. Not only that, but he'd done it without even consulting me. I could just imagine his reaction if I did something of this magnitude without consulting him. Anyway, it was too late now. The decision was set in stone, but there were a few practical implications to consider.

"Will you need to keep going into the office during your notice period?"

"They want me to go in on Monday to hand over the stuff I'm working on. After that, I'll be on gardening leave."

I was absolutely stunned at how quickly they planned to fill the Henry-shaped hole. It was obviously not a very large hole. In fact, it sounded like he was almost irrelevant to their business. I would be seriously concerned if I thought my departure from the Maths Institute would cause barely a ripple. Henry, though, didn't seem unduly worried as he poured himself a second glass of wine.

I took Beth upstairs to give her a bath. I started running the water slowly, checking the temperature carefully with my left wrist as I always did. I became mesmerised by the water tumbling from the taps. With a growing sense of alarm, I started to think through all the dire consequences of Henry's decision.

Suddenly, I felt short of breath. There was one consequence above all others which absolutely horrified me. It was not the potential loss of income. It was the fact that Henry was going to be around in the house for the next two months - possibly even longer. The idea filled me with absolute dread. He would be there all the time, checking me; correcting me; controlling me. My routine of caring for Beth and visiting mum would be under his continuous scrutiny. I would have to live my life under his constant surveillance. Henry would be psychologically and emotionally strangling me.

I started to get really hot in the face and I couldn't breathe properly. It felt as if there was a thick steel clamp around my head, slowly crushing my skull. My eyes were losing focus; my body slumping. I didn't know what was happening to me. I tried to call out but no sound came out of my mouth. I closed my eyes. That was it.

The next thing I remember was someone grabbing me and dragging me sideways. It was Henry.

"Katherine, what the hell are you doing," he shouted at me.

I partially opened my eyes. He was screwing the bath taps down hard. My eyes closed again. I didn't know what I was doing. I had no energy to think or say or do anything. It felt like I had no control over my muscles. My body was like a rag doll.

Henry pulled me again and propped me up against the hard metal towel radiator. I was sobbing uncontrollably. There was something cold and wet against my back but I didn't move. I couldn't move.

I don't remember what happened after that, but somehow I ended up lying on my bed, still fully clothed. I suppose Henry must have carried me there. I reached for my phone to check the time, but it was not on the bedside cabinet, where I normally kept it when I was in bed. I could see it was dark outside, so it must have been late but I had no idea of the time.

I could hear voices somewhere but couldn't tell what they were saying. Slowly, I dragged myself off the bed and, gripping the handrail like my life depended on it, crept downstairs as silently as I could.

"… well, she obviously isn't coping, is she?" the female voice said.

To my utter dismay, I recognised it was Henry's mother pronouncing her verdict on me.

"Ah, Katherine, you're finally up. We were wondering when we might see you," she said, as if I'd stayed in bed with a bad hangover.

"Sorry, I just woke up. How long have I been asleep? What happened?"

Henry and his mother exchanged knowing glances from which I felt excluded. It was probably deliberate.

"You really have no idea?" Henry asked, as though he didn't believe me.

"No, sorry, I don't. The last thing I remember is running the water for Beth."

"For Elizabeth."

"Yes, for Elizabeth. One minute I was checking the temperature of the water, and the next minute …"

"And the next minute *her head was under the water*."

He said these six words slowly so that I could not misunderstand them. And so that I could never forget them. It took a moment to penetrate the dullness in my brain, but he was telling me I had almost drowned our baby. He was telling me I had almost drowned Beth.

I howled with anguish; it was unlike any sound I've ever made before or since. I covered my face with my hands and shook my head violently from side to side. The next thing I knew I was banging my forehead repeatedly on the fridge door. I could feel my skin splitting on the sharp edges of the magnets holding up the baby photos, but I didn't stop. Henry grabbed me from behind and pulled me away. He tried to get his arms tight around me to hold me up, but I must have been too heavy or too limp. He let me collapse in a clumsy heap on the floor. There was a dull thud as my head hit the limestone flooring.

Chapter 27

I am sorry, but you will have to be patient with me. I am not feeling so good these days. Everything is so muddled and fuzzy since *the incident* - that is how we refer to it now: *the incident*. It is quite difficult for me to describe what I am thinking and how I am feeling at the moment. My words might be a bit slow and slurred. It is probably the pills, but Henry says I need to keep taking them. I am so very fortunate to have him by my side; to speak for me.

Henry told me what happened during the incident. I nearly drowned Elizabeth. Yes, that is right; I nearly killed my own daughter. Thank God Henry saved her from me. She is fine now, but no thanks to me. I do not see much of her at the moment. Henry says I cannot be trusted to be with her on my own. I do not like it, but I understand that he is right. It is better for everyone that way. Elizabeth stays with Henry's mother once a week which is a big help. Henry's mother is very kind and knows how to look after her properly; unlike me.

The doctors told Henry that I have mental health issues. I heard other people talking about me when they thought I could not hear them. They said that I had a nervous breakdown. Whatever it is, I do not want to talk about it. Henry says there is no reason why I should want to talk about it. I do not need any counselling or residential treatment either. Henry says we will work it out between the two of us. Anyway, the cause is obvious, he says. I have been overdoing it; that is all. I just need to be left alone so I can get better. I know Henry will help me through this. He is at home most of the time now since he gave up his job in London. He is so caring and so patient with me.

Henry lets Mrs Williams take me to the hospital to see mum whenever she can. But Henry is right; mum is dying. I have now given up all hope that she will ever recover. It is no use pretending anymore. I cannot help her. Henry says we would not be able to look after her now, even if she did come to live with us. All I can do is keep visiting her and watching her fade away. I know it is only a matter of time. How will I cope without her? What will Elizabeth do without her? We will both need Henry even more when the time comes.

Henry arranged for an au pair to come and live with us after the incident. She takes care of Elizabeth most of the time. Ingrid - she is from Denmark - is a very pretty girl. Henry chose her because she has a good education. She is very tidy and polite to me. But I do not like Ingrid. I feel like she is keeping an eye on me and reporting back to Henry. Please do not tell Henry I said that; he will think I am ungrateful and get angry. He says she is keeping an eye out *for* me, not *on* me. I suppose he is right; I should be grateful.

I do not know where my phone is. Henry says I do not need it; I am better off without it. Why would I want people calling me all the time to ask how I am feeling? I do not talk to anyone at the moment, apart from Henry and Mrs Williams and mum - although mum cannot talk back to me. I have lost contact with my new friend in Lyme Regis. I do not know how I can help her at the moment.

What can I do? I need to sort my own life out first. Do you think I should tell Henry about her?

Henry says I do not need to worry about anything now. He will organise everything for me so that I can relax my mind and body. He has all my bank details and passwords now, so I do not need to worry about the finances. That was his idea; it makes my life easier not having to worry about money. He plays golf every morning to give me some space. He has taken the pressure off me so I can focus on getting better. I know he cares for me. What would I do without him? I know I can rely on him to do what is best for me. I have let him take control of my life. I feel at peace for the first time in a long while.

I am sorry, but I have tired myself out talking to you. Henry says I need to rest now. I hope we will be able to talk again soon.

Chapter 28

I lose track of the days now. My routine is always the same. The only time I go out is to visit mum. And the visits to mum are always the same too: Mrs Williams arriving, the ring-road traffic, the hunt for a parking space, the corridors, the smell of the ward, the same visitors sitting with the same patients. I feel nothing when I see mum. My emotions are so dull. I am not sad or angry; I am just numb. Henry asked me not to discuss my mental health issues with Mrs Williams or anyone else. He says I should only talk to him about it.

While I was reading the newspaper to mum, Mrs Williams said she thought she saw mum's bent fingers twitch a couple of times. Sadly, I missed it. We stared at her hands for the next few minutes but saw nothing. When we told the nurse, she said it was quite common, so it was difficult to tell if it was really significant. Henry always tells me not to build up my hopes. He says I should prepare myself for the worst. Like every other day, I left the ward feeling empty.

One day, Mrs Williams told me she would like to go into the centre of Oxford to meet an old friend for lunch. She invited me to go with her, but I did not want to have to talk to a stranger about what had happened to me or mum. Henry would not want me to either. He said it was just easier that way. Mrs Williams totally understood. I said I would go for a walk and meet her back at the car at four o'clock.

I had not been out anywhere - apart from the hospital - for about three weeks now. As I walked along St Giles, I began to feel nervous amongst all the jostling foreign tourists and the noisy traffic. What if I fainted again? What if I banged my head again? What if I had another incident? And I was alone, without Henry to help me.

I started to panic and suddenly found myself running towards a place I knew well: the enormous Norrington Room in Blackwell's book shop on Broad Street. I always liked coming here; it was like a second home. It reminded me of a similar university bookshop where I'd spent many hours browsing as an undergraduate. I loved to look things up in the large hardback maths textbooks that, as a mere undergraduate, I could never afford to buy. I felt completely safe amongst the rows of books, and decided to stay right there, until it was time to meet Mrs Williams.

I ran my index finger lightly along the line of maths books, searching for familiar names, and found several people I worked with in the Oxford Maths Institute. I knew that my name would never appear amongst such distinguished company now. With the incident and everything else going on in my life, Henry thinks it might be better for me to start looking for a less demanding job. Maybe he is right; I should definitely think about it.

"Sorry," I said, as I bumped into someone next to me.

I did not bother to look who it was; best to avoid unnecessary eye contact.

"Katy?" a woman's voice asked.

I turned round.

It was her.

Were my eyes playing tricks on me? Surely it could not be her.

"Amy?" I said hesitantly.

She nodded and smiled.

"I couldn't quite believe it when I spotted you, Katy."

A wave of emotion suddenly engulfed me. I threw my arms around her, and hugged her like a close friend, even though our only previous encounter had lasted at most ten seconds. It felt so incredibly good to hold onto someone - and to be held in return. I realised how much I had missed human contact over the past few weeks, and did not want to let go of her.

I recognised her perfume once again. It had been one of my favourites back in the days when I used to bother wearing perfume. I still had an old bottle of it on my dressing table, but it was empty and dry now. Rather like my relationship with Henry.

As we released each other, I noticed that I had left a large tear on her cheek, but she was far too polite to wipe it away.

"Are you alright, Katy?" she asked.

It would have been easy to force a smile and say that everything was fine. I knew that is exactly what Henry would tell me to do; not to share my problems with a stranger. But Amy was *not* a stranger. I already thought of her as a friend.

"No, not really," I replied.

I could see the genuine concern on her face, and knew that she was not going to try to brush me off.

"Do you have time for a coffee?" she asked.

"I do. Yes, I do, definitely."

For the first time in three weeks, I felt ready to talk to someone. And Amy was not just someone; she was the person I most wanted to talk to right now - apart from mum.

"How come you are in Oxford?" I asked.

"You know my fiancée Jake is in the Navy?"

"Yes, your mum told me."

"Well, he's come up from Portsmouth for a few days to do some work with the Oxford URNU."

"URNU?"

"Oh, sorry, too much Navy jargon. I'm still trying to get used to all of it myself. I think it stands for University Royal Naval Unit or something like that. Jake has been up in Oxford all week helping out, and I thought it might be nice to come up here and meet him."

"I am not stopping you, am I?"

"No, no, it's fine."

It didn't take us long to move past the small talk.

"Mum said she's been messaging you for over three weeks. She was getting quite worried about you. I know she wanted to thank you for taking the trouble to return Annie's book."

"My pleasure. Look, I am really sorry I have not been in contact with your mum. The thing is, Amy, I haven't been well for the past three weeks; probably much longer if I am honest. My life is such a mess right now."

"Would it help to talk about it? I have plenty of time. Jake won't be finished until around four o'clock."

The dam broke and the last three weeks of my story came gushing out.

"Well, you've certainly been through a lot. I don't know how you've managed to keep going. I don't think I could have coped."

"I do not think I have coped. I think I have failed."

"You are here now talking to me about everything. That takes courage. If you ask me, it's a very positive step. I don't think you have failed."

My self-confidence was at an all-time low. I appreciated her encouraging words. After such a long period of feeling lost and deflated, Amy was slowly breathing a little life back into me. There was one question I desperately wanted to ask her.

"So, tell me, why did you come to the church that day?"

"I suppose I did it for mum. After what she's been through; first with dad and then with Annie. It's been a real struggle for her, but despite everything, she's somehow managed to keep her hope alive. She won't move house; she won't get rid of that car; she won't touch Annie's room - in case she comes back. It's taking a real toll on her mentally."

"I can hardly begin to imagine."

"A couple of her friends started suggesting that it might finally be time to have Annie declared dead officially. Of course, that really upset her. It got me thinking though. Was it worth one last attempt to try to find out what happened to Annie? I decided to track down that ex-boyfriend of hers. I didn't really have any idea what I would do if I found him, but it seemed like the only chance. Then, when I found him on social media, I saw his post about your daughter's christening. I was horrified to think that he had a wife and baby now. After what happened to Annie, I needed to warn you. I knew it was probably too late, but I still had to do it."

"And you didn't want Henry to know. That's why you were so secretive."

"Exactly. God knows how he would have reacted. I didn't want to spook him and ruin your daughter's christening. Also, I didn't know how *you* would react. If he'd already told you about Annie, you might be angry with me for turning up uninvited. I knew it was such a risk gate-crashing the christening. It wasn't fair at all, but I didn't know what else to do. I'm so sorry."

"Please, please, don't apologise, Amy. I'm so glad you came to the christening; I'm so glad I met you and your mum. You've both helped me so much."

"And you've helped mum too. Hearing your story, and being able to share hers with you, has given her a new perspective."

"I'm starting to see a few things more clearly now myself, especially about my own daughter. Beth is my life; I want to be close to her, but I feel so guilty about what I did. I can't forgive myself. What if I do something else stupid? What if something serious happens to her? I don't think I could live with myself."

"You shouldn't keep blaming yourself. You were under a huge amount of stress."

"I know, but she nearly drowned. I nearly drowned her. How can I not blame myself?"

Amy paused before she replied. It looked like she was weighing up carefully what she was about to say.

"Actually, Katy, when you told me about what happened with Beth, something didn't sound quite right."

"What do you mean?"

"OK, hear me out. I'm not doubting what you said, but think about it. You were running the water."

"Yes."

"Then you felt strange and Henry rushed in."

"That's right."

"And he turned the taps off."

"Yes, I distinctly remember him pushing me aside to get to the taps."

"Right, and Henry said Beth's head was under the water when he pulled her out of the bath."

"Yes, that's what he said. I don't remember what happened."

"So, my question is this: if you were still running the water, why would you already have put Beth in the bath?"

"I don't ... wait ... I'm not ..."

I clasped my hands together in front of my mouth while I thought. In my mind, I rehearsed the steps of my daily routine for Beth's bath-time. Amy had a point. Why would I put Beth in the bath before I was happy with the temperature of the water? I was acutely aware of the danger of scalding water - I'd seen the photos in baby care books. It would be sheer madness. Also, since I would need both hands to hold and wash Beth, why would I put her in the bath before I turned off the taps?

Amy was right; something didn't fit. I tried desperately to picture the exact sequence of events on that afternoon three weeks ago, but I couldn't complete the picture. It was like trying to recall a dream after it had slipped away.

"You know what; you are absolutely right. Under normal circumstances, there is no way I would ever have done that. I'm at a complete loss as to how it could have happened. Maybe I wasn't thinking straight. Maybe I was distracted by something."

"Or maybe it didn't happen," Amy said slowly.

"You mean maybe Beth was *not* in the bath."

"That's right."

"But in that case, why would Henry say ...?"

143

My question trailed off as I began to think through the implications of what Amy was suggesting. An icy cold feeling crept up my spine to the base of my skull. My eyes locked onto Amy's.

"I know; it's worrying, isn't it?" she said.

"It certainly is, if he made up that part of the story. It's more than worrying."

"What are you going to do?"

"I don't know yet. I'm so confused. I thought he was looking after me …. caring for me, but perhaps it's something else; something darker. I can't honestly say I ever know what's going on in his head. I think I need some time to process all this before I do anything."

"In the meantime, you need to be vigilant; you need to be careful. Do you have anyone close to you, that you can trust?"

That person had always been mum, but she was no longer able to help me. And Isabella was no longer in my life.

"Right now, the only people I can really trust are you and your mum," I answered.

This shocking admission demonstrated the full extent of my isolation. It also made me realise how much I still missed Isabella. I used to share everything with her. When we parted, it left a huge hole in my life. Had I been too hasty in cutting her out, without even listening to her side of the story? What sort of friend would do that? I should at least have given her a chance to explain. But it was too late for that. For the foreseeable future, I would continue to rely on Amy and her mother as my confidantes. Of course, it might be difficult to meet either of them face to face, but I could at least talk to them regularly on the phone.

But for that, I would actually need my phone.

Chapter 29

"Have you seen my mobile anywhere?" I asked Henry that evening.

I tried to sound calm about it. Any conversation with him could quickly escalate into a battle.

"Why do you need your phone?"

"No special reason. I just want to find it."

"For the moment, isn't it better not to be disturbed by people asking how you are, or about your mother?"

"I feel cut off from everyone. People at work might want to get hold of me."

"You're supposed to be on maternity leave. They shouldn't be calling you."

"Well, the hospital might need to contact me urgently about mum."

"They have my phone number now as the emergency contact."

"When did you give them your number? Why did you do that?"

"After you had your breakdown ... your incident. I thought it was for the best."

Oh, so now he was calling it a *breakdown* - and probably always had done, behind my back. Whatever arguments he came up with, I was determined not to waste the morsel of strength I'd gained from Amy that afternoon. For my own sanity, I needed to accomplish this small step forward. I would not - could not - allow Henry to stop me this time. Anyway, he had absolutely no right to deprive me of communication with the outside world if I wanted it. My mind was muddled about so many things, but not about this point.

"Please give me my phone," I said.

There was no desperation in my voice; no threat; no emotion at all. He must have realised I was not going to back down.

"OK, fine, but I don't know where it is. I haven't seen it recently."

I wouldn't let this excuse deflect me either. I searched the house from top to bottom like a woman possessed. Unfortunately, without success - or any help from him. Still, I wouldn't give up.

145

"Can you call it from your phone? I might be able to hear it ringing."

"I doubt it. The battery will probably be dead by now."

"Could you just do it please?"

He dialled my number and I held my breath. Nothing.

"See," he said.

I wanted to slap the crooked smirk off his face.

"Could you try again?"

"What's the point?"

I stared at him until he redialled. This time I sprinted upstairs and listened from the landing. I tried to calm my breathing and stand completely still. After a couple of seconds, I began to pick up the faint sound of my ringtone. It was one of those that got louder as it went on. It was coming from the spare room; now the au pair's room.

I threw the door open and yanked out the drawer of her bedside cabinet, scattering all the contents onto the carpet. There was my phone, silent now, but showing a missed call from Henry. The battery display was on red.

When Ingrid returned later, she flatly denied taking my phone or even having seen it. She claimed she had absolutely no idea how it came to be in her room. And I have to say, she looked genuinely upset by the accusation. Either she was telling the truth or she was a brilliant actor. To be fair, I couldn't think of any reason why she would take it, given that it now had a PIN code on it. And besides, her fancy smartphone was a far higher spec than my old relic. A large part of me believed her - or at least, wanted to believe her. I even began to feel sorry for her; sorry that Henry might have set her up for some reason.

One thing was for sure: my phone couldn't have found its way into her drawer by accident. If Ingrid had stolen it - for some obscure reason - then Henry would now be suspicious of her. On the other hand, if Henry had hidden it in her room - perhaps so that he couldn't be blamed for its disappearance - then Ingrid would now be suspicious of him. Either way, any mutual pact they might have against me was significantly weakened. I realised I could use that to my advantage.

Given the ambiguity of the situation - and my tendency to believe Ingrid - I decided not to be too harsh on her. I thought a more lenient approach might create some goodwill between us. And goodwill was something I desperately needed right now.

"OK, let's not worry about how my phone got in there. I've found it now; that's all that really matters."

Once my phone was fully charged, I wanted to check it in private for any missed calls or messages. I told Henry I was going for a long soak in the bath. I locked the door after me. There were half a dozen messages from Alison, to which I replied with an apology for not contacting her earlier. I promised I would call her and explain everything as soon as I could guarantee enough time and privacy. As I typed my message, I wondered if Amy would already have briefed her on our encounter in Oxford. When I saw Alison's immediate reply, it was obvious that she had. There were a handful of supportive messages from colleagues at work, including the ever-reliable Malkit. I sent him a short note, but I wasn't in the right frame of mind to reply to any of the others.

As I lay in bed, thinking about what Amy and I discussed - and the welcome return of my trusty phone - I knew in my heart that I'd taken a small first step towards the future. Quite what this future would have in store for me, I could only speculate. But whatever happened, I knew I wanted Annie's family to be an important part of my life.

The more I reflected on these wretched weeks since my incident, the more stupid I felt. I began to see that I'd been totally deceived by Henry; I'd believed him to be my saviour. But in truth, he'd been the sole architect of my personal disintegration. How could I - someone who considered herself to be reasonably intelligent and successful - have let him do this to me? How could I have been so pathetic? Perhaps one day, I might fathom it out. But for now, questions about the past would have to wait. The more pressing questions concerned the future.

It was crystal clear to me what I had to do: I had to start wrestling back control of my life from Henry. How exactly I was going to achieve that, however, wasn't quite so crystal clear. The only thing I knew for certain was that I would never be so stupid as to trust Henry again.

Chapter 30

Henry was up early on Saturday morning and brought me a mug of tea in bed. There was some kind of mixed pairs golf tournament going on, so I assumed this gesture was to assuage his guilt about being out all day - and with another woman.

While he was shaving, I sat in bed drinking my tea and chewing over my conversation with Amy. I felt something had changed in me. Something fundamental. I was stronger. I was more determined. I was on the front foot, so to speak.

As a result, I was now much more alert to Henry's devious motives. As he tucked his polo shirt into his tight golf trousers, he made a suggestion.

"You know, it might be good for you to take up some kind of regular exercise too."

Clearly, he wasn't suggesting this for my benefit, so what was behind it? Did he think I was putting on weight or losing my shape? Did he need to get me out of the house for some reason?

"Don't you think I get enough exercise running around after Elizabeth?"

"Ingrid has been doing most of the running around recently, hasn't she? You've spent a lot of your time in bed and on the sofa."

I was about to defend myself when I saw that his suggestion might work to my advantage. It would certainly allow me to escape from the house and have my own space. And the exercise would obviously be good for my body and mind too.

"Yes, you are right; it might actually be a good idea."

"There's a health club at the Berkshire Valley with all the latest gym equipment."

No! The Berkshire Valley Golf Club was *his* place. I wanted my own space.

"Gym equipment! That sounds a bit strenuous. I'm not sure I'm feeling up to that at the moment. It's only a few weeks since I had my concussion."

"What sort of exercise *are* you feeling up to then?" he said, with a touch of sarcasm.

"Well, I hadn't thought about it until you mentioned it a minute ago. I suppose I could find somewhere to go swimming. That would be really good exercise for me - and there's no danger of concussion. I used to love swimming when I was younger."

"There's a pool in the health club too, you know."

I needed to buy time to avoid being bullied into joining his club.

"Yes, that could be a possibility. Is it a full-size pool or only a spa pool though? I'll have a look on the internet this morning to see what the options are, and how much they cost."

"I'll have a chat with the manager at the health club and get some membership details for you."

"OK, thank you."

Sitting in bed with my laptop after Henry had gone, I searched the internet for regular swimming pools where I could simply swim lengths. I wasn't interested in any fancy spa treatments. The local leisure centre was the obvious choice. After looking up the opening times and various sessions on offer, I decided to strike while the iron was hot.

"Ingrid, I'm going swimming this morning. Will you be alright with Beth for a couple of hours?"

"Of course," she replied.

She looked a bit disappointed for some reason.

"Is everything OK?"

"Yes, everything is fine. I really love swimming too."

"Do you want to come with me?"

The words just came out spontaneously. Her face lit up. I couldn't remember seeing her smile before. It made me smile too.

We took turns during the lane swimming session. My technique was a bit rusty, but nevertheless I managed to splutter my way up and down the pool a few times, gasping for breath at reasonably regular intervals. I thought I was doing quite well until I watched Ingrid slip out from under her towel and dive straight in. Her beautiful slender body barely made a ripple as it entered the water. I don't think I've ever seen anyone swim so elegantly and so effortlessly. The lifeguard on duty was so hypnotised as she glided through the water below him, that he slipped off his stepladder.

The lane swimming was followed by a so-called *family fun* session, so we took the opportunity to give Beth her first brief taste of swimming. She seemed totally oblivious to the whole splashing experience, and didn't scream or cry once. Maybe it was a sign: another duckling in the making.

Ingrid offered to look after Beth while I showered and got changed first. As I sat in the café waiting for her to emerge from the changing room, I wondered if my initial impression of her had been so utterly wrong. She genuinely seemed to care about Beth and - now that I'd made a first gesture - she was extremely friendly towards me. Why had I thought she was working for Henry and spying on me? I'd been through a difficult time and hadn't been thinking straight, but I was still appalled by my poor judgement. Deep down, I knew it was Henry's fault. His poison penetrated into all my relationships.

I decided it was time to clear the air with Ingrid and start afresh. I suggested we had lunch together at the local organic farm shop, before heading back home.

"How did you learn to swim like that? You are an absolutely amazing swimmer," I began.

"Thanks. My father used to take me every day when I was a child. Then I got into the swimming teams at school and university. We had some great coaches. I always loved swimming; I still do."

"My dad used to take me every morning when the pool was quiet. I was in the team at school but didn't really do much at university; shame really, but other things sort of got in the way.

You can probably tell it's been a while since I did any serious swimming."

"I can see you have an excellent technique."

"Thanks, but I'm not very fit though, so that doesn't help."

I vaguely remembered Henry telling me he'd found Ingrid through an au pair website. He didn't involve me in the process so I never even saw her online profile. Anyway, I was getting to know the real Ingrid now in person. While we talked, I had the opportunity to study her face, and was struck by how beautiful she was; her green eyes - which didn't conform to the Scandinavian stereotype - were quite mesmerising. I could see why Henry chose her. It occurred to me that Ingrid was the same age - 22 - as Annie when she disappeared. My instincts told me that I needed to keep Ingrid safe from falling under Henry's influence. I vowed to myself that I would look after her as though she was my own sister.

We talked long after our lunch plates had been cleared away. The waitress must have wondered if we would ever shut up and leave. Back in the car, we put our seat belts on, but before I could start the engine, Ingrid cleared her throat. I sensed she wanted to say something - something important to her - so I turned to face her.

"Katy, I want you to know that … I need you to believe me. I did not take your phone."

"It's alright Ingrid, I believe you. I know you didn't take my phone. Please don't worry about it."

"I don't know how it got into …"

"I think I know who put it there … and I think I know why."

I placed my hand gently on her arm to reassure her. She looked extremely relieved, as if a huge weight had been lifted from her.

"I'll get to the bottom of it eventually, trust me."

"I do trust you, Katy, and I will do anything I can to help you."

"Thank you," I said.

Later that afternoon, I noticed that I could still smell the chlorinated water on Beth, so I decided to change her.

"I'm going to give Beth a quick bath to rinse off the water from the pool. Do you want to give me a hand?" I asked Ingrid.

"Of course, if you are sure you want my help."

I still had cold sweats every time I thought about the last bath that I'd given Beth. I sensed Ingrid was embarrassed for my sake. She obviously didn't want to intrude.

"Probably just as well … you know," I said. "Could you run the taps while I hold her?"

She knelt at the head of the bath and turned on the cold tap. Then she started to add hot, swirling the water round with her right hand and testing the temperature with her left wrist, exactly as I always did. A question suddenly formed itself in my mind.

"Ingrid, can I ask you something? It might sound a bit weird, but would you ever put Beth into the bath before you'd finished running the water?"

I wondered if Henry had told her about the incident - or at least his version of it. From the blush I detected in her face, I guessed that he probably had.

"No, definitely not."

"And neither would I."

And neither *did* I. It was simply not possible that I could have put Beth into the bathwater while the taps were still running. It had taken Amy, and now Ingrid, to help me realise that Henry's version of the incident made absolutely no sense whatsoever. It could *not* have happened the way he described it. Neither did I believe that he had made a mistake. He was so adamant and his accusation against me was so serious. It was not possible that it was simply a mistake.

In the words of a famous fictional detective: *when you have eliminated the impossible, whatever remains, however improbable, must be the truth.*

So, the truth was …

Henry deliberately lied about what happened that day.

It took some time for the enormity of this revelation to sink in. It was so utterly shocking. It was so utterly unforgivable - whatever twisted reasoning he might subsequently use to justify his lie. This was psychological abuse.

He had crossed a line.

Even in my present confused and emotional state, I could see this for what it was: the defining moment in the collapse of our relationship. The beginning of the end. The way he treated me these days was bad enough, but to use my love for Beth *against* me in such a malevolent way, that was pure *evil*; there is no other word for it. I would *never* forgive him, nor would he ever deserve my forgiveness. There was no way back from this dark place that he'd deliberately chosen to enter.

Remember that first question you asked me, right at the beginning? Why I put up with it. I gave you my best shot at an answer, but I don't suppose I ever really convinced you, did I? No? I didn't think so. Even after my feeble explanation, you probably still thought I was stupid to put up with it. Yes? And I totally understand. It's much easier to see things clearly and rationally when you are on the outside, looking in on someone else's life. And you were right of course. I can see it myself now. Just too late though. I was *so* stupid. The only defence I can offer is that I wasn't on the outside; I was stuck on the inside. And it wasn't someone else's life I was observing; it was my life. I just couldn't see what was going on around me; what was happening to me.

So, I expect you might be forming a second question in your head right about now? I know I would. My question would be: *are you still going to put up with it?* It's much easier for me to answer that question than the first one. This time it's not complicated. This time the answer is a straight *no*. No, I am *not* still going to put up with it. It's over. I owe it to myself - and to Beth - to build a new future; a safer and more certain future. A future that does not include Henry. My mind is made up now. I will find a way to break free from his spell.

It seems really weird to say this, but with my decision made, a sort of calmness descended on me. I can only explain it by saying that after weeks - if not months - of sheer hell, I finally felt like I knew where I was heading. I didn't know how I was going to get there, but at least I was now pointing in the right direction.

Chapter 31

I spent the following morning at the hospital. June couldn't make it, so I was on my own for once. I decided to use the opportunity to tell mum all about Annie, and my plan to leave Henry. I desperately wanted her to know. And even if she wasn't aware what I was saying, I still needed to tell her.

I moved close and spoke in a soft voice. My hand was wrapped around hers, so it was not easy to see if her fingers were moving, but I definitely felt something; a faint trembling. I removed my hand and watched closely; there was no movement. When I replaced my hand and continued with my story, I detected the tremor again. I convinced myself that she was trying to connect with me; to tell me she supported my decision. Knowing mum was still there for me - however faintly - gave me the strength to face my own life.

Before I left the hospital, I asked the ward nurse to reinstate me as the primary emergency contact, with June Williams as back-up. I told her she could delete Henry's name from the list entirely. It was a tiny step towards removing him from my life, but it was a first step, and it made me feel a whole lot better.

Henry didn't arrive back until well after Beth was in bed. Ingrid was in her room, on the phone to her parents, telling them about the swimming. I prepared myself for Henry's grand entrance into the living room. He walked over towards me. Instinctively I felt nervous; on the defensive.

"I got you something," he said, handing me a small rectangular white card.

It was a temporary membership card for the Berkshire Valley health club.

"I signed you up for a month's gold membership. It covers the pool and gym and all sorts of exercise classes. The first time you go they'll take a photo, and make up a proper laminated pass."

"Oh, right."

"You don't sound very grateful. I thought you wanted to take up swimming again."

"No, I am grateful, it's just that I was planning to research the various options myself, before making any firm decisions."

"Well, I've saved you the bother. We could go over there tomorrow if you like, and you could have your first swim."

I hesitated about whether to tell him. But it would be obvious from the wet stuff in the utility room, reeking of chlorine.

"Actually, I've already been swimming. I went to the leisure centre this morning."

"Oh, right, the public pool in the leisure centre in town. Isn't that a bit down-market?"

"No, it's fine. It's obviously had a bit of a revamp recently. Anyway, it's a full size 25 metre pool. The price is reasonable too."

"So do you want this membership pass or not then?"

He already had a hurt expression. I was worried it might turn into anger, as it did so often these days.

"Of course, thank you. Yes, I'll definitely try it out."

"We could go tomorrow morning … together … as a family. It is Father's Day, after all."

It was a strange suggestion, given that he'd never previously shown any interest in going swimming with me. Come to think of it, I wasn't even sure he could swim.

"Yes, that would be great."

I suddenly thought of something of someone.

"Could we take Ingrid with us?"

"Ingrid? Why? Doesn't she need to stay here to look after Elizabeth? Anyway, I thought you didn't like her. She did steal your phone, don't forget."

"No, no, I do like her. It's just that I didn't really know her before. And I know she loves swimming."

"How do you know that?"

"Because she came with me this morning. She's an incredible swimmer. And then we had lunch together, so I could start to get to know her a bit."

155

"Oh right, so you two have been out enjoying yourselves all day. I don't suppose either of you thought about all the things that need doing here in the house."

And he'd been out playing golf all day with some random woman. Fucking hypocrite.

"Don't worry; we've sorted everything out this afternoon."

"Anyway, I still don't see why we need to take her with us. She's the au pair, for God's sake, not your sister."

"Well, I would like her to come with us. I'm happy to pay for her."

There was a creak as the living room door opened and Ingrid entered.

"Don't suppose you want to come swimming with us tomorrow morning, do you?" Henry asked.

What a two-faced …

Ingrid glanced at me, and I smiled and nodded.

"Yes please," she said.

I enjoyed my swim on Sunday morning, but not as much as the previous day when it was just the three of us. It felt like Henry - and all the other middle-aged men for that matter - were judging me; contrasting my rounded curves with Ingrid's lithe body. In fact, Henry was so busy watching Ingrid, I don't think he actually did any swimming.

While we were getting changed, Ingrid touched me on the arm to attract my attention, so she could talk to me discreetly.

"I did not mean to listen, but I heard you and Henry talking before I came into the living room last night. I wanted to say thank you for supporting me, and inviting me to come with you. I know it was your idea, not his," she whispered.

"You're very welcome. We girls need to stick together."

Henry insisted that we all have lunch at the hotel next door, as his Father's Day treat. Several of his golf friends were sitting at a nearby table in the restaurant, so he put on a sociable display and we had a reasonably pleasant lunch. Afterwards, he disappeared to chat to some of his buddies, while I collected my pass from reception. On the spur of the moment, I signed Ingrid up too.

Once we were home, I decided to risk asking Henry about a controversial topic. This was a bold move for me. Had something changed in me? Maybe I wasn't so afraid of him. No, that wasn't it; I was still afraid of him. Maybe I just cared less about his feelings; or maybe not at all.

"How's the job hunt going?"

What I actually wanted to know, of course, was when I would have the house back to myself again. He'd only needed about half a day to hand over all his marketing stuff. Since then, as far as I was aware, he hadn't had a single call or email from the office. Obviously, they didn't miss him that much. And neither would I - if only I could get him to find a new job.

"Slowly. It's coming up to the summer holidays, so there isn't much around at the moment. Anyway, I still have over a month of gardening leave left."

"Yes, but that only takes you to the end of July, and then people won't start hiring again until September."

"I've been looking on all the job websites. What else do you want me to do?"

"Don't you have any industry contacts? Or what about the head-hunter who found your last job?"

"Head-hunter?"

"You know the woman who contacted you about the job in London."

"Oh, her. Well, that was a complete waste of time, wasn't it? I'm not going to contact her again."

"What about your golf buddies?"

"Christ, Katherine, I'm not going to go round begging for a job. That looks so desperate. I do have some pride, you know."

"I didn't mean asking them for a job; I just meant using your contacts. It's called networking."

"Look, in the academic world it may be about who you know, but it's different in the real world."

I objected to his assertion that his world was more real than mine. My world was a lot more real than his crappy junk-mail marketing campaigns; that was for sure. Whenever he was on the back foot, he always tried to turn his problem into my problem. But now, I saw clearly what he was doing. I almost found it amusing. It was tempting to carry on winding him up.

"I'm just trying to help, that's all," I said, not so genuinely.

"Well, you're not helping; you're nagging. Look, I know I need to find a job, but can't you leave it alone, at least on Father's Day?"

He got up and stormed off to his study. A minute later he was back staring at the screen on his phone.

"I just checked your credit card balance; it looks like they've charged you for your health club membership. I already paid for it yesterday. I'll have to phone them up and get a refund."

"Ah, no, wait, that was probably me."

"What, did you pay for it again today?"

"No, I actually bought a month's membership for Ingrid too … so she can come with me and help me look after Elizabeth."

I waited for the explosion.

"So, one minute you're nagging me about getting a job, and the next minute you're spending our money like it's going out of fashion. Fucking unbelievable!"

Actually, it was *my* money.

"It wasn't that expensive; it was only a one month's pass. You said yourself she worked really hard while I was ill. I just wanted to thank her, that's all."

"In case you've forgotten, we are actually paying her. We don't need to buy everything for her as well."

"I just thought it was a nice gesture. She really appreciated it."

"Oh, whatever …"

He was still grumbling as he shut the study door again. In my humble opinion, anyone who finished an argument by saying *whatever* in such a petulant way, had clearly lost that argument. That meant I had actually won a small battle with Henry. Normally

158

I wouldn't have cared, but today it gave me a kick. Does that sound a bit childish?

Admittedly it was a very small battle, and the win was extremely short-lived.

Chapter 32

The next day, there was no early morning cup of tea from Henry. I assumed he was still irritated with me for *nagging* about getting a job or for treating Ingrid to a health club membership. How childish was that?

Out of the bedroom window, I could see that his car had gone, which meant that I could relax for a while. I went downstairs and made tea for myself and Ingrid. She was already up and playing with Beth on the living room carpet. As I watched them together, it occurred to me that if Henry's plan had been to isolate me from Beth by hiring an au pair to look after her, then it had backfired spectacularly. His pathetic stunt of hiding my mobile phone in Ingrid's room had killed off any loyalty she might have felt towards him for giving her a job. Nice one, Henry! Ingrid and I were rapidly forming a close bond, not least through our shared love of swimming. If anyone was isolated, it was Henry. My only worry was what he would do when it finally dawned on him how badly his cunning plan had failed.

As Henry was still out, I took the opportunity to call Alison. Amy had obviously fully briefed her on our discussion in Oxford.

"By the way, Amy told me about you *not* putting Beth in the bath. I agree with her; there's no way you would have done that. Henry must have got that wrong. Either he was confused in the heat of the moment or ..."

"I don't think he was confused. I'm sure he made it up. What I don't understand though is why. Why on earth would he do that?"

"Control."

"Control?"

"Yes, it's all about having control over you."

I remembered what she'd told me about her own husband, and assumed she was talking from personal experience.

"Think about what happened afterwards. You became dependent on him, didn't you?"

"Yes. I needed him to drive me everywhere. He took over the finances; he tried to isolate me from Beth; he even took my phone."

"He took your phone? That's a classic move."

"I feel so ashamed that I let him treat me like that."

"It happened to me too. I put up with it for far too long. If my husband hadn't died, I might still be living with him, perish the thought. Look, Katy, it happens to a lot of women; a lot of successful and intelligent women just like you. Don't be too hard on yourself; don't be ashamed. He's the one who should be ashamed."

The conversation with Alison triggered a quantum leap in my understanding of Henry's behaviour. Until now, I'd assumed that each incident was just an isolated event in a difficult marriage. I'd also assumed that I was to blame for many of them. But now, prompted by what Alison had just said, I began to see a pattern. What if they were all part of some grand plan by Henry to undermine my confidence and make me more dependent on him? It was a harrowing thought. Surely it couldn't be true. A torrent of questions rained down on me like icy hailstones. Why would he want to control my life? What gave him the right? How long had this been going on? Was he planning this when he first courted me? Had our whole relationship been built on a hideous lie?

Right up to this moment, I always believed that Henry genuinely loved me when we first met - at least for the first six months. But now, I began to have serious doubts about even that. My brain started to replay those early days, re-looking at everything he'd said and done - but this time not through rose-tinted spectacles. What about our very first meeting in the café? Was that all a lie too? Had he been sitting there, just waiting for a fool like me to walk in?

"Where did you get to?" I asked Henry when he came home just before lunchtime.

"Oh, I've been at the club. Don't worry, I haven't been playing golf. I've been having a business discussion with a couple of the guys there."

Had he actually taken my advice?

"Oh, right," I said, hoping he might elaborate on his discussion, but he didn't.

"Can we have a sit down and a proper talk about something?"

"Yes, sure," I replied.

I was anything but sure. I made some tea to give me time to prepare myself for yet another fight. We sat down on opposite sides of the kitchen table.

"Don't you think it's about time we had a talk about your mother," he began.

"About what in particular?"

"About what's going to happen ... long term that is?"

"Do you mean about her stroke?"

"Yes, her stroke; whether she will recover; whether she will ever go back home; how she would manage if she did; all of it I suppose."

"I honestly don't know. Not even her consultant can tell me that. The only answer I ever get is that we just have to wait and see."

"Well, have you seen any changes in her recently?"

"Not really; her eyes flickered open a couple of times, and there were a few tiny movements of her fingers, but that's about it."

"Katherine, I think we have to face the fact that she might not recover this time."

"I know that, but like the consultant said, at the moment it's too early to say one way or the other. Mrs Williams said it took months with her husband."

"Do you think she will ever go back to her house?"

"All things considered, probably not. There's too much risk of her having another stroke, so I don't think it would be sensible for her to live on her own. Although I suppose we could find some live-in help; that's always an option."

"There's also the option for her to come and live with us. Obviously, we would have to kick Ingrid out of the guest bedroom. Actually, thinking about it, we don't really need Ingrid now, do we? You seem to be getting over your breakdown."

God, that was a lot to take in: mum living with us, Ingrid being fired, me and my breakdown. The alarm bells started jangling. What the hell was he scheming?

"What do you think we should do about your mother's house?" he continued.

He kept asking me what *I* thought, but I couldn't help feeling he was steering me towards what *he* thought. It was like he was asking me to drive, but keeping his hands on the wheel.

"June Williams is going in every day, so I don't think we need to do anything at the moment. I know it's summer so the pipes aren't going to freeze or anything, but I suppose we could turn off the water, if you think …"

"That's not what I mean."

"What do you mean then," I asked, half knowing and half dreading his answer.

"I mean, do you think we should put it on the market?"

"Sell it?"

"Well, yes, obviously. I just don't see the point in us keeping it … in her keeping it. You just said she's not likely to go back there. And she's still having to pay for council tax and utilities and everything. It would be one less thing for us to worry about too."

"There's no way I would sell mum's house; not without her agreement."

Obviously, I hadn't told him about the power of attorney arrangement, but I wouldn't sell it anyway.

"We might have to sell it to pay for her care. Have you thought about that?"

If we had to sell it, Henry would find out about mum's will. I wasn't ready for that showdown yet.

"Maybe we'll have to cross that bridge one day, but not yet."

162

He must have sensed he was making no progress with this line of argument, so he changed tack.

"Did you talk to her about taking care of her finances, like I suggested?"

"Yes, she gave me all those details a while ago. She has direct debits set up for all of her regular bills, and June Williams and I are on top of any post that she's been getting. So, don't worry, it's all under control."

Mention of the word *control* reminded me of my conversation with Alison earlier that day. It must also have reminded Henry that he was losing it.

"Oh, right, you didn't tell me that."

"Sorry. Did I need to tell you?"

"Well, it was my suggestion. It would have been nice to know you'd actually done something about it."

"OK, well I'm telling you now."

He stood up from the kitchen table and walked towards the door.

"Whatever …" he said over his shoulder.

Another win for me - not that I'm counting. Despite Henry's probing, he hadn't yet discovered any details of the private arrangements mum had put in place through her solicitor. I wondered how long I could keep that all a secret.

Chapter 33

I told mum about Henry's brazen bid to sell her house from under her. I willed her to open her eyes and tell me to refuse him point blank. But sadly, she made no sound or movement. Perhaps she sensed that I'd already made the right decision by myself.

Henry's comment about getting rid of Ingrid irked me all week. Obviously, he was jealous that we'd formed our own little circle of trust - from which he was clearly excluded - and ruined his cunning plan. I wracked my brain and came up with what I thought was an even more cunning plan of my own. On our next swimming trip, I raised it with Ingrid.

"You know about mum's illness, and that we don't have any idea what will happen to her in the long term."

"Yes, it must be very upsetting for you."

"Well, there is a chance, albeit a small chance, that she might recover enough to come out of hospital and move in with us. If that did happen, I'm afraid she would need to have the guest room - your room."

Ingrid looked worried, but I hadn't finished yet.

"The good news is that you could move into mum's house. It's not very far from here. It would give you a lot more space and freedom, and I could sort out a small car for you, so that you could get out and explore a bit. How would you feel about that?"

"That would be fantastic."

"We could go over to mum's house next week, so I could show you around.

"Great; thank you."

"Oh … and just one more thing."

"You don't want Henry to know."

Her perfect teeth gleamed through her smile.

When Henry returned home from the golf club at the end of the week, his face was flushed with excitement.

"You know how you were nagging me about using my contacts at the golf club?"

"It was only a suggestion."

"Well, I've been talking to one of my friends there; Jerry. He was a builder … he's retired now … but he's still involved in property development. He has a partnership with three other guys. They purchase development plots, get planning permission, and then sell the plots on. Obviously, the plots are worth a lot more once they have planning permission, so it's extremely lucrative. They've made loads of money over the past few years doing that."

Henry was almost breathless as he made his pitch. Needless to say, I was immediately on high alert. For a start, I'd never even heard of this Jerry before.

"So, they don't actually do any building."

"Well no. Obviously that would require a lot more cash flow. Sometimes they do if the plot is small enough - say just one or two houses - but mainly it's about adding value to the plots. Anyway, one of the four guys is moving to Cornwall, so they're looking for a new partner to replace him. They asked me if I was interested."

He sounded as excited as a schoolboy picked for the first team. I wasn't sure what to think yet. I had a lot of questions.

"Why do you think they asked you? Don't take this the wrong way, but you don't exactly have any experience of building or anything like that."

"Thanks a lot for the vote of no confidence, Katherine."

"I'm just trying to understand why they asked you. What experience do the others have?"

"Like I said, Jerry was … still is a builder; one of them is an architect; the other is a lawyer. I'm not sure about the fourth one, but he's the one moving, so he won't be involved anyway."

"Right, I see. And where do you fit into this?"

"OK, so I might not have any building experience, but I am good at dealing with people and I know about marketing."

"Yes, that's true. So how would this partnership work?"

"Well, currently they are all equal partners. Everything is split equally four ways; all the costs and the profits."

"What are the costs?"

"Well, there's buying the plot of course, plus legal fees, architect fees, planning permissions, estate agent for selling the plot. There might be other costs like rights of way for access and wayleaves for utilities … stuff like that. I don't know all the details."

"Presumably the architect does the planning work and the lawyer does the legal work."

"Yes, and Jerry finds the plots and does any site preparation work required."

"So, the other three guys put money in, but then take it out again when they get paid for their contribution."

"Yes, I guess so."

I was no expert, but it seemed to me that although the four partners were supposed to be equal, the other three would be more equal than Henry. They would get paid long before any profit was shared out - and even if there was no profit. They would be taking far less risk than Henry. And how competitive were the rates they would charge themselves for their own work? It was clear that Henry hadn't grasped any of this complexity. When I tried to discuss it with him, he became more and more aggressive. At one point, he banged his fist so hard on the kitchen table that I half expected the old pine planks to split.

"So, what do they want for you to become a partner?"

"Well, I would need to put in my share for the next project. Jerry is looking at a couple of potential plots at the moment."

Finally, we'd come to the crux of the issue.

"So, how much money are you talking about?"

"I don't know exactly but Jerry said if I was serious, I would need to commit around a hundred thousand to start with."

"A hundred thousand to start with!"

Was he out of his mind? Was he joking? There was absolutely no way he could come up with that sort of money. Then it hit me. Suddenly I understood why Henry was so desperate to sell mum's house.

"Yes, obviously we would need to find that somehow."

I noticed how he was now saying *we*.

"But we just don't have that sort of spare money, Henry."

"No, but we could extend our mortgage on this house … or we could sell your mother's house … you know … like we talked about the other day."

There was no way I would ever agree to either of these crazy ideas.

"I don't think we should start increasing our mortgage again. We've only just got on top of it. And don't forget, we'll only have my salary from the end of July, unless you find another job. I can't see anyone lending us more money currently. In fact, they'll probably start asking questions about how we can even afford our existing mortgage, when you aren't working."

"For God's sake Katherine, could you stop going on about me finding a job. I'm looking as hard as I can, but there just isn't anything suitable. Anyway, if this property development goes well, then maybe I wouldn't need a job."

He got up and started pacing around the table. As he went behind my chair, I felt quite threatened. I needed to placate him.

"Don't get me wrong; it does sound like an interesting opportunity. I just don't think the timing is right, that's all."

"The timing? Oh, for fuck's sake. Look, if I don't commit in the next couple of days, they'll ask someone else. It's now or never."

He stood in front of me, glaring at me. His face was bright red. It felt like he was trying to intimidate me. He waited for me to say yes, but I could not, and would not, agree to increase our mortgage for this uncertain venture. My answer was no, but I dare not say it.

"Well, what about your mother's house then?"

He began to batter me with the same arguments that he'd used before, but I still held firm. Obviously, I couldn't tell him that mum's house, or the proceeds from its sale, would go into trust for Beth. I was not ready to pull the pin out of that particular hand-grenade. I stuck to my line that I could not consider selling mum's house without her agreement.

"So that's it is it?" he shouted, as he began to pace the room again.

"I'm sorry Henry."

"Why are you being so fucking difficult? After everything I've done for you. This is such an amazing opportunity. What's wrong with you woman, damn it?"

He picked up his empty glass and threw it as hard as he could onto the limestone floor. Fragments of glass shot out in all directions. Henry sat down opposite me. I couldn't look at him; I kept my eyes fixed downwards, terrified that I might catch his eye.

Neither of us moved or said anything for what felt like hours. Slowly, I prised myself away from the table and went to get the brush and dustpan. I carefully cleared up all the glass and put it in the bin. Still neither of us spoke. He just sat with his head in his hands, rubbing his temples in small circles.

I felt a stinging between my toes and noticed a little smear of blood. I reached down slowly and removed a tiny piece of glass from the sole of my foot. Henry must have seen me.

"I'm sorry, I'm sorry, I'm sorry," he said.

I was so furious with him, but at the same time, I couldn't help feeling sorry for him. He looked so pathetic. Now, as dejected as a schoolboy dropped from the first team. Without saying anything, I made two mugs of tea which we drank in silence. After a while, Henry got up and left the kitchen. I heard his study door gently closing.

I sat on my own for ages, just staring into space and thinking. How could our relationship have degenerated to this level? It was too late to save it now, but could it have been saved? Could I have saved it? Anyway, it didn't matter now. I had no wish to save it. However many presents Henry might buy me or however much he might say he was sorry, his behaviour was steadily getting worse. And recently, it had taken a nasty turn. There was now a distinctly violent edge to it. He was becoming dangerous to be around.

Chapter 34

Mum was not recovering from her second stroke. If anything, she was getting weaker by the day. There was no benefit in keeping her in hospital. After lengthy consultations with the hospital staff, we agreed that she should come home and live with me. Although no-one said it explicitly, the implication was clear. She was coming home, not to live with me, but to die with me.

Only when she was back in familiar surroundings, did I really notice how wasted and pale her body had become, after lying almost motionless in a hospital bed for two months. She cast such a thin shadow of her former self; it was as if the person I'd known and loved for 30 years was only partly there. She looked so frail and vulnerable. I rearranged the guest room to make her as comfortable as possible, and became her full-time carer - with help from the hospital outreach team as before.

Ingrid moved into mum's house, but still drove over every day to help me with Beth. For such a young woman, she was an incredible tower of strength, both physically and emotionally. Nothing was too much trouble for her. I don't know how I would have managed without her during those final dark days of mum's life.

Henry kept out of the way most of the time. When I explained about the arrangement I'd made with Ingrid, he didn't really say anything. I think he understood that it would only ever be a temporary arrangement, and he could now see the light at the end of the tunnel in terms of selling mum's house. He even found a small cheap car for Ingrid - not a BMW this time, thank God - and helped move her stuff.

Other than that, I lost track of what he was doing. He always seemed to be at the golf club or in the study on his phone. At some point - I can't remember exactly when - he mentioned that one of his old contacts from OUP had helped him secure some consultancy work. It was with a small marketing services company on the outskirts of Oxford. I was far too preoccupied to ask any questions, and he probably wouldn't have welcomed them anyway.

My own life fell into a relentless routine of caring for mum. Every hour of every day exacted a heavy toll on me. By the time mum slipped into unconsciousness for the very last time, I was overcome with exhaustion and relief. I was still holding her fragile hand when the end came peacefully in the early hours one morning, towards the end of August. By a curious stroke of fate, it was exactly ten years to the day since dad died. I liked to think it somehow brought them back together again.

All the practical arrangements for the funeral kept me busy for the next few days. Mum had an impressively wide circle of friends, so the church was packed to capacity. As I glanced around from the front pew, I thought I caught sight of Isabella lurking at the back of the church, but when I checked again, she'd disappeared. Perhaps I'd just imagined it. Would I mind if she was there? Not really. At the end of the day, it was mum's funeral, so if Isabella wanted to pay her respects, who was I to stop her? And also, if I'm being honest, the less I cared about Henry, the less I found myself caring about whether anything had happened between him and Isabella.

I missed Isabella; I wanted her back as a friend.

After the funeral, came the despair and the grief. I experienced this, not in sequential stages as described in some psychology textbooks, but as a chaotic jumble of contradictory thoughts and emotions. Overlaying everything, though, was guilt; guilt, that at the precise moment of mum's death, my only feeling had been of relief. No matter how many people told me that was a totally normal and understandable reaction, I could not forgive myself. My only consolation was that I knew mum would forgive me for anything.

I did my best to keep in contact with Alison and Amy. They offered to come and visit me, but it would have been impossible to guarantee that Henry would not find out. For the same reason, I couldn't really invite them to the funeral. That would inevitably have led to a confrontation, which I could not handle in my current delicate state.

Ingrid moved back to her old room. I said she could stay on in mum's house if she wanted to, but she absolutely insisted on being close to Beth and me; a decision for which I was extremely grateful. This meant that mum's house was now empty. I was in no doubt that Henry would already be scheming about what to do with it.

Little did I know.

Chapter 35

It was now early September, and my extended maternity leave would be over at the end of the month. As I crossed off each day on my kitchen calendar, I felt the pressure mounting. I'd been at home for ten months, and my academic life was a distant memory. I was totally out of touch with all the recent research in my field. There was so much to do before the start of the Michaelmas term - and time was running out.

One piece of good news was that Ingrid offered to stay on to look after Beth until the start of the summer holiday next year. It took me a nanosecond to say yes. I told her that once I was back on top of things at work, I would find a place for Beth at one of the university nurseries for a couple of days each week. Ingrid could then use this time to explore her own interests in art history. I offered to help her find a suitable course and pay the fees. It took her a nanosecond to say yes too.

As well as my first day back at work, there was another day of reckoning fast approaching. It was only a matter of time before Henry would ask about mum's will. When he discovered that everything was going into trust for Beth - and he wouldn't be able to access a penny of it - he would go ballistic. It would be a dangerous time for me.

Might it be safer to pretend I hadn't known what mum was planning? At least then he couldn't blame me. But he might assume this meant I didn't necessarily agree with what mum had done, and pressure me to challenge the will. Fortunately, he was now earning again - admittedly not much - and I would soon be back in full-time work, so we weren't desperate for money. But still, he would be livid.

I assumed his initial priority would be to get mum's house sold. With a bit of luck, he might not focus on what would happen to the proceeds. I'd reconciled myself to the fact that, whatever memories and sentiments I might have towards her house, selling it was probably the most sensible option. Mum had always maintained her house to a high standard, and Ingrid had kept it clean and tidy while she lived there, so it was basically ready for the estate agents to value. However, I was now having second thoughts.

Before I made any final decisions, I needed Helen Franklin's advice. She said that actually she had some things to talk to me about too, and wondered if I could bring Beth into the office with me. It all sounded rather intriguing.

"Thank you for coming in, Katy. I was so sorry about your mother's illness. I've always thought of her as a friend, as well as a client. I will miss her greatly."

"Thank you. I know she greatly valued your friendship, as well as your advice."

After a few more minutes chatting, I turned to business.

"Obviously I know all about the arrangements that mum made in her will, but I did want to get your advice about a couple of specific points."

"That's absolutely fine, but just before you start asking your questions, it might be helpful for me to complete the picture for you. There are a couple of things you are not aware of."

"Oh dear."

"It's nothing to worry about. There isn't a problem with your mother's will or anything like that."

"That's a relief."

"It's just that she added a codicil."

She paused to let that sink in; mum had not changed her will, but she had added something to it.

"Oh, right. Well, I definitely wasn't aware of that."

"We both understand why your mother made her will the way that she did."

"Henry," I said, feeling no need to elaborate.

"Yes, that was indeed her main reason. Of course, it also happens to be very efficient from an inheritance tax point of view. Anyway, after she signed her will, she called me to say she was worried that if something happened between you and Henry, you might need some capital yourself. If everything was in trust for Beth, you would have nothing for your own needs."

"I told her I don't need anything; I'm fine."

"Yes, she said that. The thing is, you may be fine financially now, but what if you and Henry split up? Then you might need some money, say for a deposit to buy your own house. She wanted to make sure you are financially independent so you can make your own decisions. She was particularly concerned that once Henry found out about her will, he would make life extremely difficult for you. She was also worried that he might somehow take it out on Beth."

That last bit startled me. Mum, as usual, had a valid point. She'd obviously given this a lot more thought than I had. She was not convinced my marriage to Henry was going to last. Maybe that was actually what she was hoping for. I took a deep breath; I needed to think. Helen excused herself for a minute to organise some tea for us. When she returned, she continued to explain mum's second thoughts.

"So, she decided to leave some money ring-fenced for you. You can withdraw some of it, or all of it, as and when you need it. That is what the codicil is about. She didn't tell you, in case you tried to talk her out of it."

"Now you've explained it, I can understand why she did that."

Helen wrote something on a piece of paper and slid it across the table.

"That's the amount she has set aside for you."

I gasped in disbelief.

"So, you mean I can take that out of the proceeds, when I sell mum's house."

"No, you don't need to do that. You see your mother has already deposited that sum in a client account held by us. We can release it to you whenever you want; you have total control."

I gasped again; I couldn't believe what I was hearing.

"What ... but how?"

"Did you know much about your mother's financial situation?"

"Obviously not. I assumed mum and dad had paid off their mortgage, and I thought mum had a few savings. She did give me the details of her online accounts, but I haven't really looked at any of them. So, I guess she must have had some other money tucked away."

"That's an understatement. Would it be helpful if I went over everything with you?"

Helen walked me through all of mum's savings. I was completely blown away. It turned out my parents had been very frugal, and my dad had made some shrewd investments many years ago, which had been quietly compounding in value ever since.

"OK, now I can see why mum was so worried about Henry getting his hands on any of this."

The thought that mum and dad had scrimped and saved for their entire lives, was too much to bear. A mixture of guilt and sadness welled up inside me, until I could contain it no longer. After a couple of minutes, I managed to compose myself so that Helen could continue.

"Have you told Henry about your mum's will?"

"No, and I'm actually too afraid to tell him. He wanted to put a large amount of money into a risky business venture recently, and I said no. We haven't really been on speaking terms since. I literally have no idea how he'll react, but it will probably get extremely ugly."

"I can assure you that from a legal perspective, there is absolutely no basis for him to contest anything. However, if you think it would help you, I would be happy to go through your mother's will with you both here together. That would take the pressure off you and make it less personal; more business."

"Thank you, Helen; that's a really good idea. I'll try to find a suitable time for us both to come in, later this week if possible."

"Let me know when you can make it."

"There's one other thing I wanted to ask. What do you think about me selling mum's house?"

"Well, you can certainly go ahead and sell her house now. You already have power of attorney, so don't need to wait for probate to come through. Having said that, I can't help feeling it might be wise to keep it a little while longer … just to see what happens with Henry … in terms of your living arrangements, I mean."

"Right, yes, that might be prudent."

"I suppose you could get some estate agents round to start the ball rolling, but I wouldn't rush into accepting any offers just yet."

"OK, that sounds like a good plan. Oh, before I forget; can you let me know how much I owe you for all this legal work and advice. Will you send me an invoice?"

"Don't worry; your mother has already taken care of it."

Our business was winding up when Helen produced two white A4 envelopes and handed them carefully to me. One had the single word *Katy* written on the front; the other *Beth*. I recognised mum's handwriting immediately.

"Your mother asked me to give you these if something happened to her. She wanted you to read the one addressed to Beth, as well as your own. Shall I give you a few minutes in private?"

Before I could reply, Helen had closed the door gently behind her.

Chapter 36

I turned over the envelope addressed to me; the flap was unsealed. With a shaking hand, I pulled out a single sheet of crisp white paper, neatly folded in three, and began to read.

My darling darling Katy,
This is so hard to write and I know you will be so upset to read this letter.

I wanted you to have something from me just in case I cannot tell you myself. These wretched strokes will probably make it difficult for me to communicate with you at some stage, so I am writing this now while I still can.

My heart breaks to think I won't be with you and Beth as she grows up, but I count myself lucky that I have been with you for ten years longer than your dear father. He would have loved Beth so much, and was always so proud of you and all your achievements. You have been the sunshine in our lives and I want you to always remember that.

You know my solicitor, Helen Franklin, has all the details of my will and she will look after everything for you. She will also have a small surprise for you; it's for the best. I want you and Beth to be safe and secure, and I hope that you will be when everything is settled.

I won't write anything about Henry apart from this: he is not the man for you. I hope that you will have the confidence one day to lead your life without him. You and Beth deserve so much more.

You are an amazing woman, my darling Katy, and capable of so much. Have faith in yourself and please, please keep safe. You have always been the best daughter I could ever have imagined and you have made my life complete.

I will always be with you in your heart. I love you and always will. Look after Beth, my darling,

Love Mum xxx

I had to keep stopping to wipe my eyes with my sleeve, which was now soaking. Ever since mum's second stroke, I had racked my brains over and over, without success, trying to remember exactly what her last words to me had been. To have her words securely in this letter so I would never forget them, meant so much to me.

I now turned my attention to the letter for Beth.

"This letter is for you, Beth" I said to her as I opened the other envelope, also unsealed. As I unfolded the letter, a postcard-sized photograph fell out onto the table. It was of the three of us - me, Beth and mum - taken just outside the church immediately after the christening. I picked it up and held it close; it was difficult to focus clearly with the tears in my eyes. I knew Beth would treasure it dearly in years to come.

I placed the photo on top of the envelope and picked up the letter. I began to read it to myself, but then stopped. I started from the top again, this time reading it aloud so that Beth would hear it. Obviously, she was too young to understand what I was saying, but it seemed entirely appropriate that I should include her in the first reading. Now I understood why Helen had asked me to bring Beth to her office.

My darling Beth,
This photo is of me and Mummy with you at your christening. It was one of the happiest days of my life. You are beautiful and so lucky to have your Mummy with you throughout your life, to love and guide you. Your Mummy was my little girl and I love her with all my heart.
Have a wonderful life my little Beth and cherish Mummy. I am so sorry I won't be with you to share in all your happiness and achievements. I feel lucky to have been able to spend the first few months with you.
I love you both,
Nanny xxx

The floodgates opened and would not close.

Chapter 37

Henry could scarcely contain his excitement when I told him about the reading of mum's will at McGrew's office. He'd long since dropped any façade of sadness at mum's death. He was only interested in getting his grubby hands on her money. What a heartless bastard he was. Anyway, he was still completely oblivious to the ambush that awaited him. I didn't expect him to blow up in Helen's office, but once we were alone, God only knows what he might do. I was terrified.

"Thank you for coming in," Helen began, exactly as she had on Monday.

This time - for her own safety - I had left Beth at home with Ingrid.

"Thank you for seeing us," I replied, trying to make the occasion sound as formal and business-like as possible.

Henry said nothing and showed nothing on his face, as Helen carefully explained the arrangements mum had set out in her will.

"So, Elizabeth gets everything," Henry said, when she'd finished.

I'd asked Helen not to mention the codicil or the two private letters. Neither of us said anything.

"And who manages this trust for Elizabeth?" Henry continued.

"Katy and I do," Helen said.

She'd already explained this, but Henry was probably too stunned by what he was hearing to take in all the detail.

"Right," he replied in a dead tone.

He folded his arms and said nothing further. As we left the office, Helen tried to comfort me with a warm smile.

I got in the car and shut the door, but Henry didn't start the engine. He leaned forward and rotated his whole body to face me. I could sense the rage flowing through him.

"Did you know about all this?" he demanded.

Now it was my turn. Truth or lie.

"No, I didn't," I said.

Strictly speaking, that *was* the truth. I genuinely didn't know about *all* of it - especially the codicil - until my recent meeting with Helen. Admittedly, it was not the whole truth, but Henry didn't seem to care about the whole truth these days, so why should I?

Did I really just say that? Is this what Henry has reduced me to? Do I really no longer care about the truth?

"Well, you don't seem very surprised … or even very bothered."

"I'm sorry, but it was her money. She was entitled to do whatever she thought fit."

"Well, I don't think it's *fit* for anything. It's fucking ridiculous, that's what it is. What's the point in all that money being tied up for God knows how long … and for a baby? What's she going to do with it? We could make use of it right now. It's an insult. It makes me so fucking angry. I don't think your mother knew what she was doing when she made that will. She was still recovering from her first stroke, after all. You need to contest it."

I needed to stop him going down this destructive path.

"Mum had proper legal advice from McGrew's. I'm sure they talked it all through carefully. There's nothing to contest. And don't forget, it also avoids me having to pay inheritance tax."

"That's because you don't inherit anything," he shouted in my face. "Not a fucking penny."

He thumped the dashboard with the side of his clenched fist so hard that I felt the whole car shake. I was too afraid to say anything. I prayed that he would just start the car, so we could go home and I could have some safe space. My hands were locked onto the edges of the car seat and I stared straight ahead, not daring to look at him.

"This is all your fault," he barked.

Suddenly I felt him grab my right wrist. He was hurting me. I tried to pull my hand away but he just tightened his grip. His fingers were digging into my skin.

"If you'd done what I told you, and taken control of her finances, this would never have happened. This is your bloody fault."

He gave my wrist a sharp twist which sent a pain shooting up my arm.

At that moment, I saw Helen Franklin walking out of McGrew's reception and heading directly towards us. Henry released my wrist and slowly put both his hands back on the steering wheel. Helen glared at him as she approached my side of the car. Henry forced a smile in her direction. She tapped on my window and Henry lowered it with the button on his side.

"Sorry to bother you, Katy. I saw you were still here. Do you have a second to pop back into the office? I need your signature on something."

I opened the car door and followed her back into the office.

"I don't actually need a signature. It's just that I could see you and Henry from my office window. I wanted to check; is everything alright?"

"Not really. I don't know what to do. He's already blaming me. It's only a matter of time before he starts taking it out on Beth too."

"I'm so sorry. Is there anything I can do to help?"

"I don't think so. I'm going to have to face him sooner or later."

"Is there anyone else at your house?"

"Ingrid, our au pair, is there with Beth."

"Will you be safe there with her?"

"Yes, I should be fine once I get home."

I was shaking as I got back in the car. Then, unbelievably, Henry leaned over and kissed me on the cheek.

"I'm sorry, Katy; I'm so sorry. It's because I love you so much. If your mother loved you like I do, she would have been more generous to you. It makes me so angry to think how she's treated you."

I clenched my teeth; my head felt like a block of lead. I was too angry to feel anger. If Henry had died right there and then, I swear I wouldn't have shed a single tear. My life couldn't continue like this. I already knew that, but I had to stop just saying it; I had to *do* something about it.

"Should we have lunch at The Harrow before we go home?"

"I want to go home right now," I said in a voice that left no room for doubt.

"Right, whatever you want."

These were the last few words we said to each other that day.

I had to get out of the house before I did something I might regret. I suggested to Ingrid that we went swimming and took Beth with us. Our membership of the health club had lapsed while I was caring for mum, so we drove to the leisure centre, which had a bigger pool and which I preferred anyway. Afterwards, we sat in the busy café for ages. I was in no rush to go home.

"You look like you have a lot on your mind. Is it something I've said?" Ingrid asked.

I smiled at her as warmly as I could manage in my present state.

"No, no, absolutely not; you are one of the only people I can actually talk to and trust. I'm sorry to be so miserable. I was thinking about the argument I had with Henry this morning."

"I can understand. I never know what sort of mood he will be in. He was acting very strangely when he came over to your mum's house last week."

"Why, what happened?"

"I had my bags all packed when he arrived, but he spent ages going round the house. He said he was checking whether the house was tidy, but he was looking in all the cupboards and drawers. He got very impatient with me when I said I had already cleaned the house properly."

"Don't worry, it's not your fault. I think I know what he was looking for."

I explained about mum's will, without going into all the messy details.

"That's such a terrible way for him to behave," she said.

"Yes. I don't know what I'm going to do."

"Can I ask you something? Are you ever afraid of him?"

Ingrid was very perceptive, so there was no point trying to evade her question. Anyway, I was no longer prepared to cover up for Henry's behaviour.

"Well yes, actually I am. I have to be on full alert all the time. It's so totally draining."

"In that case … I was wondering … do you think we could move into your mum's house?"

Chapter 38

Henry left early on Friday morning. I'd been awake most of the night, mulling over Ingrid's very sensible and timely question. I knew that if I moved out and went to live at mum's house, I would never go back. Our marriage would be over. So, the question was not really whether I wanted to move into mum's house, but whether I wanted to be married to Henry.

I knew what mum thought. I'd read her letter many times. It was unequivocal. I knew exactly what she thought. She never liked Henry, and, more importantly, she never trusted him. She thought he was not the man for me. She thought Beth and I deserved much better. Her damning judgement couldn't have been clearer. In the early days of my relationship with Henry, I would have felt obliged to challenge her verdict and defend him; but not now. Now, I totally agreed with everything she'd said about him. I knew she was right.

I made my decision quickly. The answer was no; no, I did *not* want to be married to Henry. Our marriage had failed and was over. Therefore, I did want to move into mum's house.

I knew that I'd just made a momentous decision, but it felt surprisingly simple. It also brought a huge sense of release. My body suddenly relaxed and I broke down in tears. I don't know why; I certainly didn't feel sad about my decision. Ingrid poked her head around the bedroom door.

"Sorry, Katy, I thought I heard you crying. I just wanted to check on you."

I wiped my cheeks with the sheet. I was no longer under any obligation to pretend that everything was fine.

"Come in, Ingrid. Thank you. Yes, I'm all over the place at the moment."

She placed Beth on the bed next to me, and went to make some tea. I picked Beth up and held her close. That was when I noticed that my right wrist was hurting. I put Beth down and pulled my sleeve back. There was a small round bruise on each side of my wrist. If I'd had any doubts about my decision - which I didn't - these bruises alone would have sealed Henry's fate. He had hurt me; deliberately hurt me. First psychological abuse; now physical abuse. He had crossed another line.

I started to think about what might happen next. What if something more serious happened to me - or God forbid, to Beth or

Ingrid? It seemed only fair to make Ingrid fully aware of what she was mixed up in, so that she could make an informed choice. She returned with the tea and perched herself on the arm of my comfy wingback chair.

"Ingrid, you know how you asked me yesterday if I was ever afraid of Henry," I began. "I wanted to ask you the same question: are you ever afraid of him? Has he ever done anything to hurt you?"

She shook her head slowly.

"No, not so far. I don't like him, but I'm not afraid of him."

"OK, good."

"Also, I am a very fast runner."

I wanted to smile but this was far too serious a subject.

"Look, Ingrid, I don't want to worry you, but you must promise me that if he ever says or does anything that makes you afraid - or even slightly uncomfortable - you will tell me straight away ... even if he tells you not to."

"You don't need to worry about me."

I did need to worry about her, and I did worry about her. I needed to make her understand what Henry was really like; how dangerous he might be.

"I need to tell you about Annie Wilson," I began.

As I told her the story, Ingrid listened wide-eyed, shaking her head in disbelief.

"Do you think you will ever find out what happened to Annie?"

"I don't know. It's over eight years since she disappeared, so it's difficult to see how - unless some new evidence turns up."

"I am sure it is important for her mother and sister to know what happened, even if it will not bring her back."

"One of these days, I'm going to pluck up the courage to confront Henry about what he knows."

"Do you think he was involved?"

"Maybe; maybe not. I bet he knows more than he's admitted though."

"It is frightening to think how young she was when she disappeared."

"Yes, she was a young woman with her whole life ahead of her."

"Now I understand why you are worried about Beth and me. I still do not want to leave you though. We should stick together, like you said."

Later that afternoon, I called Amy. It was the first time I'd spoken to her since the funeral, and I was still liable to spontaneous outbursts of tears whenever I mentioned mum. But I found talking to Amy incredibly helpful. Despite everything that had happened - her sister's mysterious disappearance and her father's behaviour - she still had a positive outlook on life. I admired her spirit, and wished I had even half her resilience and optimism.

She was particularly excited today, as she and Jake had just set a date for their wedding - March next year - and wanted to invite me. I told her that, whatever happened, I would definitely be there. Amy was my friend, and I would *never* again allow Henry - or anyone else for that matter - to separate me from my friends.

Chapter 39

I was in bed before Henry came home that evening. He'd sent me a text message to tell me he was working late. For the first time in a long while, I slept right through until about seven thirty. When I did wake up, Henry was still not there, but before I had chance to investigate his whereabouts, he sauntered into the bedroom carrying a tray.

"I thought you might like breakfast in bed."

"Thank you. What time did you get back last night?"

"About eleven; I slept on the sofa so as not to wake you."

The conversation faltered and Henry looked decidedly uncomfortable.

"Anyway, I will let you enjoy your breakfast in peace."

I couldn't help feeling sorry for him.

"Why don't you sit and talk to me?"

"Oh, OK."

I asked him about his marketing project and we talked about my preparations for going back to work. For a brief moment, things felt almost normal between us. But then I remembered the bruise on my wrist, and all the suspicion and fear came flooding back. I couldn't trust him. I needed to keep my guard up. What did he want? What was he plotting?

I could tell that he was working himself up to say something.

"I know things have been difficult between us, especially since my job in London didn't work out and your mother became ill. I just want everything to return to how it used to be back at the beginning. I want to be close to you again. I still love you and always will."

I couldn't do it; I couldn't tell him that it was over between us; that I didn't want to go back; that I wanted to go forward - but without him. I couldn't tell him, not because there was any doubt in my mind, but because I was too afraid. I stalled.

"Yes, these past few months have been difficult for all sorts of reasons. I need time to think; to process everything that's happened; to get back up on my feet again."

"Well, now that I have a job and you will soon be back at the university, I'm sure things will settle down again."

I smiled, but without conviction.

"I suppose it's about time I got up now," I said.

Henry dutifully picked up the tray and took it down to the kitchen.

He insisted on us all going out for lunch - but for some reason, not to his usual restaurant at the golf club. The conversation was strained. I found myself second-guessing everything he said, and was constantly on edge in case Ingrid accidentally alluded to something I'd told her about Annie Wilson. I could see that Henry was trying hard, but I was extremely relieved when he finally asked for the bill.

I spent most of Saturday afternoon and Sunday morning working on the maths course I would be teaching to the first-year undergraduates from the start of term. Although I was completely comfortable with the maths, I wanted to make sure my presentation of it was well structured and easy to follow. Some of my older colleagues preferred to scatter theorems and proofs around like pearls of wisdom, expecting their students to pick them up and string them together. In my opinion, independent learning was all well and good, but it was still my job to give students some clear direction - particularly when they had only just been thrown into university life.

I was just finishing off, when Henry announced that he'd booked a table for dinner at one of our old romantic haunts. Personally, I'd always thought it very overpriced and overrated; far too many extraneous French words on the menu for my liking. However, I didn't want to upset the delicate rapprochement that had existed between us since Saturday morning, so didn't object to his suggestion.

For once, Henry left me alone to get changed. Although he never explicitly told me what to wear, he would drop not-so-subtle hints if he *didn't* like what I'd chosen. With Ingrid's help, I selected something relatively conservative for the evening. I couldn't afford to send out any misleading signals.

Henry was on his best behaviour and I quite enjoyed our meal out. At no point did he mention mum's will or her house, and I was hoping I'd heard the last on that subject.

"I really enjoyed that," he said, as we got back into the car.

He leaned over and kissed me on the cheek. I felt myself brace slightly. It was only two days since we'd been in the car together outside Helen Franklin's office.

Don't ask me why, but we had sex that night. I'm not exactly proud of myself. It just sort of happened. I didn't analyse it before, and I don't want to have to justify it now. We just had sex; that's all. Just sex; nothing more. It didn't mean anything - at least not to me. Perhaps subconsciously I knew it would be the last time.

Chapter 40

On Monday morning, Ingrid and I called in at mum's house. As we did a quick check on the rooms, I wondered what it would be like to live there. It was a lovely house in a great village location, actually slightly closer to my workplace in Oxford than where I now lived. Mum had looked after it so well that there would be nothing for me to do, but move in. Of course, the house was still full of all mum's possessions, but if I moved in myself - rather than sold the house - there would be less pressure to deal with the heart-wrenching task of sorting through her things.

Before heading over to the leisure centre, we had a long chat with June Williams in her kitchen. She was sorely missing mum and worried about who would eventually move in to mum's house. I decided not to mention that it might be Ingrid and me, until everything was definite.

When we arrived back home from swimming, there was a huge black 4x4 pickup truck parked on the road outside. My first thought was that Henry must have had some sort of mid-life crisis. But as we walked up to the front door, a slightly tubby guy with a white beard got out and approached us. He had a cheery smile and was whistling happily to himself, despite the drizzly rain that was falling.

"Good morning ladies. Sorry to bother you," he said, almost too politely.

"Can I help you?"

"Actually, I was looking for Henry. Do you know where he is by any chance?"

Ingrid opened the front door and took Beth inside. I hesitated before replying to his question.

"Sorry, I should have introduced myself … Jerry Pearce. I'm a friend of Henry's."

The oversized pickup truck and the hopeless whistling now made sense.

"Ah, yes, Jerry … the builder … from the golf club."

"That's right. And you must be Henry's *other half.*"

Don't you just hate that phrase? I know I do.

"I'm Katy."

Presumably Henry had blamed me - his *other half* - for putting a stop to his little business venture. God knows what else he'd said about me. I decided to show Jerry I wasn't all bad; it did seem a bit rude to keep him talking in the rain.

"Would you like to come in for a coffee?" I asked.

He plonked himself down while I put the kettle on. He looked perfectly at home having a woman run around making a brew for him. Years of building extensions would do that to a man. I put the coffee - *milk and two sugars please, luv* - in front of him.

"Nice house you have here," he said, casting his eyes around the room.

I was half-expecting him to start identifying projects he could quote for.

"Thank you."

"I was hoping to catch Henry at the club this weekend, but he didn't show up."

"We were out and about most of Saturday and Sunday."

"Actually, I haven't seen him at the club for ages. I don't seem to be able to get hold of him on his mobile either."

Perhaps Henry was keeping under the radar. I could imagine how embarrassed he'd feel about pulling out of their little scheme.

"Henry left early this morning. He's quite busy at the moment with his consultancy work. Can I give him a message for you?"

"I don't know if Henry mentioned the partnership we're setting up. I just wanted to show him the first plot we're buying; after all he's paying for part of it."

I sat at the kitchen table for over an hour after Jerry left, trying to digest his parting words. Henry had obviously gone ahead and agreed to invest anyway, despite my objections. Unbelievable! And now, without any means of coming up with the money, he was backed into a corner. No wonder he was avoiding the golf club and Jerry's calls. No wonder he'd tried to charm his way back from the brink, hoping to change my mind.

I was waiting with my arms firmly folded across my chest when Henry returned from work that evening.

"You had a visitor this afternoon," I said.

He must have sensed from my tone that the visitor brought bad news. Slowly, he put down his bag, took off his jacket and arranged it over the back of the chair, giving himself time to prepare his lies.

"Oh, who was that then?"

"Jerry Pearce."

He pulled a quizzical face, almost as if he'd never heard of the man.

"What did he want?"

"He was looking for you," I said simply, giving Henry his first opportunity to come clean.

"I wonder what that was about. Did he leave a message?"

"Not really. He said he hadn't seen you at the golf club or been able to get hold of you on your phone. He wants you to call him."

"OK, I'll give him a call later."

"Why don't you call him now? He seemed to be very keen to speak to you as soon as possible."

"Look, I said I'll phone him later. I've been at work all day, and I want to go for a shower and have something to eat first, if that's alright with you. I'm sure it can't be that urgent."

All his weekend charm had evaporated in an instant. After dinner, I reminded him again.

"Don't forget to call Jerry."

A small part of me was quite enjoying seeing him squirm.

"Could you stop nagging me about it? I'm going to call him in a bit, alright."

The more he procrastinated, the more I was going to push.

"Why don't you phone him now while I clear the table?"

"Oh, for fuck's sake!"

As he got up, he thrust his chair back so hard that it tipped over and clattered on the floor. He shoved it back under the table and stormed off to his study, slamming the door behind him. I was tempted to listen at the door, but it was too risky. He emerged about 20 minutes later, looking extremely red-faced. I gave him another opportunity to confess, or at least to explain.

"What did Jerry want?" I asked.

"He's still trying to persuade me to join their property business."

"I thought you said *no* a couple of weeks ago."

"I tried to, but Jerry doesn't give up that easily."

"You *tried* to? What does that mean?"

"I told him you didn't think the timing was quite right."

"So, you didn't actually say no. You just blamed me."

"You said yourself it was a good opportunity. I thought things might change; I thought you might change your mind."

"Look, Henry; we discussed it and I explained to you why I didn't want to re-mortgage or sell mum's house. You should have been straight with Jerry."

"And I explained to you why I wanted to go ahead. Why is it only your decision? Anyway, I thought we would be able to sell your mother's house once she …"

"Once she what? Once she was dead. Is that what you were going to say?"

If he was at all embarrassed by his clumsiness, it didn't stop him.

"Let's face it, Katherine, we'd already agreed that if she came out of hospital, she'd come and live here. She wasn't going to need her house again, was she?"

"For all we know, she might have recovered. It wasn't your decision to make."

"Anyway, it's all irrelevant now, thanks to your mother's will. I still can't believe she was so mean to you, and yet you don't seem to care."

Incredibly, he'd managed to blame both mum and me in one breath. I had to steady myself to keep control of my temper.

"You need to tell Jerry the answer is *no*."

"I just did, and thanks to you, I'll never be able to show my face at the golf club again. I'll be a bloody laughing stock."

190

"Perhaps if you'd been straight with Jerry in the first place, you wouldn't have got yourself into this mess."

"And perhaps if you'd been … oh, what's the point?"

He kicked his chair back under the table and stormed off towards the front door. A few seconds later, I heard his car spitting gravel across the drive.

As I left the kitchen, I saw Ingrid sitting half way up the stairs, leaning forward with her hands on her knees, ready to spring.

"Are you my bodyguard now?"

She laughed, but we both knew it was far from funny. Things with Henry were out of control. I didn't trust him an inch and, for all I knew, he still hadn't said no to Jerry. At this very moment, he was probably working up yet another scheme to get his hands on mum's money.

"I can't live like this anymore; we can't live like this anymore," I said.

"What can we do?" Ingrid asked.

"We can move into mum's house. And the sooner the better."

Chapter 41

As soon as Henry left for work on Tuesday morning, I called Helen Franklin's office and arranged to see her that afternoon. I explained the situation to her.

"So could we move into mum's house?" I asked.

"I don't see any problem at all from a legal point of view. Obviously, if you move out of your own house, you will need to decide what you want to do with it. You have a right to half of any equity that's accrued since you bought it."

"We bought it together, but Henry has always paid the mortgage."

"That doesn't change the ownership. I assume you pay for everything else."

"Yes, pretty much."

"You will obviously need to sort out who pays the mortgage and other bills once you move out."

"I haven't really thought about how Henry will manage financially. Maybe he won't want to stay in the house on his own - or be able to afford it. He might want or need to sell it or rent it out. Who knows?"

"Well, he's going to have to find a way. And then there's the question of whether this is a temporary separation or more permanent."

"Divorce, you mean?"

This was the first time I'd said the word out loud: *divorce*. So that was it; our relationship - not yet three years old - was heading for divorce.

"It would also raise the issue of custody of Beth."

Henry had never shown the slightest interest in Beth. However, I knew only too well, that he would make it difficult. He might even try to use her as a bargaining chip, so to speak. There was such a lot to think about, not least how I was going to tell him I was leaving.

I desperately needed some personal advice - as well as legal advice - and decided to turn to Alison. She wasn't my mum, but she was the next best person. When I called her, she was on her way to Portsmouth to spend a few days with Amy and Jake, and to help Amy start planning her wedding.

"Would it be alright if I came down for the day to join you?" I asked.

I'd made the suggestion before I knew it, and just as quickly, Alison said yes. We agreed to meet for lunch on Thursday at Gunwharf Quays, the upmarket shopping centre on the waterfront. I'd been there once before with mum, and really enjoyed the busy mix of shops, cafés and harbour activity. With a bit of luck, we might see one or two interesting Navy ships, as well as the green Gosport ferries relentlessly plying their trade across the harbour.

Alison and Amy hugged me warmly; they were beginning to feel like family to me. I kind of hoped it might be mutual.

"I'm really sorry to impose on your precious time together. You must have so many other things you'd rather be doing," I began.

"Not at all, not at all; it's such a pleasure to see you again, Katy," Alison said.

Amy was equally enthusiastic. After a lot of cooing over Beth and a long catch-up, especially over Amy's forthcoming wedding, I finally plucked up the courage to mention my own plan. Listening to Amy talk about Jake, reminded me what a loving relationship was supposed to be like - so very unlike my own.

"Beth and I are going to move into mum's house."

Neither of them said anything for a moment. I wondered whether my announcement had been too dramatic - or not dramatic enough.

"You mean *just* Beth and you," Alison said.

"Yes, *just* Beth and me … and Ingrid, our au pair, would come too. She's lovely and Beth is very attached to her."

"So does Henry know?" Amy asked, bringing me back to earth with a bump.

"No, I haven't said anything to him yet. I literally have no idea how he will react. That's the problem. He might get aggressive; he might be relieved."

After a lot more questions and discussion, Alison delivered the advice I was hoping for.

"Well, from what you've said, you can't carry on as you are. It's not safe for you or Beth, and your au pair is at risk too. There are a lot of worrying similarities to what went on with my husband. I put up with it for far too long. I only wish I'd talked to someone and done something about it sooner."

"I'm sure it would have been difficult to leave him when you had two young girls to look after."

"I should have left him *because* of my girls. Yes, it would have been hard initially, but we would have found a way to cope somehow. In the long run, we would have been better off without him."

"The thing is, I could just about put up with Henry if I was on my own. But that's not good enough for Beth. She deserves much better. Actually, we both do. I know that's what mum thought."

"Well, Katy, there's nothing more precious than your daughter; I know that all too well. You have to do what you think is best for her."

She dabbed her eyes with a tissue.

"I'm so sorry to drag you into my mess; it's not fair of me. You should be discussing Amy's wedding and planning for the future, not getting all sad having to think about the past."

"Don't worry; it's fine. Amy and I still talk about Annie. We don't ever want to forget her."

It was so helpful to have these two special women to talk to. I missed mum, but Alison's experience and advice were invaluable to me now. And I'd never had a sister, but if I did, I'd definitely want her to be like Amy.

"Do you have any advice on how I should tell Henry?"

"Do you have to tell him anything? Couldn't you move out while he's at work?" Amy suggested.

"I suppose I could, but I'll have to face him at some point. He will know where I am. I can't hide. I should probably be up-front about it."

"I agree," Alison said, nodding slowly.

"I would like to see the look on his face when you tell him," Amy added.

Chapter 42

I was rapidly running out of time before I went back to work, so I needed to put my escape plan into action without delay. I decided to break the news to Henry on Friday evening. As I sat at the kitchen table waiting for him to come home, I was so highly strung that I had to force my folded arms down hard against the table top to stop my whole body shaking. I had practised my speech a thousand times. My head throbbed and my eyes were stinging red.

He had crossed a line - several in fact - and now I was about to do the same. There would be no going back from here. Ingrid had insisted on taking up sentry duty on the stairs as back-up, but I knew I had to face Henry on the front line on my own.

As he walked through into the kitchen, he was holding flowers and a bottle of wine. He really had no idea what was about to happen, did he? I felt my heart sink even lower, if that were possible. Things were going to get unpleasant.

"I thought I would cook dinner for you tonight," he said.

He put the wine on the table and held out the flowers towards me. He saw my face now.

"What's the matter? You look like you've been crying."

He came towards me, ready to give me a hug.

"We need to talk," I said, putting up my hand before he could touch me.

"Why, what is it? Has Jerry been back? I told him ..."

"No, it's not about Jerry; it's about us. Look, could you just sit down for a minute and listen."

"You sound upset. Have you been feeling weird again?"

I ignored this comment; this blatant attempt to make it about my emotions. I needed to come straight out and tell him. If I tried to build up to it gradually, I might never get to the point. I took a deep breath.

"I'm going to move into mum's house for a while ... with Elizabeth."

I didn't call her Beth to avoid unnecessary provocation.

"What? Why the hell would you want to do that?"

It sounded like he found the notion quite ridiculous; almost amusing. There was a hint of a laugh.

"Don't you know why? Can't you see what's been happening?"

"No, sorry, I don't understand. I really have no idea what you're talking about."

Now, he had a hurt look on his face. I panicked for a moment, wondering if this was all just some massive over-reaction on my part. No, it was not. The fact that he was so lacking in awareness - or pretending to be - only strengthened my determination.

"Do I really need to spell it out for you?"

"Yes, I think you probably do."

He sat back in his chair with his shoulders up and his hands flat on the table, tapping his fingers impatiently. It felt like he was daring me to set out my case for the prosecution, so to speak. It would have been so easy to back down at that precise moment. I almost did. I hesitated on the brink, but then the rudeness of his tapping fingers pushed me over the edge.

"For a start, I never know what sort of mood you will be in or how you will react to anything I say or do. One minute you're giving me flowers and taking me out for dinner, and the next you're throwing things about, shouting at me and grabbing my wrist. I can never relax around you. I'm always on edge. I constantly have to work around you. It's slowly killing me."

"Oh come on, don't exaggerate. Everyone has moods. Everyone loses their temper from time to time; even you."

"That's the thing though; it's not just from time to time, is it? It's *all* the time. It's been like this for two years now, and your temper is getting worse. You really hurt me when you grabbed my wrist last week. Everything has to be done your way."

"Like what?"

"Like Mother's Day for instance. We agreed a plan for the day, and then you rode roughshod all over it doing exactly what you wanted. You humiliated me in front of your family; you made no effort with mum."

"Oh, you aren't still going on about that are you?"

"It was Mother's Day, for God's sake; don't you see the irony. You don't treat me like an equal. You play golf whenever you want. You buy whatever you want. You gave up your job without discussing it with me. You were even going ahead with your building venture despite everything I said."

"That's not true; I told Jerry I was out."

"Well, sorry, but that's not what he told me when he came round. As far as he was concerned, you were fully in. He wanted to show you the plot he'd found."

"He would say that, wouldn't he? Anyway, you got your own way about that in the end."

"It's not about getting my own way. Every time we argue, you make it my fault. You blame me about mum's will. You said some awful things about her too. I'm even worried that you will find a way to blame Beth."

I was past the point of caring that he didn't like me calling our daughter Beth.

"That's ridiculous."

"You never show any interest in Beth or say anything positive about her. You resent the fact that mum set up a trust for her, don't you?"

"I don't resent it; I just think it was a mean thing to do to us."

"Have you ever stopped to ask yourself why she did it?"

"I have absolutely no idea, but it sure sounds like you do."

There was no turning back now.

"She did it because of *you*. She didn't trust *you*. She did it to protect Beth and me from *you*. That's why she did it."

He didn't say anything for a few seconds but I could sense the anger rising in him. His face turned on me coldly.

"You lied to me. You knew what she was going to do, didn't you? That's why you weren't surprised or bothered. Now I understand. You two cooked this up together with that bloody solicitor, just to spite me."

He picked the wine bottle up by its neck and slammed it back down. Fortunately, the pine table-top absorbed the force and the bottle didn't break. I wasn't going to be deterred this time.

"You're not listening to what I'm saying. She didn't do it to spite you. She did it to protect Beth and me *from* you. It was her idea, but I supported it. I still support it."

Ingrid walked into the kitchen. She must have heard the thud of the bottle.

"Sorry, I just need a clean teaspoon for Elizabeth," she said.

Henry glared at her and then at me. He got up and started pacing up and down. I caught Ingrid's eye for a second. She left, but I knew she would be right outside. He was still on his feet in front of me.

"After everything I've done for you, this is how you repay me. Remember who paid the mortgage; who helped you when your mother had her stroke; who looked after you when you had your breakdown; who hired the au pair; who got you back into swimming and into the health club.

"Yes, and I pay for everything else; you did next to nothing when mum was ill apart from trying to figure out how you could get your hands on her money; and you were responsible for my breakdown …"

"What did you just say?"

"You caused my breakdown. I know for a fact that I did *not* put Beth in the bath and nearly drown her. There is no way I would have done that. You made it up."

"That's absurd. Why would I do that?"

"To make me weak; to make me dependent; to control me. That's why you shut out all my friends too. And what you did with Isabella … it's despicable."

"I told you; that never happened."

"I don't believe you; I don't believe anything you say."

"I'm not listening to any more of this crap. You've taken leave of your senses," he shouted.

He threw the bunch of flowers in my face and stormed out of the kitchen.

"I *am* leaving tomorrow. With Beth. With Ingrid," I shouted.

A moment later, I heard the front door slam.

Chapter 43

Ingrid peeped cautiously round the kitchen door.

"It's safe … come in … he's gone," I said.

She started to pick up the flowers carefully one by one, trying to align the stems back into a bunch.

"Please leave them. I can do that."

"You just sit there for a moment," she replied.

I put my hand on her arm.

"Thank you for being around just now."

"It's no problem. I didn't really do anything."

"You did more than you think. It really helped me knowing you were right outside."

"So, you finally did it, Katy. You told him we're leaving and moving into your mum's house tomorrow."

"Yes, I guess I did. Oh, God, have I done the right thing? Is this all just some terrible nightmare? Will I wake up tomorrow and regret it?"

"No, it was definitely the right thing to do. So, what do we do now?"

"Well, we need to start thinking about what we're going to take with us. We only have two small cars, so we'll need to make several journeys each. I have no idea what Henry is going to do now; whether he'll even be here tomorrow. Obviously, he's not going to give us any help."

Our thoughts quickly turned to practical things. Mum's house was fully furnished, and Ingrid had stayed there recently, so she had a detailed knowledge of exactly what was where. She hadn't been in mum's room, but we wouldn't be touching that for now. Ingrid could move back into the bedroom she'd used previously, and I could share the other slightly larger one with Beth.

It occurred to me that I should let June Williams know what was happening, rather than surprise her by turning up with two car loads of stuff first thing tomorrow morning.

"Hello, Katy, how are you? I was just wondering whether I might see you this weekend."

I smiled to myself.

"Well actually, yes … yes, you will. In fact, I'm calling to tell you that someone will be moving into mum's house tomorrow."

"Oh, right, so you've already rented it out. Is it someone nice?"

"Well, I'm hoping you will like them."

It was a bit mean to tease her like this, but she soon forgave me when I explained. In fact, she sounded excited, and very happy to hear that Ingrid, whom she described as *that lovely young Swedish girl* - actually Danish - was joining us. A few minutes after I hung up, June phoned back to offer the services of her grandson and his trusty white transit van. I was about to decline, when it occurred to me having her grandson around might be a good idea if Henry showed up.

Kevin turned out to be an extremely helpful young man. He was a stonemason by trade, and obviously worked out in the gym too. At one point, I caught Ingrid blatantly admiring his toned body as he lifted a heavy box of books. She was so embarrassed.

Henry didn't come back on Friday night, nor did he leave a message. I did feel a slight pang of concern for his welfare and wondered whether I should call him, but immediately saw the folly in that. There was still no sign of him on Saturday as we picked up the third load for the day. I left a brief note saying I might come back on Sunday to collect a few final things, but without specifying a time. I signed off with the single word *Katy* - no *love* - but wrote a small '*x*' before thinking about it. I briefly considered redoing the note without the '*x*', but decided to leave it as it was.

By early Saturday evening, we were totally exhausted. June had thoroughly cleaned the house - even though it was already spotless - and stocked the fridge with a few essentials, so we didn't need to go shopping. I was about to order a takeaway for us all, when June announced that she had a home-made lasagne waiting for us in her house. She totally spoilt us.

Kevin quickly dispelled my prejudiced idea of *white van man* as he talked eloquently about the restoration work he was doing in one of the Oxford college chapels. Ingrid was so fascinated that she basically invited herself on a personal guided tour. I tried to make a joke about her having to wear a hard hat, but she was no longer listening to me. Kevin also knew a thing or two about the construction of the Andrew Wiles Building, which was now home to the Maths Institute. Discovering I worked there, he asked me to explain what the Penrose Tiling entrance stonework was all about. I did my best to oblige with the help of a pencil and napkin. It wasn't that complicated, after all.

As we ate and chatted into the late evening, I started to feel relaxed; a feeling I'd almost forgotten over the past three years. The only slightly awkward moment came when I clumsily tried to offer Kevin some money for his help. He wouldn't hear of it.

"Any friend of gran's," was all he said, and I understood.

As we stepped out of June's porch, I half expected to see Henry's car lurking somewhere nearby. There was no sign of it. I opened the front door of mum's house and immediately felt at home. I reminded myself that this was our home now. After I put Beth in her cot and Ingrid went for a shower, I opened the door of mum's room and sat on her bed for a while. My fingers stroked the soft light blue mohair blanket that she always arranged artistically when she made her bed each morning.

"Well, I finally did it. You always knew; you were right. Thank you for your letter; thank you for everything. I love you," I whispered, dissolving into floods of tears.

After I went to bed, I lay awake for ages worrying, partly about what had happened in the past 24 hours, but mainly about what was going to happen in the next 24. I knew that although I'd moved out, I was still not free of Henry. Not by a long shot. If anything, things would probably get worse before they got better.

Midway through Sunday morning, as I unpacked my clothes, I realised that I'd forgotten all my knickers. I already had a long list of other items that would be useful to pick up, so decided to risk a trip home - to my old home, that is. I drove past the house to check if Henry was there, but his BMW was nowhere to be seen. As I put my key in the front door, I wondered if he might have changed the lock in retaliation, but it opened without a problem.

I was back outside and had just finished packing up the car when Henry returned. He parked his car directly in front of mine, blocking it in. Someone had to speak first.

"I assume you saw my note about coming back today for more stuff," I said.

"No."

"Didn't you see it? I left you a note in the kitchen."

"I haven't been here."

"Oh, right."

"I've been at my parents since Friday night."

"So, they know about us."

"They know about *you*; yes."

So, this was how he was going to play it: *I* was the problem. It was all my fault. The stilted conversation was so awkward, I wanted to make my excuses and leave. But that would mean having to ask him to move his car. How difficult was he going to be?

"Do you want to come in for some tea before you go?" he asked.

I felt like I couldn't refuse, so I nodded and followed him into the house. He made two mugs of tea in silence, and set them down on the kitchen table. We each quietly pulled out a chair and sat down on opposite sides. I felt it was his turn to say something first.

"How did your move go?" he asked.

"Yes, fine. Mrs Williams' grandson helped us out with his van. We totally forgot loads of things, which is why I had to come back this morning."

"Oh, right."

"There's the note," I said, pointing to it.

He looked across and back again but said nothing. I picked up my mug of tea and sipped at the rim a couple of times. In the stony silence, the sound was deafening.

"I was just trying to look after you." Henry said.

I didn't want to reply; I didn't know how to; it was far too risky. One wrong word and he might get angry with me or violent again. One wrong word and I might end up sleeping with him and agreeing to move back in. I said nothing.

"I want to carry on looking after you."

Why did this promise from Henry feel like a threat?

"Look, I think it's best if we both have some time and space," I said after a long pause.

The conversation stopped dead right there. We finished our tea in silence.

"I should probably be going."

"I'll move my car."

"Thank you."

There was no eye contact between us as I went outside and got into my car. As I drove off, I looked in the rear-view mirror, but Henry was already nowhere to be seen.

Chapter 44

Later that afternoon, there was a knock at the door. I looked through the spyhole that mum had fitted when she first moved in, and was astonished to see Henry's father. All sorts of thoughts buzzed through my head as I opened the door. Had Henry done something? Done something to himself?

"Don't worry, Katy; I come in peace. I just wanted to see how you're holding up," he said.

Did Henry tell him I'd had another breakdown or something? He sounded genuinely concerned, so I invited him in and offered him a drink. As we chatted, he didn't mention Henry at all. After about fifteen minutes, he stood up ready to take his leave, but I sensed that he hadn't quite finished.

"Look, Katy, I know Henry can be difficult … I'm not trying to defend him or anything, but he's had trouble with relationships ever since …"

He started shaking his head and his words tailed off, but I couldn't miss this opportunity.

"Ever since what?"

"Oh, no, forget it; it doesn't matter."

"Ever since Annie Wilson," I said slowly.

The blood drained from his face and he sank slowly back down. If the chair hadn't been directly underneath him, I think he would have slumped right down onto the floor.

"He told you?"

"No, he didn't. He's never even mentioned her. But I found out anyway … it doesn't matter how."

"Right."

"And he doesn't know that I found out. You must promise not to tell him that I know about Annie Wilson."

I realised it was a bit late asking him not to tell Henry. Henry was his son after all. Why wouldn't he tell him? Oh God, I'd done another stupid thing.

"You have my word."

I had no option now but to trust his word.

"What happened between Henry and Annie?" I asked.

"They met in Lyme Regis during the summer holidays. He got to know Lyme when he was a student in Exeter, and he often drove down there, even though he'd moved to London by then."

Henry's father told me everything he knew, which wasn't much, as Henry was apparently always so secretive. He then described the distress that Annie's disappearance and the police investigation had caused for everyone. I didn't learn anything new, but his story was at least consistent with everything Alison had already told me.

"Annie's disappearance had a huge impact on Henry. He couldn't face staying in London, so he moved back to Oxfordshire. He became very withdrawn for a while; didn't even want to play golf. He refused to talk about Annie."

"Did he go out with anyone else after that?"

"Not as far as I'm aware … oh, no, hang on … I think there was one girl. She might have been an artist or something."

"Was her name Isabella, by any chance?"

"Sorry, I don't think he ever told us her name."

On his way out, Henry's father asked me to promise not to tell Henry about our conversation. I gave him my word.

After the best part of a year on maternity leave, it was now just over a week until I would be back at work full-time. I knew it was going to be a massive shock to my system in all sorts of ways, not least the separation from Beth. I had total confidence in Ingrid though, and June Williams was right next door if she needed back-up. To ease myself back in, I planned to visit my college and the Maths Institute on Tuesday with Beth, and then again on Thursday, but without her. My Tuesday visit would allow me to deal with all the mother and baby-related questions, leaving Thursday to focus on my academic work.

On the Monday morning of my final week, Ingrid and I went swimming. Now we were living in mum's house, the golf club was much nearer than the leisure centre, so we'd renewed our memberships at the health club there. There was always a small chance we might bump into Henry, but that might happen anyway given that we still lived only a few miles apart.

The first person we bumped into was not Henry, but Jerry. Ingrid took Beth into the changing rooms while I stayed outside to talk to Jerry.

"Shame about Henry," he said, catching me off guard.

I had no idea what he meant.

"First, he reneged on our business agreement, and now he's cancelled his membership at the golf club. You certainly have been putting your foot down, haven't you?"

I wasn't planning to wash our dirty linen in front of a loose-mouthed man like Jerry.

"I'm sorry; I'm going to have to go. My friend will be wondering what's happened to me."

Although my encounter with Jerry was rather unsettling, it did at least confirm that Henry had now pulled out of their venture. The news about him quitting his beloved golf club was a bit unexpected, but I could see why his face would no longer fit. His ego wouldn't be able to handle the humiliation. I almost felt a little sorry for him. But only a little.

After lunch, I forced myself to sit down at my laptop and tackle the mammoth task of letting people know about my change of address. I didn't want any of my correspondence to end up in Henry's hands.

Then there was the issue of paying bills. I needed to transfer all the payments on mum's house into my name; that was relatively easy. The challenge would be to get Henry to pick up the bills on our old house, now that I was no longer living there. I thought about sending him an email but felt that was too impersonal at this early stage of our separation. Later that evening I summoned up all the courage I had and called him. I felt sick as I waited for him to answer.

"It's me," I said.

"Yes?"

Even from this one short word, I knew he was cold to me.

"I just wanted to talk to you about a couple of things," I began, as pleasantly as I could manage.

"Like what?"

He didn't seem open to small-talk, so I plunged straight in.

"Well, it's about the bills and things. Obviously, I'm going to have to pay for everything at mum's house."

"So what? That's your choice."

"So, I can't afford to keep paying for everything at your house too."

"*My* house? When did it become *my* house?"

I didn't want to be sucked into an argument about ownership of the house. That would have to come later.

"Look, you know what I mean. Now I've moved out, you need to start paying for the council tax and utilities yourself."

"Oh right, so now you want me to pay for everything else, as well as the mortgage which, in case you've forgotten, I've paid every damn month since we bought the house."

"No, I haven't forgotten. I might not have paid the mortgage, but I did pay for everything else. That's just how we agreed to split it. But I'm not living there anymore."

"So, I'm just supposed to pay for everything from now on."

"Well yes, if you want to keep living there. Or I suppose, if you prefer, we could just sell the house and split the proceeds."

Oh God, I shouldn't have said that. I knew I was about to lose control of the argument.

"And where the hell am I supposed to live? It's alright for you in your nice cosy little house you inherited from mummy. What am I supposed to do? Do you expect me to live on the street?"

"You could buy something else, or rent, or stay with your parents. Or you could buy me out and stay in the house if you want. It's up to you."

"That's so kind of you to allow me to stay in the house I've been paying for."

"Look, Henry, I don't want to keep arguing like this. It's up to you where you want to live. Just let me know what you decide. But in the meantime, you need to pick up the bills for the house you're living in."

"Do I now? We'll see about that," he said, and hung up on me without any warning.

My head was pounding with rage after he cut me off so rudely. Why did he have to make everything so difficult? And what the hell was *we'll see about that* supposed to mean. My knee-jerk reaction was to cancel all my direct debits relating to my old house. He'd have to do something when they turned the electricity off.

However, provoking Henry at the moment was probably not the best strategy. Instead, I carefully composed an email giving him all the relevant details and politely asking him to pick up the payments. I decided to wait until the following morning before sending it, in order to give him some time to cool off. If my email didn't work, I would ask Helen Franklin for her advice about using a more formal process.

Chapter 45

I suggested to Ingrid that she came with me on Tuesday when I went into Oxford. The idea was to show her around my college in the morning, before she met up with Kevin for lunch and the private tour he'd been volunteered to give her. I wasn't convinced the outfit she chose was entirely appropriate for climbing over stone walls, but I decided to trust her judgement.

It was great to see my colleagues again and realise that, not only did they still remember who I was, but they were genuinely looking forward to my return the following Monday. I didn't mention any details about what was happening in my private life, until I met Malkit loitering outside the Whitehead Library.

"Hey, Katy, great to see you again. It seems a long time since the christening … when was that now?"

"Twenty-second of March."

It was a date I would not forget in a hurry.

"Oh, right, very precise. I'm sure Beth is still looking absolutely gorgeous."

I laughed.

"Still using that old line are you?"

"Absolutely. Anyway, what have you been doing for the past six months?"

"Do you have time for a cup of tea?"

I completely trusted his integrity and loyalty. He would never gossip about me. I told him about mum's illness and my issues with Henry - but not about Annie Wilson as that was not my story to share.

"Well, I am sorry to hear you have had such a difficult time since I last saw you. You must be very tough to handle all that, and still be returning to work next week. Anyway, I am glad you are coming back. We have missed you. I have missed you."

"I've missed you too."

"I hope you do not mind, but when I heard you were coming in today, I collected a few recent papers and articles together. I thought they might be useful to help you catch up," he said.

He pulled out a thick folder from his bag.

"Thank you; that's so thoughtful of you. Yes, a lot to catch up on. Talking of which, how's your research going?"

Malkit talked me through his latest work - deep in the bowels of quantum field theory - and I was pleasantly surprised by how much of it I understood. Perhaps I hadn't lost my touch, after all. Or maybe he was just very good at explaining things simply. Beth fell asleep as soon as he started talking, but I don't think it was about the maths.

As we parted, I gave him a huge hug. I think I caught him by surprise, as he didn't quite know how to react, and looked slightly embarrassed.

"You are a good friend, Malkit," I said, trying to alleviate any lingering weirdness between us.

"You too."

"I will be back in on Thursday afternoon. Maybe we can catch up again then if you're around."

"Yes, of course."

Ingrid had also experienced her share of weirdness. Apparently, Kevin had mentioned his girlfriend a number of times during the guided tour, which not surprisingly hadn't gone down too well with Ingrid.

"Oh, well, there are plenty more fish in the sea," I said.

This turned out to be one of the few English sayings that Ingrid hadn't heard before, and my clumsy explanation did nothing to comfort her. However, a few minutes later I noticed her busily messaging on her phone, and her gloomy expression miraculously lifted. I spared her blushes by not asking any questions.

Having still heard nothing from Henry, I called Helen on Wednesday afternoon. Although she agreed I was within my rights to simply stop paying the bills, she did strongly counsel me to avoid confrontation if at all possible. She said she'd seen too many relationships escalate very rapidly from rather difficult to extremely toxic over money arguments. Based on her advice to keep a written record of my interactions with Henry from now on, I sent a polite email reminder, rather than calling him again.

Late on Thursday morning, I was deep in discussion with my professor in the Maths Institute. We'd had a really good talk and I was feeling extremely positive about being back at work the following Monday. He'd enthusiastically endorsed my plan for the lecture course I would be giving, and had some exciting ideas for research areas we could work on together.

Suddenly, I heard my phone vibrate and saw Ingrid's number. I knew she wouldn't call me like this unless it was extremely urgent. Immediately, I assumed something had happened to Beth.

"It's my au pair. I'm really sorry, Roger, but do you mind if I take this?"

"Not at all; go ahead. I need to dig out a couple of research papers to show you anyway. I'll be back in a few minutes."

I answered Ingrid's call.

"Hi, Ingrid, is everything OK?"

"Henry has taken Beth. I don't know what to do."

She was distraught; sobbing.

"Taken Beth? When? Where did he take her?"

"He just turned up at the front door. I told him you weren't here. He demanded to know where you were. I didn't want to tell him, but he said he wouldn't leave until I did. He was standing in the hall shouting at me. I was holding Beth and she started screaming. He said he was taking her home with him. I couldn't stop him. I'm so sorry, Katy. I don't know what to do."

My mind was racing. I couldn't think straight. I feared the worst.

"It's not your fault, Ingrid. I will deal with this. Right, go and find June Williams, and tell her what happened, just in case Henry comes back."

"She's already here. She heard the shouting and came round just as he was driving off."

I called Henry's phone but it went to voicemail. There was no point leaving a message. I told my professor I had an emergency at home and needed to go out for a couple of hours. The drive was a total blur. I had to keep wiping the tears from my face. I couldn't breathe properly. My only thought was for Beth. I needed to get to her as soon as possible. I tried not to think about Henry's motives.

Before I knew it, I was skidding to a halt on the gravel behind Henry's BMW, my front bumper right up against the back of his car. He must have heard me but he didn't come out. I hadn't brought the front door key with me, so I had to knock. He made me wait. What a fucking bastard he was. I was about to hammer on the door again, when he finally opened it.

"Where is Beth?" I screamed in his face. "I want to see my daughter right now."

I tried to push past him to get to Beth, but he put both his arms up and blocked the doorway.

"Calm down, calm down. *Our* daughter is fine. She's just in the living room."

"Don't tell me to calm down, you monster. What the hell did you think you were doing taking her like that? Do you have any idea what I've been going through? And Ingrid … how could you do that to her; she's only a girl?"

"Well now you know what it feels like to have your daughter taken away from you. And you don't like it, do you?"

"How could you do this to Beth? Why are you taking it out on her?"

"You leave me. You take my daughter. You refuse to talk about our relationship. You demand I pay all the bills. What am I supposed to do?"

"This is between me and you; it does *not* involve Beth."

"Well actually it does involve her. I am her father; I have as much right to be with her as you do."

"Don't pretend for one minute you actually care about her. You've never shown the slightest interest in her before."

"She's still my daughter."

It was so obvious what game he was playing. Of course, he had absolutely no interest in her. He was simply using her to upset me. I needed to keep my focus.

"What is it you really want, Henry?" I said.

My bluntness caught him by surprise.

"I just want to talk, that's all. Why don't you come in and we can sit down in the living room?"

He stepped aside. I rushed over to Beth and picked her up out of the carrycot.

"How did you get her here?" I asked.

"In the car of course."

"But you don't have a baby seat in your car."

"She was in the cot on the back seat."

"You know that's not safe. How could you be so bloody stupid?"

"She's fine."

"No thanks to you. And she's soaking. How exactly were you planning to change her?"

"I would have found something," he said.

I glared at him. My emergency bag was in the car. I changed Beth on the small mattress from the cot and threw the stinking wet nappy in Henry's direction. After I'd put her into a dry outfit, I sat her securely on my knee with both my arms wrapped firmly around her. There was no way I was going to let go of Beth again.

"Right, so what do you want to talk about?" I said.

"I want to know if this move to your mother's house is permanent. I mean, are you ever planning to come back here?"

"No, I'm not planning to come back," I said firmly. "It's permanent."

I didn't even need to think about it; my head and my heart were in complete unison.

"After what's happened this week … and after what you did just now … I am *never* coming back."

I started shaking. I waited for him to explode. But he didn't say or do anything. He just sat there with his jaw firmly locked. I could see the muscles in his neck pulsing and his temples throbbing. The suspense was killing me.

Slowly, I stood up and collected my things together, all the time holding Beth tightly with one arm. At any moment, I expected Henry to grab me and stop me leaving. He didn't move. He didn't even come to the door as I left. As I reversed my car away from his

BMW, I noticed the vertical crack my bumper had made in the middle of his number plate - right by the backward 'E'. I prayed that it wouldn't swing loose before I could escape.

I drove out of the village and a mile or so up the hill, and then turned off the engine. I needed to think. My mind was in overload. I tried to forget the past and the future and focus on the present: what to do right now. I phoned Ingrid to let her know we were safe, and on our way back to mum's house.

She was waiting there with June Williams when I returned. I didn't expect Henry to show up again, but in the unlikely event that he did, Ingrid was to keep the door locked and June would call the police if necessary. On a practical note, June suggested I upgrade the security on the front door with a new 5-lever mortice deadlock, chain and spyhole. She said she would ask Kevin to install them for me.

First thing on Friday, I called Helen Franklin to tell her what happened. Her suggestion was to keep talking to Henry - politely but firmly - and work things out between the two of us, if at all possible. She reminded me that resorting to legal action would be extremely messy, not to mention costly.

Late on Friday night I checked my phone and noticed there was a reply from Henry, regarding him paying his own bills from now on. I opened it with trepidation.

It said simply *OK*.

Chapter 46

Ingrid and I went swimming on Saturday morning, as I desperately needed to relax after all the stress of the previous week. I'd also heard there was a mother and toddler group that met at the health club on Saturdays, and thought we could take Beth after our swim.

When we arrived home, Kevin was already in the process of chiselling out a slot in the door frame for the deadlock rebate. There were wood shavings everywhere - including in his hair. I volunteered Ingrid to get the vacuum cleaner, while I took Beth inside and fed her. It was only sometime later that I realised Ingrid was still talking to Kevin, and progress on the lock had slowed considerably. When Ingrid eventually came into the kitchen, she had a huge smile on her face, which she made absolutely no effort to conceal. I was intrigued.

"Did he mention his girlfriend again?" I asked, without really thinking.

"Yes," she said.

"Oh, sorry."

"No, it's fine. He said his girlfriend was not happy when he told her about giving me a private tour. She asked him why he hadn't done the same for her, and he told her it was because she had never shown any interest in his work. Apparently, that did not go down well. Anyway, they ended up having a huge argument, and sadly, they split up."

Ingrid didn't look too sad.

Sunday was my final day of preparation before going back to work. I tried to focus on what I was supposed to be doing, but my mind kept wandering off down long dark tracks. My number one concern was Beth, and how to keep her safe from Henry. The question that was troubling me most, was what Henry would demand in terms of custody and visiting rights? I was sure he wasn't remotely interested in Beth, but I was also damn sure that he would make it an issue, if for no other reason than to be difficult. Or even to bargain with me about something else - probably money. Of course, since he now knew Beth was the main beneficiary of mum's will - albeit via a trust - he might suddenly become much more interested in her. I was well aware that there was nothing I could do to permanently exclude him from her life, so this was going to be an ongoing nightmare for years to come.

Always at the back of my mind was Helen's advice. I was committed to being constructive, but there was no guarantee Henry would be the same. At least on the financial side, he seemed to have accepted my proposal of a way forward - or so I thought.

Literally, the moment I was about to switch off my phone and try to get a good night's sleep, a message pinged up. It was from Henry:

I've made all the mortgage payments since we bought the house, and am now paying all the other bills as well. So I should get all the equity in the house, if and when we sell it. Agreed? H.

Damn it! This was the last thing I needed at eleven o'clock on Sunday as I was climbing into bed. I couldn't believe it. No, actually, I could believe it. I knew he'd timed his message deliberately to disturb my last night's sleep before I went back to work. What a bastard! His financial logic was absurd, so I would certainly not be agreeing to it. But tempting as it was to bash out an angry reply with my jabbing index finger, I forced myself to hold off. For now, I just forwarded his message to Helen Franklin and told her I would try to call her on Monday afternoon. This issue required a considered response.

Facing a lecture theatre full of bright first year maths undergraduates was always going to be daunting, especially on the first day of term. I was well aware that the slightest stumble on my part would be greeted with sharp intakes of breath from those ultra-keen students; the ones who'd already worked through the recommended textbooks, even before they'd arrived in Oxford. I was like that myself, not so long ago. At school, I just seemed to be good at maths, which meant I enjoyed it and worked harder. Which meant I became even better. Virtuous cycle, I think they call it. What started the cycle, I have no idea; it doesn't really matter now. It just kind of happened. Anyway, I guess I don't need to explain or apologise.

My first lecture seemed to go quite well. There were certainly a lot of nodding heads - or were some of my students just dozing off? Afterwards, there was a short queue of what looked like autograph hunters. They were simply the keenest of the keen, wanting to impress me with what they thought were clever questions, and share a few extra maths moments with me. I was happy to oblige. As a fresh undergraduate, I'd done exactly the same.

As I strolled back to college reflecting on my first lecture, and on my academic life in general, a disturbing thought began to form in my mind. For the rest of the day, it lurked there, growing and taking shape. It wasn't until my drive home that it crystallised with such clarity, that I couldn't fail to grasp its significance. I might finally have stumbled on the root cause of Henry's problem with me.

He was jealous.

He was jealous of my education, my academic achievement and my career.

He resented my intelligence and my success.

He felt inadequate in those areas.

He needed to find some other way to get the upper hand.

He needed to control me.

It was all about control.

I replayed some of his hurtful words and actions, and saw how many of them supported my new theory. His systematic approach to extinguishing my close circle of bright friends was a prime example.

It was Alison who first shed a ray of light onto Henry's scheme to undermine me; to make me more dependent on him; to control me. She helped me recognise that there was a disturbing pattern in *what* he was doing. But until this moment, I hadn't been able to work out the underlying *why*: why did he need to control me?

Now at last, maybe I understood. Of course, just because I understood the reason, didn't mean I would excuse or tolerate his behaviour. His actions were still loathsome, whether or not he had some twisted motive. However, this new awareness somehow gave me more confidence, and that had to be a positive step. For one thing, I could stop worrying, once and for all, about whether I was to blame for everything.

Any sense of self-satisfaction with my theory was quickly dashed by one of its obvious implications. If I was indeed as intelligent and successful as I thought, then why on earth had I let Henry walk all over me for so long? Why hadn't I figured out what was going on and done something about it much earlier? Perhaps I wasn't so smart after all. I tried to console myself with the thought that I was not alone. From the extensive reading I'd done recently about coercive control, I was only too well aware of how many other intelligent, successful, professional women had been taken down this sinister path. Why did any of us let it happen?

I remembered how Annie had been described by her mother; her passion for books and reading. She was clearly an intelligent and talented girl. Was it just a coincidence that Henry had picked on us two academic types? I somehow doubted it. More than likely, he'd deliberately targeted both of us for the same reason. The more I thought about it, the more I became convinced of the accuracy of my hypothesis.

Thank God that Amy had come to Beth's christening. Her small action was the proverbial flap of a butterfly's wing that had dramatically changed the course of my life.

I hadn't managed to catch Helen Franklin during the day; the one time I called her office, she was in a client meeting. Thus, Henry's message about the equity in the house was still unanswered. Late that night, he sent me an irritating reminder, with an even more irritating assumptive close:

Since I haven't heard anything from you to the contrary, I assume you agree that I get all the equity in the house. H.

Stupidly, I didn't let it go this time. I should have ignored it, but I couldn't help myself.

No, I do not agree. I will talk to my solicitor and let you know when I have an answer. K.

I decided to use '*K*' to mimic his '*H*'. I knew it was childish but that's what happens when you resort to messaging instead of talking. And I didn't add an '*x*' this time. Within a minute, I had another message:

If that's how you want to play it, I will talk to my solicitor about the bills and equity - and also about custody and visiting rights - and let you know when I have an answer.

After I read his threatening message, I shouted and swore so loudly that Ingrid came rushing in to see what was happening. The phrase *see you in court* was reverberating in my head, as I told her about my latest exchange of fire with Henry. The only positive from this rapidly increasing level of hostility was that, if there had been any lingering fog surrounding my true feelings for Henry, it had now cleared.

I no longer thought of Henry as my husband and the father of my child.

I now thought of him as the enemy.

Chapter 47

I had an appointment with Helen Franklin late on Thursday afternoon to discuss strategy and next steps.

"So, you've been exchanging messages with Henry," she said rather sternly.

Her tone reminded me of my old headmistress, Cynthia Horseface - as we used to call her. I told Helen I wanted a clean break from Henry: he could keep the house and all the equity in it - which wasn't a lot anyway - and he didn't need to pay me any maintenance for Beth. In return, I wanted to minimise his involvement in Beth's life. I was convinced that he would make no effort anyway, but it would be good to have something in writing.

Over the next few weeks, our solicitors argued things back and forth, until they eventually hammered out an arrangement that

Henry and I were equally dissatisfied with. During the entire process, Henry tried every trick in the book to frustrate me.

Here's just one sample. The only thing I requested from our garden was the small conifer - *pinus mugo* - that mum and I bought together shortly before her first stroke. I wanted to replant it in her garden now in memory of her. He cynically claimed that he'd already dug it up and thrown it into the garden-waste bin. Given that he never did anything in the garden unless I asked him at least three times, I was convinced that he dug it up only *after* my request. What a *pinus* he was - pun intended.

As the end of the Michaelmas term approached, the settlement was finally signed off. Henry couldn't afford to keep the house on his own, so it was under offer. All I had left to do was sign a couple of documents to complete the sale. At no point did Henry ever ask about Beth or visit her. For her sake, I felt a little sadness; for my own, only relief.

Ingrid and I went swimming at the health club every Saturday now, followed by the mother and toddler group most weeks. We occasionally managed a swim on Sundays too - that is, when Ingrid wasn't out with Kevin. Beth was now attending my college nursery one day a week, freeing up Ingrid to pursue her own interests. Rather than enrolling on a course as she originally planned, Ingrid wanted to get some work experience. With a bit of help from me, she found a part-time volunteering role at the Ashmolean Museum. This arrangement was really convenient for both of us; our offices were only a five-minute walk apart, so we could travel to and from Oxford together most days.

And despite all the distractions in my personal life, I felt my first term back at the university had been a success. The feedback on my lectures was overwhelmingly positive - probably thanks to my posse of *mathletes* - and I had started to get my teeth into an interesting new research problem.

To cap it all, Alison had invited Beth and me to spend part of Christmas with her and Amy in Lyme Regis. She'd invited Ingrid too, but she was going to be in Denmark with her own family over the holiday. We fixed some dates and I marked them on my trusty

Country Living calendar. As I put it back on the peg rail in the kitchen, I smiled to myself at the thought of being down there by the sea with such good friends.

After a truly harrowing few months, things were looking up. I was beginning to enjoy my new life. It felt like I'd finished with my old life.

Unfortunately, my old life had not finished with me.

It started the day before I was due to drive down to Lyme Regis. Ingrid had already gone to Denmark, so Beth and I were in the house on our own. I was in my bedroom, trying to make a final decision about which five coats to pack, when I noticed a shiny red BMW turn into the drive. It may have been a different colour, but it had the same tiresome registration: H3 NRY. I wondered where he'd found the money. Perhaps he'd taken out a loan, which he was hoping to repay from the proceeds of the house sale - a bit premature in my opinion.

Rather than rush downstairs, I waited half-hidden by the curtain. I hoped he might only be dropping off some paperwork for me to sign, so I wouldn't actually need to speak to him. However, a few seconds after he got out of the car, there was a knock at the door. I walked very slowly down the stairs, trying to compose myself - I thought I would let him wait this time. I opened the front door a little, but left the security chain on. He stared at the chain and raised his eyebrows. If he was expecting me to remove it, he had another think coming.

I decided to let him speak first.

"You need to sign these forms," he said, with neither preamble nor politeness.

"Just leave them with me and I'll post them back when I've had a look at them."

"I don't want to risk them getting lost in the Christmas post. Can't you just sign them now?"

"It depends what they are."

"You know, just legal crap."

I held out my hand through the opening in the door. After a brief standoff, he reluctantly passed me a brown envelope. I looked inside and saw a couple of thick documents.

"It's going to take me some time to read through all this."

"Can I come in while you go through them then?"

I had to make a split-second decision.

"I would prefer it if you didn't. I'll ask Mrs Williams to come round to look after Beth, and then we can go and talk outside."

That's what I should have said.

"OK, but only for a few minutes while I look through these documents."

That's what I actually did say.

"That's all I want to do. I'm not here to argue."

"Right. Let's go into the kitchen."

Out of habit, I made us both a mug of tea, and then started flicking slowly through the forms. Everything seemed fine, so I signed them all without any argument. As I looked up from the final flourish of my signature on the last document, I noticed Henry was staring at my calendar on the other side of the kitchen. Scrawled in felt pen between 23 and 27 December, it said in large red capital letters: *LYME REGIS.*

I felt a wave of panic shooting through my body. He suddenly looked back at me.

"Why Lyme Regis?"

"Beth and I are having a few days by the sea, that's all."

"Where are you staying?"

"Why?"

"Just asking, that's all. I used to go there with my mates when I was at Exeter. I imagine it's changed quite a bit since then though."

Here was my opportunity.

"When were you last there?"

"Haven't been back since I graduated."

His response - another lie of course - was unbelievably casual. There was absolutely nothing in his body language or facial expression or tone of voice. It was as if Lyme Regis meant nothing more to him than a place he had vague memories of as a drunken geography student.

It was insulting. The man had no shame. I just couldn't let him get away with it.

"Not even to see Annie Wilson's mother?" I said slowly.

Now there *was* a change. He looked down for a second and put both his forearms out on the table in front of him. He gripped his mug of tea tightly with both hands. It was almost as if he wanted to strangle it. I could see the cogs whirring as he tried to work out what lies to tell next.

"Who told you about Annie?"

"It doesn't matter who told me. The only thing that matters is what happened to her, and what you know about it."

"Did my father tell you about her?"

"No he didn't, and anyway, who told me is not relevant. I want to know what happened between you and Annie. Tell me what happened, Henry."

"Why should I tell you?"

"You know why. You should have told me when we met."

"Look, I just don't want to talk about it."

"Why not?"

"Because I don't. I've had to live with this hanging over me for nearly ten years now."

"Hanging over you! You selfish bastard. It's always about you. What about Annie's mother? How do you think she's lived with it? Do you ever stop to think about her?"

"Of course I do."

"But you never bothered to go and see her."

"She wouldn't want to see me. I know she would only blame me."

"And would she be right to blame you?"

"No, I didn't have anything to do with Annie's disappearance. I wasn't anywhere near Lyme Regis when it happened; I was in London. I wouldn't do anything to her. I wouldn't hurt her."

"Why should I believe you?"

"Because I loved Annie … and she loved me."

His words took me totally by surprise. I don't know what I was expecting him to say, but it was certainly not such a fervent declaration of mutual love. It completely knocked the wind out of my sails. I lost my momentum and didn't know what to say next.

"Look, I'd rather not talk about it anymore. I spent hours and hours back then answering endless questions. Everyone assumed it was my fault. I can't go through that again. I really loved Annie and I know she really loved me. I'm sorry it happened, but there's nothing I can do to bring her back. I would if I could, but I can't. So can you please just drop it?"

His voice was cold and controlled. I didn't know how to respond to what he'd just said. All I remember is a terrible empty feeling. Anyway, he didn't wait for me to say anything. He just gathered up the signed forms from the table and slid them back into the envelope. He took his mug over to the sink and put it on the drainer, unrinsed. And then he was gone. I was still sat there, too stunned to react.

I didn't move from the table for nearly an hour. The terrible empty feeling in the pit of my stomach wouldn't go away.

For months, I'd wanted to confront Henry about Annie. I'd imagined so many different scenarios, but in each of them, there had been some great new revelation; some final definitive explanation of what happened to Annie; at least something I could share with Alison that might help her find peace. But I'd discovered absolutely nothing new. Her disappearance was as unexplained now as it always had been. I had failed.

Another part of me had perhaps hoped for some sort of confession from Henry; an admission that he had caused her disappearance or even death. But again, I had absolutely nothing to suggest that. I knew that I had totally wasted the only opportunity I was ever likely to get to interrogate Henry. I had completely failed. I had let Annie's mother and sister down badly.

The only scrap of new information I'd extracted during my brief and feeble questioning of Henry, was his repeated statement that he loved Annie and she loved him. It made her disappearance even more mysterious and pointless. How could it possibly help Alison to know that? Was it even worth telling her? It would only pile more agony onto her existing mountain of grief.

On top of this overwhelming sense of failure, there was something else gnawing away at my guts. It was the way Henry had declared so emphatically his love for Annie and her love for him - twice. I began to wonder if this was a message aimed at me. I tried to convince myself that I was reading too much into his words, but I couldn't get them out of my head. I tried to convince myself that it wasn't true, but my heart told me it was. His message was starkly clear; absolutely brutal.

He had loved Annie more than he loved me; their love had been stronger than ours.

I started to question everything again; every last shred of what remained of our tattered relationship. Did he still love her when he met me? Did he ever really love me or was I just some sort of inferior replacement for Annie; a second best? It made me feel sick in my heart.

I told myself that none of this mattered now; that it was irrelevant what Henry said or thought; that I didn't care whether Henry loved me - or had ever loved me. But it was no use. I did care. It hurt me deeply that the last three years of my life had been based on such a fundamental lie.

I desperately needed someone to talk to. I really needed mum. Not for the first time since moving into her house, I willed her to walk into the kitchen at that very moment. She would feel my sadness immediately. She would know exactly what to say. I closed my eyes. I could hear her words.

"Is everything OK, darling? You look a bit upset," she would say.

She would put her arm right around me and pull me towards her until our cheeks touched, just like she always did. I craved the warmth of her skin; the smell of her hair.

"I don't think Henry ever loved me," I would say.

"What makes you say that, Katy?"

"He basically just told me. Not in those exact words, but he told me how much he loved Annie. He repeated it right in my face. He was giving me a message."

"Whatever he said, I don't think he knows what it means to truly love someone."

"He used to tell me how much he loved me when we first met."

"But his actual deeds didn't match his false words, did they?"

"No, not recently anyway. He only told me he loved me after he'd been horrible to me. It became so meaningless. He probably never truly loved me."

"He probably never truly loved Annie either. He just told you that to be cruel to you. You know that's what he's like; a nasty piece of work."

"Yes, I can see that now. It's precisely the sort of thing he would do."

"Anyway, why do you even care what he says? You are free of him now. You and Beth are so much better off without him. You have such a bright and exciting future ahead of you both. You mustn't keep thinking and worrying about what he says. You need to keep looking forward, not back. Try to focus on your new life."

"I am trying, mum, and I will keep trying."

"I love you," she would have said finally.

She would have stroked my hair back, and kissed me tenderly on the forehead. Everything would have been alright then.

Oh God, I miss her; I miss her so much.

Chapter 48

I knew I wouldn't be able to sleep - far too much going on in my head - but I got into bed anyway. I also knew I wouldn't be able to concentrate on my bedtime book, but I opened it up at the bookmark anyway. Two weeks after starting it, I was on page four.

I hadn't even read a paragraph when I heard a faint crunching noise; it sounded like something or someone on the gravel outside.

My first thought was: what the fuck does he want now? Why can't he just leave me alone and let me get on with my life? I was furious.

But I was also afraid. I turned my bedside light off and crept over towards the window. It was dark and I couldn't see anyone. I held my breath for a few moments and then I heard another noise. This time I was a little bolder and opened the window slightly, just enough to put my head out and get a better look. A shadow moved across by the tree.

"I know it's you Henry. What the fuck do you want now?"

"It's me, Katy."

I recognised Isabella's voice instantly. But I could also hear tears in her voice. She sounded distraught. It had to be Henry's fault; something he had said or done; something bad; something evil. I was in absolutely no doubt.

"I'll run down and let you in."

I'd rehearsed this encounter so many times; what I would say to Isabella if I ever saw her again. It usually started with some sort of frosty greeting, followed by a brief opportunity for her to apologise and - if I was feeling particularly generous - for her to explain. But that all seemed so pompous and stupid now. I honestly didn't care what had happened; whether she and Henry had slept together. That was yesterday's news; old news; the past. Henry was part of the past. Now I only cared about the future, and I wanted Isabella to be in it.

I opened the door and she took a tentative step forward. I threw my arms around her and pulled her in close. There were tears in my eyes now too.

"Oh Isabella, I've missed you so much."

"I'm so, so sorry about what happened, Katy."

"Come in; come in. None of that matters now. Tell me what's happened."

I could see she was shivering. God knows how long she'd been wandering around outside in the cold December air, trying to pluck up the courage to knock on my door. I led her through into the kitchen and put the kettle on. I grabbed one of my mum's old tartan travel rugs, and wrapped it loosely around her shoulders. She sank down in the slightly sagging armchair.

"It's Henry," she began.

"Now why does that not surprise me?" I replied.

What she said next did surprise me.

"He tried to rape me."

I collapsed down on the arm of the chair and put my hand on top of hers. The shock took my breath away for several seconds.

"Oh no. Oh God, Isabella, I'm so sorry."

"It's my own stupid, stupid fault."

"I'm sure it's not your fault. What happened?"

Isabella started to tell me, but she was so shaken that her account was disjointed and incoherent in places. I managed to piece together the basics of the story. After Henry's argument with me at mum's house, he went straight round to see Isabella. He told her that he'd finally finished with me. Gave her the whole sob story about how I never understood him; never appreciated him; never loved him. He told her that he loved her; always had; wanted to be with her now.

I was already stunned by what she'd told me, but it was nothing compared to what came next. She was talking rapidly by now; she needed the momentum to get through this trauma.

"He'd been pouring large glasses of wine for us both. I'd definitely had too much to drink. Suddenly he lunged towards me, put his hands round the back of my neck and started kissing me all over my face. He caught me totally off guard. I should have pushed him away then. But before I knew it, he was pushing me down on the sofa and forcing himself on top of me. I tried to slide away, but I couldn't move. He started taking off my dress; he ripped it. I kept saying no, but he just didn't stop. He pulled my bra down and started touching me. It was horrible. I freed one hand and slapped him as hard as I could, but he just laughed. He said he knew I wanted him again. Next thing, he put his fingers inside my knickers. That was it. I panicked. I reached behind me, picked up my glass and threw my wine in his face. In the process, I must have smashed the glass into his nose. There was a large gash and blood running down his face and dripping onto his shirt."

"Oh my God," was all I could say.

"That made him stop, thank God. He stood up slowly and just stared at me. I don't think I've ever seen such an evil look. I was too scared to say or do anything. I honestly thought he was going to kill me right there and then. But then he just started to cry. He kept telling me how sorry he was and how much he loved me. But then he started to twist things around to make it all my fault. He said I'd invited him in and encouraged him; that I'd offered him wine and got him drunk; that I'd attacked him with a broken glass. I couldn't believe what I was hearing. That's when I told him to leave or I would call the police."

"And did he?"

"Yes, but only after he threatened me. He said if I spoke to anyone, he would tell his version; it would be his word against mine; that no-one would believe a woman like me."

"He actually said that? A woman like you?"

"Yes. He knows about my depression; my suicide attempt; all the bad stuff that's gone on in my life. He's right; no-one would ever believe me."

"Well, I believe you," I said.

"Thank you, Katy. I'm so sorry to burden you with all this, but I didn't know who else to turn to."

"No, you definitely came to the right place. I've witnessed Henry's dark side; not in exactly the same way as you, but I can at least begin to understand what you've been through. Anyway, you are safe here with me for now, but we have to decide what to do next. I assume you are going to report him to the police."

"Probably … I don't know yet … I haven't decided. I'm so confused. I've no idea where he went afterwards. He'd had a lot to drink. He left his car at my house. He could be anywhere now … a bar … hospital … back at my house. I can't go home, Katy; I can't go home."

"I know. Stay here with me."

"Thank you; you are such a good friend."

By now, we were both cold and exhausted. The adrenalin from the shock was wearing off. Isabella was shaking again and visibly drooping. I thought she would be much better off lying down under a warm duvet. I couldn't put her in mum's room, and although I could have given her Ingrid's room, I suggested she came in with me for company. I sensed we both still had a lot of talking to do. I made more hot drinks and we took them upstairs - but not before double-checking the door and window locks.

"I want to tell you what happened six months ago," she said, once we were settled side by side in the bed.

"Honestly, I don't need to know; that's all ancient history as far as I'm concerned. I don't give a damn about Henry now; I don't care what happened."

"I want to tell you anyway; I want you to know the truth. It's important to me."

"Well, if you're really sure."

"You know Henry and I used to be an item, don't you?" she began.

"Henry never actually told me - turns out there were a lot of things he never told me - but I kind of figured it out."

Partly from my conversation with Henry's father; partly from my instinct.

"I think that's one of the reasons he was so keen for you and me to be close friends. So that he could keep an eye on me; keep track of my movements, if you know what I mean."

"Yes, I know exactly what you mean. He likes to have control."

"Control; yes, exactly. Control is exactly the right word. Anyway, even though he'd started going out with you - and then you got married and everything - I was worried that he still had a thing for me. He was always a bit too touchy; a bit too friendly. I didn't encourage him, or at least I didn't mean to."

"I'm sure you didn't, but he fooled himself anyway."

"Yes, probably. So anyway, one afternoon … a Friday afternoon when I was back early … he just came round unannounced. We had a drink or two and then he started to … well,

229

it was like tonight, only I didn't say no then. I let him. I was stupid and weak. I hated myself while I was doing it, and I hated myself afterwards. Most of all, I hated myself for betraying you. I felt so disgusted; so ashamed. I still do."

"Look, what's done is done. I appreciate you telling me what happened, but I honestly don't care. Henry is dead to me now. I have no feelings for him at all."

Isabella hadn't finished yet; she obviously wanted to get the whole story out. It had been bottled up for six months.

"Afterwards, he said it would be better if neither of us said anything to you. He said there was no point telling you what happened; that you wouldn't believe it, and even if you did, he would deny it. He said that all it would achieve would be losing you as a friend. He said it was best if you didn't know; it couldn't hurt you if you didn't know. He wanted me to promise. But I couldn't keep it from you. I had to tell you."

"You were very brave to come and see me. You did the right thing."

"I'm sorry I screwed up so badly. I'm sorry I screwed up our friendship. I hope one day you might be able to …"

I turned to face her.

"Isabella, I have forgiven you. I do forgive you."

I leaned forward and kissed her gently on the cheek.

"Thank you. Your friendship means a lot to me."

Our emotional energy was almost spent. Neither of us said anything for a couple of minutes. But I did have one more question.

"I am curious though. What happened after you told me about it … you know, that Saturday afternoon. You just disappeared off the face of the earth. I tried to call you but you never answered."

"Henry came round to see me the next day. He …"

"He what? He saw you on the Sunday? He told me you weren't there; he said you'd already gone away. He really is such a fucking liar."

"Yes, he came round. He told me that you hated me for what I'd done, and hated me even more for telling you about it; for rubbing it in your face, is what he actually said. He told me you said we could never be friends again. I couldn't stand it. I couldn't stay there. I couldn't face you. I just had to drop out of sight. I went to stay with an old artist friend of my parents in Antibes."

"I assume you know what Henry said was all lies."

"I do now."

"So, what made you come back?"

"It was when I heard about your mum. I knew how close you were to each other. I just wanted to be there for you at her funeral - and to speak to you if I could."

"I was convinced I'd seen you."

"But when I got there, I couldn't face you. I knew you would still hate me."

"I didn't hate you. If only we'd talked then."

"I realise that now. Anyway, I decided to move back to my house a few days ago. I thought that after six months, we could … we might … I don't know what I thought … friends …"

Isabella's voice trailed off and I heard her breathing deeply. I left her to sleep and I must have drifted off shortly after. The next thing I remember is hearing Beth rustling about.

While Isabella made tea for us, I went and sorted out Beth. Then we got back into bed, with Beth between us, and sat up against the pillows, talking for ages. Isabella really couldn't decide what to do about reporting Henry's sexual assault. I understood her reluctance - not least, the cut on his face wouldn't look good for Isabella's case - but I urged her to contact the police anyway. She promised that she'd give it some serious thought, but I wasn't convinced. I had a lot of sympathy for her; like me, she wanted to exorcise him from her life. I had no sympathy of any kind for Henry. For all I cared, he could bleed to death in a ditch.

Isabella said she was planning to stay with her parents in London over Christmas and Boxing Day. I offered her the use of the house for as long as she wanted, while I was in Lyme Regis. I gave her a spare key and introduced her to June Williams next door. I also reminded her to be vigilant, and to call the police immediately if Henry showed up.

"Right, I suppose I'd better get going then," I said, once the car was packed.

Isabella had been holding Beth for a while and they looked extremely comfortable together. It was so sad that she hadn't been in Beth's life until now. I planned to make up for that as soon as I was back.

"I'm so glad you are in my life again, Isabella. I've really missed you."

"And thank you so much for everything you've done for me. You are a real friend, Katy."

I strapped Beth into her seat and had one final long embrace with Isabella. We both had tears in our eyes as I said a final goodbye through the open car window. I prayed that Henry had finally understood the message from both of us - if not, a brief glance in the mirror at his own face would help him understand.

Chapter 49

The clouds had been clearing as I made my way down to Lyme Regis, and the sky was now a crisp winter blue. There was so much going on in my head, that I was outside Alison's house almost before I knew it. I couldn't tell you a single thing about the drive down - apart from the sky.

Alison ran out to greet us.

"Happy Birthday to you my beautiful little girl," she said to Beth.

I was quite impressed, but not at all surprised, that Alison remembered it was Beth's first birthday. She helped Beth out of the car seat and held her in her arms; they both looked entirely at ease.

It was so much easier to load and unload all the baby stuff now that I'd bought the car I actually wanted: a chunky old second-hand Volvo estate, a bit like dad's. I regarded it as a statement; a statement of my independence and freedom.

"I've put you in the same room as before, if that's alright with you."

"That's perfect, thank you," I said.

Then I remembered that it was Amy's room and she would be home for Christmas.

"What about Amy? I don't want to put her out of her room."

"No, it's fine; she insisted you and Beth have it. It's a bit bigger than the guest room."

"But what about Jake?"

"Unfortunately, he won't be able to make it. Apparently, there's something going on in the Gulf. His leave was cancelled and he had to fly out to join a ship there. I'm afraid that's just how it is in the Navy. Things are always changing."

As we passed Annie's room, I noticed the door was slightly open. Alison saw me glancing across the landing.

"I've been doing a little bit of sorting in Annie's room. I thought it was probably time now."

"I'm sure that can't be easy for you."

I was dreading the same task ahead of me with mum's room. Alison quickly changed the subject.

"Do you want me to fix that at the top of the stairs for you?" she said.

She was pointing to the adjustable stair gate I had brought, one of the many useful items I wouldn't have been able to get in the impractical little car Henry previously chose for me.

"If you don't mind ... or it could just go across the bedroom door."

She picked it up and headed for the landing.

"It may as well go at the top of the stairs so Beth can wander around anywhere up here. Right, I'll leave you to it. I've put towels in the bathroom if you want to freshen up. We can have some tea when you're ready; I've made a cake."

I could hear her setting up the stair gate, giving it a couple of trial openings and closings, and then heading down to the kitchen. I changed Beth, quickly splashed my face in the bathroom, and then followed Alison downstairs. I thanked her again for inviting us, and for all the work she'd clearly done in preparation for our visit. She'd even made a little birthday cake for Beth, exactly as mum would have done. We sat at the kitchen table talking for ages. It was so good to have someone like Alison - an experienced mother and wife - to talk to. When I told her about my latest encounter with Henry, her supportive words were almost identical to mum's in my earlier imaginary conversation. Alison understood me.

First thing next morning, after the best night's sleep I could remember in a long while, we parked down in town and went for a walk along the front. We followed the Cart Road down to The Cobb, just as I had on my visit at the end of May. It was much quieter now. There were only a couple of joggers and a handful of dog-walkers about - and not a single ice-cream cone to be seen anywhere. As we ambled back, watching the small waves breaking on the shingle beach, we bumped into one of Alison's elderly friends. I wondered why she seemed so surprised that I had a baby, until I realised that she thought I was Amy. When she discovered her mistake, Alison's friend was mortified; she blamed her glasses. Amy arrived at lunchtime and we had another good laugh about it with her.

Late in the afternoon, Isabella called to let me know she'd just arrived at her parents' house. She'd gone home first to pack a few things; fortunately, no sign of Henry or his car. She wanted to know if my offer to stay for a few days after Christmas was still open. I assured her that it was, and that I was looking forward to spending a lot more time with her as soon as I was back from Lyme.

I started to relax into Alison's family routine. It made a pleasant change from rushing around with Henry from one tedious drinks party to the next.

"There's something I'd like to do a bit differently this year," Alison announced after breakfast on Christmas morning.

I could tell from the slight wobble in her voice that it would relate to Annie.

"Yes, mum?" Amy said.

"I would like us to unwrap our presents in Annie's room."

No-one asked why; no-one needed to.

"Yes, that's a really nice idea, mum."

Alison's presents for everyone else had already been placed on Annie's bed, and we added our own presents to the small pile. It was a very emotional event; I could imagine even sea-hardened young Jake wiping a tear from his eye when he thought no-one was looking.

Alison gave me a lovely leather-bound copy of *Little Women*; she said she remembered me talking about Beth's name. Once again, I couldn't help admiring the similarly beautiful books in Annie's bookcase. I walked over to them and ran my finger along the titles. I was pleased to see that *Northanger Abbey* had been re-united with its Jane Austen siblings. I caught Alison's eye and we smiled at each other.

Without thinking about it, I slid out the copy of *Mansfield Park* - for some reason I'd never read that one. I opened the front cover and saw the now familiar AW initials. I started to flick through the first few pages, trying to get a sense of the story's opening. I assumed it would be about love and money; families and fortunes.

As I turned the pages, I noticed that the book was falling open by itself about three quarters of the way through. I wondered if Annie might have strained the book's spine a little when she last read it, but then I spotted what I thought was a bookmark poking out. I put my finger into the opening and some sheets of lined paper, folded neatly in half, fell out onto the floor right in front of Alison. She bent down and picked them up, then opened them slowly. The blood drained from her face and she sagged down at an awkward angle, only just making it onto the edge of Annie's bed. She started shaking violently and tears began to stream down her face.

"It's a letter from …," she sobbed.

She closed her eyes and sighed deeply, unable to continue. Amy sat down on the bed beside her and looked at the letter.

"It's a letter from Annie," she said.

No-one spoke for what seemed like several minutes. We were all too stunned. Someone had to read it. I knew it would be impossible for Alison. She passed the letter to her daughter.

"Amy, could you …?"

Amy wiped her eyes with the back of her sleeve. She held up the pages, trying to blink her streaming tears out of the way. She took a couple of deep breaths.

"Annie has written the date at the top … Saturday 12 May."

Alison gasped with horror. Amy couldn't continue. She knew what that date meant. We all knew what that date meant. An icy shiver ran up my body. It was a … no, I couldn't contemplate such a terrible thing. If it was, it would destroy Alison for ever.

It was a suicide note.

I looked at Alison and then at Amy. Their faces told me they were thinking the same thing.

"Please, you have to …" Alison whispered.

Amy began to read again, wiping her eyes and sniffing deeply every few seconds.

"Dear Mum,

I have to write this all down. It's the only way I can do it. I don't have the strength to tell you in person. And writing is something I know I'm good at. I remember you told me that the day I wrote my first story at school.

But this is not a story; it is the truth; it is my truth.

I can't live like this any longer."

Amy's body slumped forward, her arms dropped, and she stopped reading. She didn't need to read any more of the letter; we all knew what was coming. Part of me didn't want to hear any more, but another part of me insisted that we must hear Annie's story through to its tragic end.

I couldn't bear to look at Alison, let alone make eye contact with her. I didn't know how anyone could survive the pain of hearing their daughter's suicide note.

Eventually Amy lifted the letter up in front of her eyes.

"I can't live like this any longer."

She stopped again.

"Please don't blame yourself for making me go back to university after dad died. It was the right thing for me to do. And please don't blame yourself for what has happened since. All the bad decisions were my decisions. I've made such a mess of my life over the past year - since I met him. He has ruined my life. I hate him with every bone and muscle and feeling in my body. He is crushing me; he is suffocating me. I need to be free of him.
But I have his ..."

Suddenly she choked and stopped again. After a moment, she said the next word without looking at the letter.

"... baby."

There was a cry of anguish from Alison, followed by an awful wailing, the sound of which I don't think will ever leave me.

"But I have his baby inside me now. I know I have been a stupid fool. I should have told you and Amy what he was like. I should not have shut you out. I'm so, so sorry. But he put a barrier between us, and between me and my friends. I felt so isolated. I had no one to turn to, except him. I needed to be able to think without him crushing my spirit. I didn't know what to do. I was at the end. That's why I came home this weekend on my own. I needed to see you and be with you.
I have decided what I am going to do; what I have to do."

Amy stopped again. The next few words might provide the vital clue to her disappearance. If it was suicide ... no, I couldn't think about that.

"I am going to go back to university tomorrow and study hard and get the best degree I possibly can to make you proud. Then I am going to come home and have my baby here, if you will have me. I want to stay with you until I have sorted out my life properly. My baby needs her mother and her grandmother and her aunt."

Amy was reading faster now; the excitement in her voice building word by word. Alison began to raise her head.

"But my baby does not need him as a father. I am going to finish things with him as soon as I get back on Sunday. I will tell him I never want to see him again. I am not going to tell him about the baby. I don't want him to ever know. I need your help and Amy's help. Promise me that he will never know. I will surround myself with my friends again and they will help me keep him away. He will pretend he loves me like he always does after an argument, but it's a lie. It's always been a lie. I should have seen that from the start. You can't love someone and treat them the way he treats me. I hate him.

I know in my head and in my heart that this is the right thing to do. I feel much stronger already for writing this letter to you, mum. I will leave it for you to find when I go back to London tomorrow. I know you will understand.

I am going to go out for a walk now down to The Cobb, to clear my head in the wind and the rain, and think about the future.

I love you mum. Please tell Amy I'm so sorry and I love her too. I want you, Amy and me to be a family again, and I want to bring up my baby with my family.

All my love,
Annie xxxxx"

Amy lowered the letter slowly, and folded it again carefully. No-one spoke. What could we say? I think we were all so exhausted and so deep in thought. There were so many emotions coursing through my body and mind that it was impossible to comprehend or process any of them.

My first and over-riding sensation was one of immense relief. Annie's handwritten letter was emphatically *not* a suicide note. It spoke not of death, but of life. It was a note about the life that Annie was looking forward to with her baby and her family. Of course, that would not make it any less painful for her mother and sister. But it was full of love for her family and hope about their future life together. This love and hope might one day form into tiny seeds of comfort for her family.

Annie's letter was so passionate, yet so clear. She was deeply troubled, yet so sure of her decision and her plan. I knew Alison would treasure the letter for the rest of her life; it might help her get through the darker moments. Amy too would never forget the words that she'd been brave enough to read to us.

I tried hard to push all thought of Henry out of my mind. I was so appalled by his behaviour and disgusted with his lies - especially his most recent lie about loving Annie - that I didn't want to waste another second on him. This was Annie's moment; her only opportunity to tell her final story. I would not allow it to be sullied by any thought of him. Annie must have felt the same; she couldn't even bear to mention him by name in her letter.

After the relief came the almost unbearable sadness. Not only had one young precious life been cut short, but a second innocent life had been snatched away before it had begun. Alison had grieved for her daughter for eight years; now she would have to start the process all over again, but this time for her daughter and unborn grandchild. Annie's child would have been seven years old by now. Amy's grief at the loss of her sister and a niece or nephew would be no less painful.

We remained in Annie's room for well over an hour; any fragments of attempted conversation soon died out. No-one touched their presents. Eventually Alison said she needed to go down to the kitchen to finish preparing lunch, otherwise it would be ruined. I joined her there, but we only talked about the meal. Then Amy came down and we went through the motions of Christmas lunch together, but it was just food and fuel to us. The wine was left

239

unopened and the crackers lay silently in their boxes; corpses in coffins. Even Beth was subdued; perhaps she sensed the mood. After Annie's revelation, I felt guilty for having a baby in the house.

The afternoon and evening dragged painfully by. We had no energy to analyse or discuss Annie's letter with the gravity and dignity it deserved. Alison went to bed with a terrible migraine. Amy and I took it in turns to check on her until the weeping abated.

Early on Boxing Day, I heard Alison in the kitchen and looked at the clock on my phone; it was twenty past five. It was too dark to see outside but from the chill in the air, it felt like it would be a frosty morning.

"Sorry, did I wake you?" she said, as I arrived downstairs slightly bleary eyed and still in my dressing gown.

"Don't worry, I couldn't sleep either."

We just looked at each other and burst into tears. I went over to her and hugged her with all the love and support I had in me.

"I would like to go down to The Cobb this morning," she said.

"Yes, it would be good to have a walk in the crisp cold air."

Just after eight o'clock, I drove us all into town. I could feel the wind biting at the back of my neck, as I strapped Beth in her pushchair and covered her with a warm blanket. Even Alison's dog, Rusty, looked cold. I was glad I'd brought my thick down jacket with me. We set off at a brisk pace along the seafront, trying to warm ourselves up.

When we arrived at the first set of steps leading onto the upper part of The Cobb, Amy said she would like to walk along the top to get a better view. Alison was happy to stay on the lower path with Beth, but she suggested I join Amy if I wanted to. As Amy and I mounted the steps, I was alarmed to see how steeply the top surface of The Cobb sloped down from left to right, and how rough and uneven the stone paving was. There were countless trip hazards, and no safety rails of any kind on either side. And as if that wasn't bad enough, I could see a few patches of night frost lingering on some of the smoother stones.

It was chilling to think of Annie wandering along here on her own, in the rain and the wind and the fading light. Her eyes would have been drenched with spray; her mind overflowing with emotion. *Local girl feared drowned*; that's what the newspaper cutting said. Standing up here on the top of The Cobb, it wasn't hard to believe how Annie suffered a tragic accident in this dangerous place. Losing her balance; tripping or slipping; banging her head on the stone paving; tumbling into the waves; disappearing into the water. Perhaps she was already unconscious when she hit the water; if not, she would have been screaming. But no-one would see her in the water; no-one would hear her screams - unless they too were on top of the wall. I could see it happening right now with my own eyes but there was nothing I could do to help her. There was nothing anyone could do.

Local girl feared drowned was the inevitable result. No, hang on, that headline doesn't tell the whole story, does it? The truth was so much worse.

Local girl and her unborn baby feared drowned.

I suddenly felt light-headed and started to sway. Oh God, I was going to faint again. I took a couple of deep breaths and tried to steady myself.

"I think I'll go back down and walk with your mum," I said to Amy.

"I might just stay up here for now," she replied.

"Be careful."

"Don't worry; I will."

I descended the steps and rejoined Alison.

Further along, we reached the point on The Cobb where a set of projecting stone slabs had been built directly into the wall, forming a roughly diagonal staircase with large gaps between each slab. As the wall of The Cobb sloped inwards towards the top, the steps followed the curve. The whole thing looked like a complete death-trap. For a moment, I wondered if Annie could have fallen here, but the lower part of The Cobb below the steps was quite wide; there was no way she could have ended up in the water from the bottom of the steps.

"I wouldn't fancy going up or down those steps," I shouted to Amy.

She approached the edge cautiously, and looked down.

"No, neither would I," she replied.

"Granny's Teeth," Alison said.

"Sorry?"

"Granny's Teeth; that's what these steps are called."

"Oh yes, I can see why."

Suddenly, at that moment, we heard a shout … and then another. Someone was shouting, but the wind was taking the sound away. It got steadily louder. Finally, we could hear what they were shouting. It was a name.

"Annie!"

"Annie!"

We all stopped and looked behind us. Someone was running along the top of the wall towards Amy. I recognised him immediately from the slightly lop-sided run. It was Henry.

I would like to tell you that I analysed the situation rationally and then calmly decided what to do. But that would be a complete lie. It all happened so fast - but weirdly in a kind of slow-motion way. I know that doesn't make any sense, but that's what it felt like at the time. I didn't analyse or decide anything. I didn't say or do anything. I was completely frozen to the spot, totally speechless.

For Alison and Amy, the confusion must have been a thousand times greater. Neither of them had ever met Henry; neither of them knew who this person was. And it was Amy that he was addressing as Annie.

Henry stopped just before he reached Amy. He was out of breath. He looked down at me. I could see the panic in his eyes; he looked slightly demonic. The gash on his nose looked angry. He turned back to face Amy.

"You aren't dead. You survived. I can't … that's …"

Oh God, he really did think he was talking to Annie.

242

"Oh Annie, please believe me; I wanted to help you. But I panicked. After you tripped and fell, I wanted to jump in after you but I just couldn't do it. I was scared; I froze. You know I can't swim. It would have been hopeless anyway. I wouldn't have been able to help you. I would have drowned. There was nothing I could do. I'm so sorry, Annie."

"So why didn't you go and get help?" Amy said coldly.

Amy was tough. She was going to keep this up. She was going to pretend she was Annie, to see what he might say next. Alison and I didn't intervene.

"I wanted to. I was going to. But you'd already disappeared. I couldn't see you anywhere in the water. And it was too dark. I started to go crazy. I couldn't think straight. I was panicking. Before I knew it, it was too late. You'd gone."

"You still should have tried to get help … the police or the lifeboat or someone."

"I know; I know I should have. But I wasn't thinking straight, was I? And if anyone found out I was there, they'd assume it was my fault; that I'd done something to you. They did that anyway, even when they thought I wasn't here. So, I ran away; I drove back to London. I'm so sorry, Annie?"

"I don't know what to say to you."

"But you survived; you're here now. Can you forgive me? Please forgive me."

Alison had heard enough.

"Well, *I* will never forgive you; *never*," she said.

"I'm not asking you; I'm asking Annie," Henry said aggressively.

"Well Annie isn't here; you left her to drown," Amy said.

Henry's mouth dropped open.

"What? What's going on? Who the hell are you then?"

"I'm Annie's twin sister, Amy. You let my sister drown, you bastard."

Amy took a step forward and kicked him as hard as she could in the balls. He staggered forward and fell to his knees, groaning.

Amy kicked him again, this time in the stomach. He rolled onto his side.

"Get away from him, Amy," I shouted. "He's dangerous."

Amy clambered down the Granny's Teeth steps as quickly as she could, using her hands and bum to steady herself at various points. When she reached the lower causeway, she pulled out her phone.

"I'm calling the police."

Henry raised himself back onto his knees and then stood up. He looked very unsteady.

"It's not my fault," he shouted. "It's not my fault Annie died. I loved her and she loved me. It's not my fault."

He moved to the top of the steps and started to stagger down them. Alison's dog went mad, barking and snarling at Henry. I had never seen Rusty like this before. Alison let go of his lead and he bounded up the steps and locked onto Henry's right ankle. Henry swore, and with the other foot, aimed a wild kick at Rusty's head. His foot skidded off but became entangled in the dog's lead. Henry bent down and tried to untangle it, but lost his balance in the process and fell backwards. The back of his skull hit one of Granny's Teeth with a horrific thud. He tumbled off the steps, landing in a crumpled heap on the hard stone at the bottom.

"The police are on their way," Amy said.

I took Beth's blanket from the pushchair, folded it up and placed it under Henry's head. I don't know why I did that; I don't know how I managed to do it; I just did it. Then I picked Beth out of her pushchair and placed her deep inside the front of my down jacket to keep her safe and warm. I clung onto her and hugged her as if our lives depended on it.

Chapter 50

Nine months later, Beth and I were back in Lyme Regis. It was the end of the summer but the weather was still fine. Most of the bustling crowds had left for the season, so it was a great time to be there. Amy and Jake were coming over from Portsmouth to stay with Alison too.

Ingrid had also just arrived after being in Denmark with her family for a couple of weeks. She persuaded me to join her in a spot of sea bathing in the bay, but as soon as I tested the water with my toes, I realised it was a rash decision. Five minutes later, I was wrapped in my towel with my down jacket over the top, sitting on the beach, watching Ingrid swimming through the waves.

I began to think about that last Boxing Day.

Henry died later that night. He never regained consciousness after his fall. His parents were by his bedside. I was at the hospital too, but let them make all the decisions. I was in no fit state to decide anything.

You probably want me to give you a detailed description of my feelings when he died. But I'm afraid I can't. And I don't think it's because I was confused or anything like that. I think the reason that I can't describe my feelings about Henry's death - and I know this is an awful thing to admit to anyone - is that I didn't have any feelings about it. I didn't feel sad or relieved or guilty - I didn't feel anything. It was like I'd been given some kind of anaesthetic which numbed all my emotions.

Everyone assumed it was because I was in shock - and I let them. But that wasn't the case at all. The truth was that, to me, Henry was already dead. His despicable lies and treachery had made him a stranger to me; a stranger for whom I had no feelings whatsoever now. So, his death was like the death of a stranger; something you might hear on the news - or perhaps read about in the *Dorset Echo* - and then forget about just as quickly.

Does that make me a cold, heartless, unfeeling, unforgiving person? I hope not. I admit that I'm probably a bit colder now compared to the naïve young woman who smiled at the cute guy in the café. But I still have deep feelings for Beth, for mum and dad, for Annie's family, for all my close friends - so I can't be completely hardened. It's only Henry I feel nothing for.

I realise I will never be able to extricate myself fully from his web. Nor would I necessarily want to. After all, there were some high points. He gave me a beautiful daughter that I love dearly. He introduced me to Isabella - complicated as that friendship became. There were some - albeit too few - happy times. I will still be holding onto those treasures, long after the bad memories have faded away.

Of course, once Beth is old enough, she is bound to ask about her father and grandparents. If and when that time comes, I will be sure to answer her questions carefully. Will I tell her the truth? Yes. The whole truth? I don't know yet.

And what about the enquiry into Henry's death?

I went straight to the hospital in the ambulance with Henry, before anyone could ask me anything. When Amy came to collect me in the early hours of the morning, she told me what happened after I left The Cobb.

She and Alison took Beth home, and shortly after, a policewoman came and spoke to them there. It turned out that an elderly gentleman who was walking his dog on The Cobb at the time, had witnessed the event - or at least the latter stages. He told the police that Henry had been shouting at us, and then got tangled in the dog-lead and fell down the steps. It sounded like the fact that Henry tried to kick Rusty, had made this dog-loving witness rather unsympathetic, to say the least. The policewoman already seemed to be treating it as an accident - there was absolutely no suggestion of foul play - but she did want to know what Henry was doing there, and why he was shouting at us.

Alison and Amy told her about Annie's disappearance, and about my tumultuous relationship with Henry. They said they could only assume he must have followed me to Lyme Regis and tracked us down. And that he was still trying to abdicate any responsibility for his actions against Annie and me. In the heat of the moment, he lost his balance and fell from The Cobb. It was an accident. That was what they said - and that was all they said. Nothing about Annie's letter; nothing about her baby; nothing about Henry's confusion between Amy and Annie; nothing about his cowardice when Annie was drowning. They also felt it was not their place to say anything about Henry's sexual assault of Isabella - that was her decision.

When I got back from the hospital, the three of us stayed talking around the kitchen table until the morning. Sleep was out of the question. Alison and Amy were feeling guilty about withholding key parts of the story from the policewoman. But I assured them they'd done the right thing, and that I would stick tightly to their version of events. After all, Henry was dead, and it was indeed an accident. None of this additional information would bring him back or change anything. It would only re-open old wounds, even deeper this time. There would be a new enquiry with everything raked over once again: Annie's state of mind; her pregnancy; her drowning. In my opinion, this was a gross invasion of her privacy. Annie's secret was sacrosanct. It would also devastate Henry's parents to know what he'd done - although I have to be honest, that wasn't my primary concern. So, we kept things as simple as possible.

The coroner recorded Henry's death as an accident.

From this point onwards, I tried hard not to think or talk about the man who had damaged so many lives. I changed Beth's surname to match mine - my maiden name of Harrington. I began to re-establish links with my old friends and, to my joy, discovered that many of them were as enthusiastic to do so as I was. One of my first weekend away trips was to see Elena in Cambridge; the friend who had covered for my first trip to Lyme. When I met these old friends in person, a few sidled up to me - once they knew I was not grieving at all - and whispered *I never did like him* - or something stronger.

Although Isabella was now safe to return to her own house, she stayed with me for almost three weeks. She was really taken with Beth; I decided to make her an honorary godmother. We never ran out of things to talk about. Perhaps unsurprisingly, she decided not to report what had happened to her. It was her decision. Why relive it? There was no point now. He couldn't do anything to anyone else.

Beth, Ingrid and I all had an amazing time at Amy's wedding in March; Jake and his friends looked particularly dashing in their formal Navy uniforms. Alison spent a week over Easter with me in Oxfordshire and - with some welcome help from June Williams - I finally summoned the strength to sort through mum's clothes and possessions. Even so it was hard; almost every item had a look or a feel or a touch which made the loss of mum fresh and raw again. Things like her hair brush on the dressing table; the same brush she had used for as long as I could remember; the same brush she had used on my hair when I was a little girl. It still had strands of mum's hair on it now. All these items, I kept. I was not ready to lose those memories. I offered June mum's finest set of china, to thank her for all her help over the previous year, and she gave it pride of place in her glass-fronted cabinet.

The powers that be at the Ashmolean Museum were so impressed with Ingrid's work and knowledge that they offered her a permanent - but currently only part-time - role there, starting in October. She asked if she could continue staying with me, and without a moment's hesitation, I said yes. Beth had become very attached to Ingrid, as had Kevin - although their budding romance was proceeding with all the pace of a frozen glacier. Given all the mistakes I'd made in my whirlwind romance, I decided not to interfere.

So here we were, back in Lyme Regis. As Jake helped Amy step out of the car, I could tell straight away that she was expecting a baby. My excitement for her was like that of a sister. Alison would be a grandmother after all. I thought of them as my family too. Beth and I had a new family now.

While we were all together, Alison said that she would like to remember Annie by going down to The Cobb once again. It was where Annie had died; we knew that now. None of us had been back since the other death there; the death that no-one mentioned or mourned. This time we all climbed onto the top of The Cobb. When we reached the far end, Alison handed out the bunches of flowers she had been carrying.

"I brought these flowers to scatter in memory of Annie," she said. "And I thought it would also be nice to remember Katy's mum too."

She loosened her bunch and started to cast the individual stems into the sea. Amy and I followed her example. Almost imperceptibly, the flowers began their own journey, drifting gently out to sea.

About the author

I was born and brought up on the edge of the Peak District in England, and then lived in Oxfordshire for a number of years, before moving up to the Lake District with my family.

My career path has taken me from the academic world, into international business and back to teaching. I now split my time between writing, teaching, and walking in the hills.

Alex Fallows

Printed in Great Britain
by Amazon

44017496R00145